Raging

Holly Kelly

Clean Teen Publishing

THIS book is a work of fiction. Names, characters, places and incidents are the product of the author's imagination or are used factiously. Any resemblance to actual persons, living or dead, business establishments, events or locales is entirely coincidental. NO part of this book may be reproduced, scanned, or distributed in any printed or electronic form without permission. Please do not participate in or encourage piracy of copyrighted materials in violation of the author's rights. Purchase only authorized editions.

RAGING

Copyright ©2016 Holly Kelly
All rights reserved.

ISBN: 978-1-63422-195-5
Cover Design by: Marya Heiman
Typography by: Courtney Knight
Editing by: Cynthia Shepp

For more information about our content disclosure,
please utilize the QR code above with your smart phone
or visit us at www.CleanTeenPublishing.com

To my husband, James. Your strength and determination in the face of adversity is only one of the millions of reasons why I'm grateful to be your wife. If fate is so kind, I look forward to growing old with you—preferably on a beach in Fiji.

CHAPTER 1

1128 AD

Tana hummed as she meandered along the cobblestone streets of a quaint village—completely unaware that her life as she knew it would end that day. She reached the fountain. It bubbled in a blooming, sparkling flow. She loved water, relished the feel of it. In fact, she'd like nothing better than to jump in the fountain and drench herself. She doubted the villagers would appreciate their water being polluted by her. Instead, she filled her bucket to brimming and started back through the narrow streets. Dipping her fingers in the fluid, she smiled as she touched the coolness, swishing it through her fingertips. Water always made her feel at ease. It was safe; it protected her from herself.

"Tana," a voice shouted behind her. "What are you doing here? On the prowl for another lover?"

Tana stiffened. As she pulled her hand back from the bucket, steam rose as the water coating her fingers bubbled and hissed. Before anyone could see, she stuffed her hand into the folds of her skirt.

She turned to find the glaring eyes of a group of young women. In the center stood Lettie—a seventeen-year-old girl who relished taunting her. Lettie stood tall,

Raging

a beauty with raven-black hair, and steel-grey eyes that held the hatred of a much older woman. And in Lettie's eyes, the hatred was well earned. She blamed Tana for the dissolution of her engagement to Gabriel. And to be honest, Tana *was* the reason. But it was not intentional. The love that sprang up between them came completely unexpected. Gabriel was determined to marry her, but his family refused to allow it. Tana was, after all, a red-haired devil, without family, without means—at least not in this world. She did have a father, but if she told them who he was, they'd think her a liar. Or mad.

"No, Lettie. I was just fetching water."

"Oh, really?" Lettie looked beyond Tana's shoulders.

Tana looked to see who might be approaching when the bucket slipped from her grasp. She turned back to see Lettie holding the water as it sloshed and splashed over the cobbled stones at her feet. "I don't think there's enough water here to clean the soot and filth from you." Lettie shook her head and laughed. The other women laughed in chorus with her. "No, there's not nearly enough water here." A wicked smile spread over her face. "But perhaps it could help," she said, and then swung the bucket, splashing its entire contents across Tana's face.

Tana sputtered and wiped the wetness away. "You..." she said though clenched teeth. Her anger rose, boiling beneath her skin. "You are a hateful, spoiled child," Tana continued. Clouds of mist swirled around her.

"Yeah, and you..." Lettie's voice dropped away as her eyes widened. "You're..." she said in a whisper, her eyes searching the steaming mist, "…a witch?"

Tana glanced down to see steam rising from her skin. Horrified, she looked up to meet Lettie's eyes, which were narrowed to slits.

"You *are* a witch," Lettie said.

"No. No, I'm not," Tana stammered. Her heart pounded as fear crept in.

"Yes, you are! And I bet you used witchcraft on Gabriel. That explains how he could have feelings for a twit like you—you daughter of Satan." Lettie ran forward and lifted the bucket above her head. Tana attempted to raise her hands to block, but she wasn't quick enough. The sturdy, wooden container came down on her with a crack as pain exploded in her head. In agony, she collapsed to the ground.

"Witch, witch, witch…" the girls around Lettie chanted. Doors from nearby houses squeaked open. The voices swelling as a crowd gathered.

Tana looked up. "I'm not a witch."

The angry faces around her told her they didn't believe her. And why should they? She'd always been an outsider among them—never accepted, never trusted. And here she was, covered in water, steaming like a hot griddle.

An old man with a shiny head and shaggy beard leaned over and picked up a rock. Tana turned away just in time for it to miss hitting her in the face. Pain sliced across her shoulder. Almost immediately, another strike hit again, and then again and again. Stones pelted

Raging

Tana's body as she curled into a ball—attempting to shield herself from the onslaught of increasingly large stones.

"Stop," she shrieked. "Please, st—" Pain stole her voice as hurt accompanied a crack in her side when a rock the width of a dinner plate dropped on her. She was sure that one broke a rib or two.

She had done nothing wrong. She was innocent. And here they were stoning her. If she were human, they might succeed in killing her.

In the midst of pain and despair, Tana's control snapped.

Heat radiated from her. She could feel it surfacing—burning from within. When she rose to her feet, the shower of stones ceased. Through a reflective puddle of water, she could see the glow of fire dancing over her skin.

Anger flowed through her as she glared at her attackers. Her hair whipped around her face as the wind picked up. The terror-stricken faces of those surrounding her gave her a certain satisfaction. Without remorse, she let the flames swell.

Let them burn.

After all, they had tried to kill her first. It was time to see how they liked it.

Clarity struck for a moment when the frightened eyes of a small child peeked around the skirt of his mother.

What am I doing?

Closing her eyes, Tana attempted to calm the flames

that delighted in seeking out tinder and flesh to burn. Her hands clenched into fists, shaking with effort. But the fire would not be calmed. It was too late.

"Run," she whispered, her breathing ragged. She raised her eyes to the crowd and shouted, "Run!"

Chaos erupted as the villagers fled, some simply running away, others running toward loved ones they wished to save.

Tana herself rose and sprinted to the outskirts of the village. She needed to get as far away as she could. She should have been relieved when she reached the exit at the wall surrounding the town, but what lay before her didn't comfort her—in fact, it was a nightmare. A dry, grassy meadow spread out before her. Nothing looked more flammable, but she couldn't turn back. That would be worse.

Taking a deep breath, she sprinted, racing across the field. Fire licked the dry tinder and ignited. She knew there was a pond not far from this field. She must get there! That was the only way to stop this.

The sky darkened with smoke and the landscape looked surreal—like someone had painted over it with an orange glaze. Distant screams erupted from behind as the village burned. *Please don't let anyone die. I didn't mean it. I was angry. I don't want to be responsible for more deaths. Please, make it stop!*

Finally, she reached the tall trees, where the moisture still clung to the grass and the leaves on the foliage were green. Air burned in her lungs as she gasped for breath.

Raging

Smoke rose and swirled around her legs as they continued to pump, driving her to her destination. She could hear the fire crackling behind her as it raged—drying up the moisture and catching on the tinder as smoke filled her nostrils.

"Please, make it stop," she sobbed. "Father, if you can hear me, make the fire stop!"

"Tana!" a voice cried out, and she skidded to a stop. "Gabriel?" Her heart pounded as terror shot through her. A moment later, she could see him as he raced from the trees. Gabriel had grown up in the village near her woods. They'd spent many a day fishing, hunting, and simply enjoying each other's company. And then, just this summer, they'd finally admitted they loved each other. He was the most important thing in her world. She wanted to spend the rest of her life with him.

He stepped away from her, his eyes widening in horror. "Tana, you're on fire!"

Tana glanced down at her hands. Yellow flames danced over her entire body. "I can't stop it, Gabriel! You need to run. Run far away from here."

"I won't leave you," he said as he took a hesitant step forward.

"You have to," she shouted. "I can't stop it. I can't stop the fire." The crackling increased, as did the dancing flames, swelling and growing as they took on a life of their own. "Run, Gabriel! You have to run!" He finally seemed to realize how dangerous the situation had become, and he sprinted into the trees.

She pressed her hands to her forehead as fire filled her vision. "Not fast enough. He's not running fast enough," she sobbed, dropping to her knees as the intensity of the fire increased. There was no chance of reaching the pond now. She was beyond help. An ear-shattering explosion filled her vision as white light blinded her eyes. She may have been blind to the scene, but she could feel it—the explosion coming from her. The fire incinerated everything around her. Puffs of moisture struck like pinpricks into the flames.

She knew exactly where the moisture came from. It came from life—the trees, small animals, and rodents. A shout and a stabbing pain drove her to her knees. That shout… Oh, please no! But even as she was desperate to deny it, she knew who it was.

Gabriel.

She could feel the moisture of his body evaporating in the wake of her inferno. She was killing the one human who had shown compassion to her. The only man she had ever loved. She could feel the moisture from his living, breathing body succumb to the inferno. And then it faded, and he was gone.

"No!" she screamed as wails tore from her lips at what she'd done. Moments later, she felt many more screams of fright rising and then quickly being snuffed out. The explosion had reached the already burning village. "No, please, no more." She collapsed to the earth. "Father—"

"Tana, my child." The deep voice she had longed to hear resonated over the crackling flames. Tana's eyes rose, landing on the tall, dark silhouette of her father, Hades. She turned on her stomach and pushed herself off the ground, the black, burnt grass pressing into her hands as she looked up. The fire raged around him. He regarded her somberly, the fire retreating at his approach. "What have you done?"

"I didn't mean it. I…I tried to stop it."

"Tried? Well, stop it now!"

Closing her eyes, she attempted to focus her thoughts—instead, Gabriel's face came to mind. She could feel the heat rising with her despair, and the flames continued to spread.

"Tana!"

"Father, please! You need to stop the fire."

"No! *You* need to stop it, Tana! I cannot save you from yourself."

"Please, I don't know how."

"Tana. Stop the fire, or I will have to stop you."

"Me?" She looked up at the man she called father. "What do you mean?"

"If you cannot control your powers, you are a danger to all those around you. I cannot allow you to continue as you have been."

Tana dropped her face into her hands. But she *had* tried to stop it! She'd tried over and over. Even now, she could feel the flames building, but she was helpless to stop them. The more she tried, the more desperate she became, and the more the flames grew. Even thinking about it…

Heat swirled around her. She could feel the flames rise. Chancing a glance, she opened her eyes. Light filled her vision—a dancing array of yellows and orange.

"Tana!" The sharp tone of her father cut through to her. She'd never heard him sound so angry. The wall of flames parted as his face appeared before her—furious, filled with condemnation. He blamed her for her weakness. Contempt rolled off him—as hot as the fire engulfing him. Finally, Tana weakened and the flames diminished. Numbness seeped up her limbs as darkness filled her vision. Unconsciousness soon overtook her.

Icy cold greeted Tana as she gradually awakened. A murmur of mumbling voices prodded her.

"Won't her mother be angry?" an unfamiliar voice said, the clear words tinkling like glass.

Tana's heart clenched at the mention of her mother, and her body trembled. She couldn't think about her. She wouldn't.

"Her mother is dead," her father said. "Tana killed her."

"No!" the woman gasped. "I can't say as I've seen a more innocent-looking young woman."

A sob racked Tana's chest as guilt and despair washed over her. *I didn't mean to. It was an accident.* She wanted to scream, but her tongue sat thick in her mouth and her body didn't respond to her. As desperate as she was to defend herself, she could not yet move.

"Skadi, looks can be deceiving. This daughter of

mine has murdered hundreds. Those deaths, whether Tana accepts responsibility or not, are blood on her hands. Now, will you help me?"

"I *can* help you. But I wonder why you don't simply destroy her."

"She's my daughter. If I have her destroyed, she will be in my domain. And despite the fact that I *can* show her mercy in the Underworld, I dare not. I rule with equity. It would not be right to show her leniency simply because she shares my blood. She would face endless torment, wallowing in pain and sorrow for all eternity for the innocent lives she has stolen."

"I understand. But still, I hesitate to do what you ask. She's a powerful goddess. Her consciousness will endure, and her prison would be endless torture."

Prison? Endless torture?

"Either way, she will be tortured. I cannot abide the thought that I would be the one to administer it."

Please, no! Have mercy.

Tana's fingers began to burn—not hot, but cold. Feeling came gradually, like the stabbing pain of a thousand needles. Wetness seeped into her back, bringing with it agony. She clenched and unclenched her hands, attempting to generate some warmth. "Father…" she said, finally managing to speak. A puff of white, misty air billowed from her mouth.

"Tana," he responded. "You're awake."

"P-please…" she begged through chattering teeth. "D-don't to this."

"My mind is made up, my child."

"No, F-father. You're supposed to protect m-me; you're supposed to help me."

Pain shone in his eyes when he turned away. Knowing he regretted his actions didn't help. It didn't lessen the bitter feeling of betrayal.

"Skadi, do it now."

"No!" Tana shrieked as the ground below her rumbled and cracked. "Father! You do this and I'll n-never forgive you!" Pain as she had never felt before washed over her as ice water flooded the hole she was sinking into. She gasped, her muscles clenching—screaming in pain as fury burned in her. "I swear I will escape, and when I do, I will come for you, Father. You will feel pain a thousand times worse than what you inflict on me! I promise you'll regret what you do today."

Icy water washed over her, covering her face as she spoke her last words—and down she sank. The burn of cold engulfed her, more painful than anything she could have imagined. She flailed her arms, trying desperately to reach the surface, but some unseen force pushed her down. In less than a minute, her lungs screamed for air. And then as fast as a cracking whip, she could no longer move. Her eyes looked toward the surface—frozen in place. Bubbles around her stilled, like a cruel constellation spread out above her head. And this was how she remained for nearly nine hundred years—locked in her icy prison, with nothing to think on, save regret and revenge.

Chapter 2

Present day

Drakōn stood with his feet braced apart in defiance of the god who stood before him. "Your wife is a goddess. She no longer needs guards. My business is concluded."

"So you are just going to ignore the threat of destruction the world faces?" Xanthus asked.

"You mean the threat to the humans. The prophecy states that it will take four women to save them. Last I checked, I wasn't a woman."

"No, you're not, but they could use your help." Xanthus sighed. "The humans are not all bad. You have to admit that Gretchen and Sara are both good and selfless women. They grew up among the humans. They think of themselves as humans."

"The land-walkers are not my problem," Drakōn said.

"So you'll just let them all die?"

"I have no desire to see innocents suffer, which is why I have to go. My daughter…" Drakōn's voice trailed off, hesitant to continue.

He could see the surprise in Xanthus' eyes. Xanthus knew him well enough to know that he never talked about his child.

"You were in Panthon Prison in her stead," Xanthus bluntly said.

"Yes," Drakōn said. His eyes narrowed as his jaw tightened. "I fear for her. There is no one left to accept punishment for her now. If she makes another misstep, the council will seize her. I cannot allow her to suffer as I did."

"How do you expect to protect her?" Xanthus asked. "You know if you return to the sea, you will be hunted down and destroyed."

"It will take a lot more than a Dagonian warrior to take me down."

"For you, they'll send an entire battalion."

"Let them," Drakōn sneered.

"Drakōn." Xanthus put his hand on his friend's shoulder. "You…" His voice dropped away as confusion clouded his features.

Drakōn slapped Xanthus' hand off him. "Don't touch me."

Xanthus shook his head. "Drakōn Sumur, always pushing people who care about you away. You may not want to admit you have friends, but you do. And we'll be there for you if you ever need us."

Drakōn growled, not liking to admit Xanthus was right. He'd done his best not to forge close relationships, but regardless, he knew that Xanthus and the others cared about him. If he were ever in trouble, he need only ask, and they would be at his side. And by the gods, he'd do the same—but not at the expense of leaving his daughter in danger.

"Maybe you will survive the soldiers and protect your daughter." Xanthus shrugged. "But I'm letting you know, if I have to come down there and avenge your death, I won't be happy."

"We wouldn't want the god of war unhappy, now would we?"

"God of war…I really wish you all would stop calling me that."

"It's true, isn't it?" Drakōn said, knowing full well it was. Triton had destroyed Ares and given his powers to Xanthus. But the former Dagonian wasn't accepting the title—regardless of the fact that he had the power.

Drakōn knew Xanthus would eventually accept who he was. All it would take would be a tyrannical lunatic killing innocent people, and Xanthus would not be able to stop himself from intervening. In fact, if he remembered right, Xanthus was conspicuously absent while the rest of them watched the recent news filled with terrorist threats. And somehow, miraculously, the situation saw a peaceful resolution. Coincidence? Not likely. Drakōn didn't believe in coincidences.

"War needs no god," Xanthus said. "Now, god of peace, that I could accept."

"What about *god of threaten the innocent and I'll shove my fist down your throat and rip out your heart?*"

"That's a pretty long title," Xanthus chuckled, "but it works too."

"Yeah, I thought you'd like it."

Xanthus smiled and clapped him on the back. "I don't like goodbyes, so I won't offer you one."

"Till we meet again," Drakōn said.

"Till we meet again," Xanthus answered.

Moments later, Drakōn stepped onto the beach. Human families gathered in groups—some sitting on towels soaking up sunlight, others playing with a thing called a Frisbee, and then there were some splashing in the surf. He'd have to go farther down the beach to be alone when he transformed. The humans would surely notice his tailfin if he entered the water within sight.

Their laughter made him smile as he walked away from them. Humans were such complex creatures. Yes, they polluted the oceans and made life in the sea more difficult, but they were often playful and tender. Much of the harm they did, they did out of ignorance.

A sudden pain radiated from the back of his head. Something had hit him. He looked down to see a Frisbee in the sand and a boy running toward him.

"I'm so sorry, sir," he said as he raced to him. "Are you alright?"

Drakōn rubbed the back of his head, bending over to pick up the human toy. Familiarity struck him when he looked at the Frisbee. It resembled a láka—a toy he'd often played with as a boy.

"I'm fine," he answered. The child looked to be about ten years old, wearing tattered shorts with patches in the seat. He greatly resembled the human woman Sara had

Raging

hired to do mending—though Drakōn had no idea why Xanthus' wife would need anyone to do mending for her. She was a goddess after all. Therefore, she had no need for repaired clothing.

"Are you Mary's son?"

"Yeah, I'm Steven," he answered and nodded his head in the direction of a slightly younger boy. "And that's my little brother, Paul. My mom's up at the house fixing some curtains."

Drakōn tried not to look surprised. The draperies in the house had only been recently replaced. He was suddenly humbled, realizing why Sara had hired the woman. She was obviously helping her, but she didn't want to damage her pride by offering charity.

"So where's your father?"

The boy's face fell. "My dad died in Iraq two years ago."

Oh right, the human war. "I'm sorry, son."

He shrugged. "It's okay."

Drakōn could see in the boy's face that it was definitely not okay. "Did your dad play Frisbee with you?"

A spark lit his eyes. "Yeah, all the time. My dad gave me this," he said, lifting up the toy.

"It's a nice, sturdy one. It sure left its mark on me."

The boy laughed, lightening Drakōn's melancholy mood. "Be glad you have good memories of your dad," Drakōn said. "My dad didn't care about me at all."

"How could a dad not care about his son?"

"Not all dads are as good as yours was. Cherish your

memories."

"Steven!" a child's voice called from behind. "You have to see this!"

Drakōn turned to look behind him and froze. It looked like someone had pulled a plug in the sea. Only moments before, the shore had lain a few feet away, now it looked to be a mile from where they stood. Suddenly without water, fish flopped, stranded, and seaweed lay flat against the ground. He should take the boy and his brother and run, but he knew it wouldn't matter. With the loss of that much water, there was no hope of outrunning this. A giant tsunami was on its way.

"Sara!" Drakōn shouted.

A moment later, she stood at his side—her white hair blowing in the breeze at odds with her eternally youthful face. "What's the emergency?"

He gestured toward the exposed seafloor and said, "We need your father."

Shock flashed across her features as she shouted, "Dad." She put her arm around Steven and gestured for Paul to come to her.

Drakōn could feel the power of a god suddenly at his back, but he couldn't take his eyes off the swell in the distance.

"Great gods on Olympus," a deep voice rumbled—Triton's voice. "It's not just this beach that's threatened, but the entire Eastern seaboard will feel the effects of this. I don't have the power to protect all the humans, but I will protect all I can."

Raging

"Whoa," Steven said, just as his younger brother ran to his side. His eyes were wide as he gaped at the figure with a trident in his hand. "You look like Poseidon."

"Poseidon is my father. My name is Triton."

"Is that a tidal wave?" Paul asked, "Are we going to die?"

"It's a tsunami," Triton answered, "but I'm here to protect you."

"How many others can you protect?" Drakōn asked.

"If I expend all my strength, I can cover about a thousand miles of beach."

The colossal wave drew closer and seemed to reach higher into the sky as it approached.

"What if you had help?" Sara asked.

"Only another sea-god would be of use to me, and I'm sorry, my dear, but the powers you get from the sea are too weak to help much."

"How about Drakōn?"

Triton shook his head, "A Dagonian wouldn't be any more help than you."

She raised her eyebrows, her eyes locked on Drakōn.

Drakōn's knees went weak when he realized she knew.

"I don't know what you expect of me," Drakōn said. "My powers have been taken from me."

"Not taken, Drakōn," she said. "Locked away."

"What are you talking about?" Triton asked. "No one can lock away another god's powers."

"Drakōn's mother can," Sara said, "and she did."

"Who is your mother?" Triton asked him.

He shook his head. "I don't know. I only know she abandoned me to the sea when I was just a babe."

"Your mother did not abandon you," Sara said. "She hid you away before Zeus got to you."

"What?"

"Zeus had been stealing power from the gods for many years, plotting to overthrow all the pantheons. Your mother is a powerful Sumerian goddess, and your father is the son of Poseidon—his firstborn. Your parents found out you were in danger, so they both agreed to hide you from Zeus. Your father didn't abandon you, either. He is doing his best to protect you."

"Drakōn is my brother's son?" Triton asked.

"Who is this brother? I thought you were Poseidon's firstborn."

Triton shook his head. "No, his firstborn son is Proteus. My brother's a trickster, a shapeshifter. He could transform into any person or creature he wished. My father couldn't control him, so he gave up on him years ago. We have no idea where he is now or what shape he's assumed. I haven't heard from him in years."

"I'm sorry to interrupt," Sara said, "but I think it's time for you and Drakōn to stop this tsunami." She gestured to the colossal wave building in the distance. "I'm going to take Steven and Paul back to the house."

"But I don't—" Drakōn began, his voice cutting off as Sara touched him. He collapsed to his knees as power washed over him, flowing through his veins. He'd never

Raging

felt anything like it.

"There," she said, suddenly breathless. "Now I really have to go. These boys are terrified."

"No, we're not," Steven said, puffing out his chest.

"Well, we're going back to the house anyway." With that said, she and the two boys disappeared. Drakōn guessed Sara figured the children had seen enough strangeness today that one more thing wouldn't matter. Perhaps she meant to erase their memories.

Standing on shaky legs, Drakōn asked, "What do I do?"

"You have yet to learn to use your powers, so I suggest lending them to me."

"You're not taking them from me!" he said, suddenly furious.

"Calm down," Triton said. "I can't steal your powers. They will remain rooted in you, but you can channel them to me."

"How?"

"It takes skin-to-skin contact. Keeping your hand on my shoulder should do it. And when you feel me draw power from you, don't resist. It will be difficult and you won't want to let it go, but you have to trust me. I can't take your power without your consent."

Drakōn narrowed his eyes. The sea-god was asking him to trust him? Drakōn had little trust in others. But then, he'd been watching Triton from afar for centuries. He had always acted honorably and was quick to defend the weak. That was why Drakōn had secretly admired

Triton in a society that had loathed the sea-god.

Lifting a shaky hand, Drakōn placed it on Triton's shoulder. Power flowed from him, weakening him. His first impulse was to fight the theft and remove his hand, but he allowed his power to flow to Triton. Raising his eyes, he was shocked to see the wave towering above them—impossibly tall. His heart dropped when the wave crashed, but it crashed in on itself. The level of the sea sank down and down—barely splashing a few drops beyond the original shore. Within several long minutes, the sea was back in its place.

Drakōn dropped to his knees at the same time Triton did. "Were you able to stop it all?" Drakōn asked.

Triton sighed, breathless, "Yes."

"I have to admit that it was impressive, Your Majesty."

"It wouldn't have been nearly as impressive if you weren't here to help. Sara's right. You are powerful."

Drakōn looked down the shore to find it deserted, with towels and other items stirring in the breeze. It looked like the humans ran for cover. "So none were hurt?"

Triton sighed and shook his head. "I'm sorry to say it, but I couldn't save everyone. Those curious humans, who foolishly ventured into the empty sea, were covered by it.

"How many?"

"Ninety-four."

Drakōn wondered how he could know the exact number, but Triton was an old god. Thousands of years

Raging

ruling the Atlantic had to teach you something.

Moments later, Drakōn found himself lying against the back of a plush couch beside Triton. Sara brought them glasses of seawater to drink. "Here, this should help restore your strength."

As Drakōn drank the water, he felt as if life filled his body once again. His energy returned and his trembling body calmed. "Thank you," he said, cracking a grin at Sara. She continually impressed him. And he was not easily impressed. Xanthus was a lucky man to have married such a woman.

If he could ever learn to trust a woman enough to marry her, he'd want one like Sara. But that possibility was about as likely as being struck by lightning—at the bottom of the sea.

Sara patted him on the shoulder and whispered, "Don't leave. I need to help my father, but I'll be back, and I need to speak to you alone." She looked up at Pallas as he stepped through the door. "I need to talk to you too, Pallas. Later."

"Sure," he said as he brushed past her.

And then she was gone.

Pallas rushed to sit next to Drakōn. "Dude, you have to see this." He picked up the remote and switched on the TV.

"Scientists are baffled." A young woman holding a microphone stood on a dock overlooking the sea. "The largest tsunami in the history of the world disintegrated before the eyes of millions."

"I sure hope Triton doesn't get in trouble for what he did," Pallas said.

"Who told you it was Triton?"

Pallas shook his head. "That human boy has been chattering on and on about how he saw Triton and how he saved everyone from the giant wave."

"If Zeus finds out about what he did," Drakōn said, "Triton could be in real trouble. I mean bigger than that wave, trouble."

"Zeus shouldn't even be king—the traitor." Pallas stood and paced the floor. "Triton and Nicole are the rightful heirs—that is, until Petros is restored to the throne."

"Right." Drakōn shook his head as he stood. "Try telling that to the millions under Zeus' control."

Pallas cracked a smile. "We have Odin."

"What?" Drakōn said. "The king of the Norse pantheon? Sara restored his memories? Why?"

"King Petros and Odin are cousins and were extremely close. Our pantheons were the tightest of allies—until Zeus stole the throne from Petros and erased everyone's memories. Odin now remembers everything, and he's furious. He's pledged to do all he can to bring down Zeus and restore Petros to the throne. He's even vowed to cut off Zeus' head, pound it flat with Thor's hammer, and then give the head to Hel to burn with the refuse of the Underworld cattle. Zeus' body, he says he'll impale on the pinnacle of his palace to feed the birds of prey that migrate there. The Norse gods are quite imaginative and

Raging

brutal. This is a very good development."

Drakōn sat and smiled weakly. "Yeah. It is. Remind me to never get on Odin's bad side."

Pallas sat beside him. "Yeah, me too."

Chapter 3

Skadi stepped across a vast field of ice. It covered many square miles in a wide circle, and shone like glass rimmed with shards—like the teeth of a gaping mouth, open wide to consume its prey. She could feel sparks of life below—criminals trapped. She and Hades had a mutually advantageous agreement. She was in charge of imprisoning the fiery fiends of the Underworld, and he oversaw the imprisonment of those in her icy domain. As goddess of ice and snow, her power alone kept these dangerous prisoners at bay.

Hades actually got the better end of the deal. There were fewer inhabitants in her domain than his. His lake of fire held a mere three prisoners of hers. On the other hand, Skadi's lake of ice held dozens.

Skadi slowed as a life force brighter than the rest glowed from below her bare feet. She stooped to peer down. The frozen features of a young woman looked up in horror—an expression she'd worn since being frozen nearly nine hundred years before. Pressing her palm against the ice, she whispered, "You are my one regret in this field, Tana." Skadi shook her head. "I know what you've done, but I can't help but feel your punishment is

Raging

unjust. If I could free you, my child, I would. But your father will not allow it. I'm truly sorry."

Tana could feel the tears burn behind her eyes, but the icy prison would not allow them to be released. Her warden knelt above her as she had so many times before—speaking words that only succeeded in angering Tana.

If I could free you, I would. But your father will not allow it.

Her father was cruel, her father was a coward, and her father feared what others thought more than he cared for his own daughter.

If I ever get out of this prison, I will show him who he should truly fear. He will regret what he has done.

Her vehement threats fell on deaf ears once again. Turning her anger inward, Tana could feel the spark that demanded to become an inferno. Despite the rage that burned inside, the icy prison surrounding her did not diminish, did not succumb to the heat. Instead, the fire raged in her heart, burning away all the compassion and goodness inside of her.

In rare moments of clarity, Tana feared the day she was unleashed. For no one around her would be safe from her wrath.

"Goodbye, T—" Skadi disappeared.

That was strange. She obviously hadn't left of her own accord. She was in the middle of her farewell. But who would have been rude enough to transport a goddess without her consent?

Holly Kelly

Blinding light flashed as the smell of electrically charged air burned Skadi's nose. In moments, her eyes adjusted to the light. She stood in a tiny stone room. Blue sky peeked through small windows, which circled a room with a heavy wooden door. Skadi moved toward one of the open windows and looked out. Clouds spread out like a carpet hundreds of feet below the window.

She turned away from the dizzying sight and shouted, "How dare you bring me here without my consent! Who are you? Show yourself!" Even as she asked the question, deep down, she knew and dreaded the answer.

Footsteps sounded from outside the wooden door just before it opened. Her heart sank at the sight. Zeus—king of the Greek gods—entered.

"Hello, Skadi." Zeus smiled, but there was something off about the smile—sinister, with a hint of madness.

"Why have you brought me here?" she asked.

"You have a unique and rare gift. I'm sure you know that there are no gods or goddesses in the Greek Pantheon that hold power over ice and snow. Yet, I can't help but notice that snow falls in my kingdom. Why is that?"

Confusion hit Skadi. Why did she make it snow there? She couldn't remember. Why could she not remember? A goddess's memory should be infallible. "I...I'm not sure. As long as I can remember, I've sent light flurries to Greece. You've never complained before."

Zeus chuckled. "Truly, I don't care whether the humans get snowed on or not. But it has come to my attention that I cannot produce snow, nor can I stop

Raging

you from dumping it in my realm. This is completely unacceptable!"

"I'm sorry, Your Highness. I will cease immediately."

He narrowed his eyes and shook his head. "You don't understand. That's not what I meant. I mean that it is unacceptable for a goddess to have powers I do not."

"But… but you're a god of lightning and thunderclouds."

"No, my dear. I am the king of all the gods—"

"The Greek gods," Skadi clarified. "My king is Odin."

"Greek, Norse, Sumerian, Celtic…it doesn't matter. Soon, I will be king of all the gods."

Laughter bubbled from her chest. "You've got to be kidding."

"Not at all. You see, I've discovered how to steal power from the gods. Soon, no one will stand against me."

"You have plans to overthrow my king?" Skadi wasted no time as she pulled out her bow and had an arrow fired off in less time than it took to blink.

Caught off guard, Zeus found himself with an arrow through the heart. Roaring, he stumbled back, falling against the wall. Skadi attempted to transport, but she found herself blocked. Wasting no time, she leapt to the door and yanked it open. Perhaps shooting a powerful god through the heart was not the smartest thing to do. But he crossed the line when he threatened Odin.

Stone steps wrapped around the outside of the tower, and Skadi had to fight dizziness as she looped around and around in her descent. In minutes, she could hear footsteps in pursuit. How did he recover so fast? She knew her arrow would not be fatal to a god, but she'd hoped it would have slowed him down longer than it did.

"You filthy Northling!" he snarled. "I'll teach you to have respect for your king."

"You'll never be my king," she shouted.

"Then you will die," he said as he slammed into her, pushing her over the edge. Powerful winds whipped around them as they fell.

But no…they weren't falling. It felt as if they were, but the tower was not flying by her view as it should have been. Skadi could see the tower steps hovering in place. The wind must be holding them suspended.

Zeus locked his hands around her throat as he glared at her. "I am in need of your power, Skadi."

"You can't have it," she sneered.

"I'm not asking your permission," he said with a smile, and then whispered strange words as he looked behind her.

A cold wind whipped her back as pain flared in her fingers and toes, traveling up her limbs. She watched in horror as she realized the pain came from the fact her body was slowly turning to ice. In minutes, she could feel the icy burn traveling to her torso and then up her neck to her head.

A wicked laugh was the last thing she heard before she fell. Seconds later, her icy form shattered against the ground below.

Raging

Something was different.

The warmth within Tana had been contained inside her heart for hundreds of years, but now she could feel it inching through her veins—barely perceptible, but after being suspended so long in eternal sameness, it was unmistakable. The warmth continued to grow for the next few hours. If she could summon some anger, she might be able to break free from this prison.

She focused her mind on her father, his contempt, his disappointment, his unwillingness to accept any blame…

He should have trained her. He should have guided her. Instead, he'd show up whenever she was out of control, and even then, he didn't help her. He didn't even use the situation to teach her. He had simply condemned her. And then her mother…

No—she never thought about what happened to her mother.

Anger melted into despair.

No!

It wasn't her fault; it was her father's. He was the one to blame for what happened that day. If he had trained her to channel her anger, her mother would not have burned.

Tana screamed inside at the memories—her mother burning, her hair a fiery halo around her head, her white wings charred black. She could hear her mother's last words, tearing from her lips in agony. "It's not your fault."

No, it wasn't her fault. There was only one to blame. Hades.

And she would see him pay.

Her anger heated the ice surrounding her, and finally, it began to melt. At last, she could turn her eyes and look around her—bringing into focus the things that had only been seen in her peripheral vision. There was a man on her right and a woman on her left. They were still frozen in place. Her bubble of melted water grew, and she ached to breathe air. She refused to take the water into her lungs; that would likely hurt worse than the lack of oxygen. As the pocket of water expanded, it nearly reached the surface. Pounding her fists against the icy top, she fought to break free.

The sound of approaching steps caused fear to strike her heart. What if it was Skadi? Her escape plan would be thwarted before she got a chance to free herself. Tana pounded harder as an unfamiliar figure stepped above her. She continued to beat the ice.

A flash of lightning burst from the figure, branching out around her as the ice exploded. Chunks of ice slammed against her, stunning her. She floated, dazed for a moment, before she became aware of a strange sensation—a breeze on her back. Lifting her head into the air, she opened her eyes to blue skies with fluffy white clouds. She took the first breath she'd breathed in nearly a thousand years. Greedily sucking in gasp after gasp, she relished the feel of the life-giving air.

"Here, let me help you out," a warm voice said. Tana

Raging

looked up to see a tall figure dressed in a white robe. His face was incredibly handsome and his shoulders were heavily muscled. Should she trust him? But even as she thought it, she dismissed the possibility that he could be a threat to her. After all, he'd freed her.

She reached up her hand, and he pulled her from the water to stand on the icy ground.

"Thank you," she said, breathless. As she stood on her feet, her legs trembled.

"I'm Zeus," he said as he grinned.

Tana's eyes flew open wide. This was the king of the gods. "Um, hello, Your Majesty. My name is Tana," she answered, giving a weak smile.

"I know. You look so much like your mother."

"You knew my mother?"

"Yes, we had quite a…special relationship."

Tana felt warmth flood her cheeks.

"That was," he said with a frown, "until you killed her."

Tana's heart broke on his words. Did Zeus love her? Would he now punish her himself? "I'm sorry; I didn't mean to hurt her. It was an accident."

Zeus shrugged. "It was her own fault for giving up her immortality. But because I have a bit of a soft spot for her, I'm sorry for what I have to do. Truly, it has nothing to do with what you did to your mother."

"What do you have to do?" she asked.

"I'll be taking your powers."

"My powers? Wait, you'll take my powers away? I

won't have them anymore?"

"No, but not to worry," Zeus said. "You won't remember a thing. You'll have a new life, a life as an ordinary human."

"A life as a human? That's the extent of my punishment?"

"I think that is enough."

A tear leaked from her eye as she dropped to her knees. "Thank you. Oh, thank you."

"That's not the usual response I get," he said.

"I don't want my powers," she said as she brushed her damp hair from her face. "They've given me nothing but grief. But I…I have to do something first."

"Sorry, Tana—"

"No, you don't understand. I have to. I seek revenge on my father."

"Hades?" Zeus' eyes widened.

Tana nodded. "I swore that he would suffer. I want him dead."

"You want Hades tortured and destroyed?"

Tana nodded, her eyes burning with hatred. "Yes. It's something I have to do."

"No Tana, you don't." A slow smile crept across Zeus' face, and then he laughed. "I'll kill him for you. I promise. Your father will suffer greatly before he dies. But first, I'll be doing something for you."

"What?"

"Giving you the life you've always dreamed of."

Chapter 4

"So you finally decided to pay me a visit." Drakōn frowned at the beautiful goddess before him.

"I'm sorry," Sara said. "I wouldn't have made you wait if it wasn't important."

"Yeah." Drakōn growled. "I don't appreciate Xanthus keeping me prisoner. I can tell who runs things around here."

"I'm sorry you—" she began, and then apparently censored her words. "I'm sorry. But what I have to say is really important."

"Please don't tell me you need me to save the world because I have my own world to save."

"Your daughter."

"Yes." His eyes widened in surprise, and then narrowed when he realized she knew something. "What is it? What do you know?" he asked, not wanting to avoid learning anything that might protect his child. He remembered the fateful day—the day he learned he had a daughter. It was the same day he was taken away to be imprisoned in her stead. Hearing the circumstances of the crime, he became incensed. His child had only defended herself. But there wasn't much justice for females—especially when the family bringing charges was politically connected. Though he'd never met her, he gladly took her punishment. He couldn't bear the thought of any child of his being held at Panthon Prison.

"Your daughter is safe," Sara said. "And I can see clearly she will remain so—for the next several years, at least."

Drakōn looked closely at Sara, trying to determine if she were lying. He trusted her, but the fate of the human world was at stake—a big motivation for her to be untruthful with him. And although Drakōn no longer wanted to see the humans destroyed, the importance of his own child far outweighed the importance of the humans.

He searched her face—she seemed to be truthful. Still, he could guarantee it with a simple question, "Do you swear on the River Styx?"

Sara calmly answered, "I swear on the River Styx."

Drakōn relaxed. "Okay then, why did you need to talk to me?"

"I want you to protect a woman."

"Here we go again." He shook his head and sighed. "What woman?"

"The daughter of Hades. Her name is Tana."

"Who would dare threaten the daughter of Hades?"

"She has many threats."

"Why doesn't she go to her father for protection?"

"Her father is one of her greatest threats."

Drakōn swore. "You want me to protect her from

the most powerful god in the Underworld?"

"Yes, and I need you to also protect her from Zeus."

"Absolutely not," he shouted. "You're sending me on a suicide mission."

"If you don't succeed, she'll destroy the world."

"I…" Drakōn shook his head, raking his fingers through his black hair. "So she'll wipe out the entire human race?"

"Not intentionally."

"Oh, this keeps getting better and better. How will she do it?"

"The power she was born with is immense, yet she doesn't have the ability to control it. Zeus is now siphoning her powers, but the connection between them needs to be severed. When her powers return, that will be the time of greatest danger. If left unchecked, the world will be consumed by the fire she unleashes."

"Why unleash that power? Or even better, why don't you just have me kill her?"

"You remember the prophecy?"

He nodded. "'Gather the daughters who join the four corners, and go to the place where the mountain touches the heavens. There, you must free the king by the fourth new moon. If you fail, the wind will drive fire across the land and the earth will crumble into the seas. All mankind will perish.' As I understand it, the daughters who join the four corners are the keys to unlock the prison of the forgotten king of the Greek gods—King Petros."

"Yes," Sara said. "Tana is one of the daughters the

prophecy speaks of."

"Wait," he said, his eyes wide. "I know you are the daughter who joins the sea and the earth, and Gretchen is the daughter who joins the Underworld and the sea. So this woman joins the house of the Underworld and which other realm?"

"The skies," Sara answered. "She is also the daughter of Eos—goddess of dawn."

"So what are Tana's powers?"

"Wind and flame."

"That's a dangerous combination. You think I'm powerful enough for this impossible assignment?"

"Yes," Sara said simply. "Your powers make you uniquely fit for this assignment."

"But I haven't even learned to use my powers yet."

"You will."

Drakōn shook his head as doubt mingled with frustration in his head. "Why do I feel like a pawn in an intricate game?"

Sara looked down, color warming her cheeks.

"You know something," Drakōn growled.

Sara avoided his gaze.

"Tell me what you are hiding," Drakōn said, "or I will do nothing to help you or the humans."

Sara sighed as apprehension set in. "It's the Fates."

"The Fates?" Drakōn said, feeling like she was withholding the whole truth.

Sara sat down, wringing her hands in her lap. "I only recently learned that…"

Raging

"What?" he coaxed gently.

She looked him in the eye. "For years, the Fates have been meddling in the lives of all of you. Putting you in each other's paths. Influencing events." She sighed. "Doing what they can to save the world."

"How could you have not known that until recently?"

"It's hard to explain." Sara frowned.

Drakōn shook his head. "You're not making sense."

Sara sighed. "Xanthus made me promise not to tell anyone, so I can't explain more than I have."

Drakōn's breath caught as a thought popped into his head. "It's you."

"Me?" Sara paled.

"This isn't about the other Fates. It's about what you can do. You don't just see the past…" He looked her over with growing awe. "You can travel there."

Sara swallowed as she avoided looking at Drakōn. She was trembling.

Drakōn felt sympathy for the goddess. If certain individuals were to realize how powerful she truly was, she would definitely be a target. A huge target. "I promise on the River Styx," he said, "that I won't reveal your secret to another living soul."

Sara visibly relaxed as she closed her eyes, as if offering up a prayer. "Thank you," she said, opening them.

"I understand your fear," he said.

Sara nodded. "I need to be more careful about revealing too much. You seemed to figure that out too easily."

"I don't think you need to worry." Drakōn smiled. "I'm exceptionally smart."

Sara cracked a smile. "And humble."

Drakōn chuckled. "To tell you the truth, I figured it out when you mentioned the fact that Xanthus made you promise not to tell. He's extremely protective of you."

Sara nodded. "That's good to know. I mean that… that was how you figured it out."

Drakōn smiled. "Okay, so where do I find this goddess of wind and fire?"

Sara sighed and her expression lightened. "In the Florida Keys, diving for gold."

"What? That doesn't make any sense."

"Tana doesn't remember who she is. She thinks she's human."

"Let me guess—Zeus."

"Yes. He's taking her power for his own. Beware, Tana doesn't trust easily. The betrayals she experienced in her life cut her deep. She may not remember them, but they taint every aspect of her personality."

"So who do I tell her I am?"

"You'll be a customer."

"What? Is she a prostitute?"

Sara smacked him on the shoulder. "No! Of course not."

"Good, because I don't sleep with land-dwellers."

Sara shook her head. "She runs a business for those looking to dive for treasure."

Raging

"You mean underwater? You know, she just might notice I have a tailfin in the water. Land-walkers may be stupid, but they're not that stupid."

Sara shook her head. "What am I going to do with you, Drakōn? First, humans are just as intelligent as the gods, and second, since your powers have been unlocked, you can keep your human form in the sea if you want to. It's completely under your control now."

"Great. How am I supposed to swim with legs?"

"Well, Tana also teaches swimming lessons at a pool she owns. You might want to sign up."

"Swimming lessons... Do you even know how insulting that is?"

"It's a great way to get to know her. Who knows, you might even enjoy spending time with her."

Drakōn narrowed his eyes. "There's something you're not telling me."

"Wouldn't you like to know?" She smirked.

"Yes, actually, I would."

"Well, too bad. Your assignment is simple. Keep an eye on Tana, keep her safe, and keep the world safe."

"You don't ask for much, do you?"

"Don't worry. I'm fairly confident you'll survive."

"There are worse things than dying."

Sara's smile faded. "Yes, there are."

Chapter 5

Tana's body glided through the water. It caressed her like a gentle lover. Surfacing just before she reached the edge of the pool, she flipped and pushed off with her feet, shooting through the water once again.

She'd really missed this. This was the first fair weather in the Keys in the last several weeks—the first time she'd been able to lose herself in the water, forget her troubles, and focus on absolutely nothing but her rhythmic strokes. As she approached the other side, something looked different. A shadow darkened the surface.

She shot up out of the water and glanced up.

Holy crap...

There were no words to describe this man. He stood insanely tall, built like a brick wall, and had the most piercing brown eyes she'd ever seen. If she were an artist, she'd want to sculpt him.

"Excuse me," she said, frowning, "but you're not supposed to be here. The pool is not open until one o'clock."

"Are you Tana?"

"Who wants to know?"

Raging

Anger flashed in his eyes, and for a moment, they seemed to glow. No. She had to be mistaken. Eyes didn't glow.

"Are you always this rude to people?" he asked, scowling at her.

"Do you always break into places that are closed and locked?"

"The door wasn't locked."

"Liar. I know it was locked because I locked it behind me."

"Some guy named Eric let me in."

Tana pulled herself out the water and stepped onto the pavement. "He shouldn't have done that."

"Listen," the man said, his eyes taking a quick glance down her body. He shifted uncomfortably. "I just wanted to ask you about private swimming lessons."

"Who are you?"

"My name is Drakōn."

"Drackin?"

"No, Drakōn."

"Okay, Drake," she said, looking him over. She would have thought he might have grown up on the beach. He was a bit more muscular than a swimmer, but his body glowed with a healthy tan, and she could smell the sea on him. "Why don't you tell me what you really want?"

He glared at her and stepped forward. "I would like to take swimming lessons. Why is that so hard for you to understand?"

"I can smell the sea on you. You've been swimming

in the ocean recently."

He jerked back in surprise. "You can smell it?"

"I practically live in the ocean. Of course, I can."

"Why?" he asked, as if the idea shocked him.

"Why do I spend a lot of time in the water?"

He gave a quick nod. This man was a strange one. The situation screamed that he was interested in her, but his body language gave her mixed messages. Heck, she didn't want a relationship anyway. She had no use for them. Falling in love now just meant a broken heart later.

"I feel safe in the water," she said, surprising herself at her honesty. She was usually a closed book. The only explanation she had for giving him a truthful answer was that he'd caught her off guard. Yes, that had to be it.

He nodded, accepting her answer. "Can you give me private lessons?"

"You really don't know how to swim?"

He narrowed his eyes. He obviously didn't like her question.

"Okay," she answered. "Come back tomorrow, six AM—sharp. I'll give you an hour lesson, and then we'll go from there. Oh, and I'm not cheap—a hundred dollars an hour. If you don't like it, you can join the regular class. I teach a beginning class to older kids, but most of them are pre-teens."

"The private lessons are fine," he said through his teeth.

Her eyes followed him as he turned and left. "What have I gotten myself into?" she whispered as her betraying

Raging

heart fluttered in excitement.

Stepping into the locker room, she showered and dressed quickly. She had a mystery that needed revealing. But first, she had someone to chew out.

"Eric!" she shouted as she exited the locker room and entered the concession area.

"Yeah, boss," he answered stepping up to the counter.

"Why'd you let that man in?"

"He wanted to take some private lessons."

"And…"

"And I thought you might want to give him some."

"Listen, I know you're new here, so I'll give you a pass this time. When I'm out here, or walking the perimeter of the pool, I'm fine to talk to patrons. But when I'm swimming laps, I'm not to be disturbed."

"Oh. Sorry." He looked really worried. In fact, his green eyes took on a sheen.

Tana sighed, attempting to relax. "It's fine. Don't worry about it. Just don't let it happen again."

"Sure thing, boss." He blinked and gave half a smile.

"I'm going to be diving today," she said.

"On the diving board?" he asked, his brows furrowed.

Tana shook her head. "No, in the ocean."

"Oh," he said and nodded.

"Natalie is going to be in charge. If you need anything, you can talk to her."

"Sure thing, boss."

"Oh, and one more thing."

"Yeah?"

"Stop calling me boss. My name is Tana."

"Oh, okay."

A few hours later, Tana put on her gear as she sat on the deck of her trawler—anchored about twenty miles southeast of the Keys.

"What are you hoping to find down there, 'cause I have a feeling you aren't looking for gold?" Malia frowned down on her. Her blue eyes sparkled; her face haloed in long, blonde hair.

"Nope, I'm looking for something much better," Tana answered.

"What?"

"Proof that I'm not crazy."

"That's impossible," Malia said with a chuckle, "because you are crazy."

"Ha, ha, ha." Tana rolled her eyes as she hung her beloved camera around her neck. "You're so funny."

"What do you think you saw?"

"You'd think I was nuts if I told you."

"Now you seriously have to tell me!" Malia whined.

"Nope," Tana said. "I'll let my camera tell you for me." She pulled out her underwater camera and opened the file that would have showed all the pictures that had been taken on it—if she hadn't downloaded them and deleted them last night.

Malia crossed her legs and sat down beside her. "What am I supposed to be seeing?"

"Nothing. I just want you to see that all the files are empty."

"Okay, now why would you want me to see this?"

"So you'll know that the pictures I take are the real thing. I haven't doctored anything and loaded it on here."

Malia scrolled through, checking all the files, and found them empty. "Okay, you've convinced me. But why don't you just take me down there so I can see for myself?"

"Nope. I can't guarantee that it's safe."

"Whoa, whoa! What do you mean by it's not safe? Then why are *you* going down there?"

"Because I know what I'm looking for and I know where to hide."

"I don't like this, Tana." Malia pushed the camera away.

"I'll be fine," Tana said. "I promise."

Malia frowned at her, obviously not convinced.

"Listen, I've gone down there a couple of times before. I know what I'm doing. And if I sense any danger, I promise I'll get out of there right away. I only hope it's still there. With the weather the way it's been, I've had to wait weeks to come back," she said as she muscled her body into her wetsuit.

"Is it an artifact?"

"Nope."

"A school of sharks?"

"Uh-uh."

"A new species of sea creature?"

She shrugged. "You could say that."

"Grrr! You are driving me crazy!"

"Listen, I'll be fine. And you'll have your answers soon enough."

"Okay, but you have thirty minutes. If you're not up before then, I'm coming down to get you. Are we clear?"

"Crystal."

Moments later, Tana entered the water and swam down beneath the rising bubbles. She took regular breaths through the mouthpiece as she searched the surroundings. There wasn't much to see on her initial descent, but then a rocky mound emerged from the deep. She would have turned on a light, but she didn't want to scare away the reason she was there.

Grasping onto the rock, she guided her way around and into a small tunnel—barely big enough for her and her gear. She could have gone around the rock and avoided the tunnel, but the first time she dove here, she was almost spotted. This way would keep her hidden.

The light increased, signaling the end of the tunnel. Glancing at her watch, she noted that she'd been down for nearly five minutes. That gave her about fifteen minutes to take pictures, five more minutes to get back to the boat, and five minutes to spare before Malia started freaking out.

The dark silhouette of a stone building came into view. The first time she saw it, she was sure she was seeing the ruins of a structure that had once resided on land, but that was before she saw it, or rather—her.

There seemed to be no movement. What if she didn't show herself again? What if no one was home?

Raging

Or worse, what if she had moved on?

Her heart pounded as a flutter of movement came from the window. Tana grabbed her camera. *Please let there be enough light.* She couldn't chance using a flash—at least not yet. If she got desperate enough, she might chance it and then swim her butt back to the surface as fast as she could.

Raising her camera, she got the place into the frame and began taking regular shots. If she showed her face for only a second, Tana didn't want to miss it.

Darkness passed like a ghostly apparition across the window. Only Tana was sure it wasn't a ghost. And then it turned.

A beautiful face framed in black wisps looked out the window. Tana's heart took off in a sprint as her finger pressed the shutter button as fast as she could—hoping to get that perfect shot.

And then she was gone.

Tana sighed into the mouthpiece, releasing the air she'd been holding. And then she shrieked—bubbles passing out of her mouth as the figure swam outside. Fumbling to raise the camera again, she pushed the shutter button, and finally got the camera lifted with the woman in the viewfinder. But this wasn't just an aquatic humanoid creature. She continued to press the shutter. This thing had the head, arms, and torso of a woman, but she also had the tail of a fish. Tana had discovered a freakin' mermaid!

The creature turned as if sensing someone watching

her, and her eyes locked on Tana. Horror flashed across the mermaid's face and she shot through the water, escaping faster than Tana could imagine possible.

Tana made her own escape, turning back and snaking through the tunnel. Swimming toward the surface never seemed to take her so long. All she wanted to do was get on the boat and show Malia what she found. Malia would completely freak at the pictures!

Finally, Tana surfaced and pulled herself up the ladder. Ripping away the mouthpiece and face mask, she took quick, gasping breaths and said, "Ma-Malia."

"Tana, what happened?" she said, pulling Tana on deck. "I knew it!" She shook her head. "I knew I should have come."

"No," Tana said, still breathless. "It's good. It's… perfect. You need to see this."

"What is this about?" Malia furrowed her brows and frowned.

Tana pulled her into the cabin and sat on a bench. She opened the view screen and scrolled through the shots looking for the eyes of the woman. And there they were. "Here!" She shoved the camera into Malia's view.

Malia narrowed her eyes and searched the screen. "Is that…a… What is that?"

"Here, let me find a better shot," Tana said, scrolling across several more. The full picture of the mermaid came into view—the image unmistakably clear.

"Holy…" Malia's voice dropped off in shock.

Raging

Tana nodded her head, her own eyes wide at the impossible image. "Yeah."

"What are you going to—?"

Something rammed into the boat. Tana and Malia tipped over against the wall of the cabin.

"What was that?" Malia asked, her breathing ragged as she froze in place.

"I don't know," Tana breathed as she looked out the window of the cabin. The sun shone bright, the mild weather at odds with the horror of the situation.

"Maybe the mermaid didn't like getting her picture taken," Malia said.

Tana braced herself as another slam hit the side of the boat, along with a loud crack. It sounded like the hull had splintered. As soon as the boat righted itself, she scrambled to the helm. "They're going to sink the ship!"

"They?" Malia asked.

"Yeah, I think the mermaid went for reinforcements."

"This is like that freakin' scene from that *Pirates of the Caribbean* movie—you know, the one where the mermaids sink the ship," Malia said as they both made their way to the helm. "I don't think it ended so well for them."

Tana hoisted the anchor and started the engine; it came alive with a roar. Without hesitation, she slammed it into gear and the boat lurched forward. "This isn't a movie."

"Could have fooled me," Malia answered.

The boat shuddered and groaned as Tana ran it as fast as she could. There were a few more bumps as something slammed into the craft, but nothing as strong as the first two hits. Whatever was trying to sink them looked to be having a harder time causing damage while they were moving. The thought had only just passed through her mind when they were hit with incredible force. The entire boat tipped, the waves washing over the side. Malia screamed and tumbled across the floor while Tana held on to the wheel. She really hoped they wouldn't capsize.

Thankfully, the boat rocked and then righted itself. Up ahead, the shore came into view. Tana felt a hint of relief, but they weren't out of danger yet. Smoke billowed from below deck as she put pressure on the engine. The island swelled in size at their approach. The sooner she got to dry land, the better. Another boom and she dropped to her knees. This time, it wasn't a collision.

She had blown the engine.

The boat glided, slowing to a stop. The silence was deafening after the roar of the engine quieted. Water lapped gently against the boat.

Malia sobbed quietly. "We're going to die, aren't we?"

Tana didn't answer as she looked at the shore—still a half a mile away.

The trawler rocked as something bumped against the side. Her blood turned to ice when she heard a sound, faint, but unmistakable. A low growl came from behind her on the left. The wheel shuddered in her grip. Tana realized a moment later that her shaking hands were the cause.

Raging

Stepping toward the door of the cabin, Malia put a hand on her and whispered, "Don't go out there."

"Shh, I have to see," Tana answered.

As she poked her head outside, her heart clamped painfully in her chest as terror gripped her. The first thing she noticed was his eyes—black and filled with hatred. He pulled himself out of the water. He was insanely large, muscular, and had murder in his eyes as he pinned her with his glare.

As he pulled himself up, she could see he was bare from the waist up, and black from the waist down. It almost looked like he was wearing some kind of black wetsuit—except for the pelvic fins. Tana backed away.

This was a merman, and he was furious.

In a moment, the creature howled as something seemed to pull him down. He caught himself in his descent and grabbed the post of the railing lining the deck with his hand. The muscles in his arms bulged as he struggled against the pull of who knew what. Finally, he couldn't hold on any longer, and he fell back with a splash into the sea.

It probably wasn't the smartest thing to do, but curiosity could cause a woman to do pretty stupid things. Without hesitation, Tana rushed forward to see what had gotten to the merman.

As she leaned on the railing, she could see bubbles churning in the water. Fins and the occasional arm splashed into view. It looked like there were two of them— one fought the other. Within moments, the creatures disappeared and the sea calmed. Tana continued to search for them, but they didn't return. All was quiet.

She didn't know how long she stood looking at the water when Malia approached.

"Is it gone?" she asked.

"Yeah," Tana said, still unable to take her eyes off the water.

"What was it?" Malia asked.

"A really ticked-off merman."

Malia mumbled under her breath and crossed herself. "I'm never going near this place again. Do you hear me?"

Tana nodded, keeping silent. Her mind churned even more than the water had moments before. She was sure the merman had intended to kill them, but it seemed another merman stopped it. Why did he protect them?

Malia must have called for help because only minutes later, a rescue vessel pulled up alongside. The adventure was over—for now.

Tana knew she had to be crazy, but she also knew she wouldn't be able to leave this alone. She had every intention of going back.

Chapter 6

Drakōn held the unconscious Dagonian in his arms. Blood seeped from his nose, drawing sharks within sight. He could leave the man and continue on his way. But floating helplessly in the sea would be a death sentence. And from what he had seen, the Dagonian was simply protecting his mate.

If Drakōn hadn't agreed to protect that woman, he'd have let the Dagonian kill her for what she did. Hades, what was she thinking, sneaking up on a Dagonian home? And then taking pictures? That was unforgivable!

The rage in the Dagonian's eyes told Drakōn he would have likely torn Tana apart. His stomach sickened at the thought—not that he hadn't carried out his share of human executions over the years—but the thought of Tana dying at his or anyone else's hands caused a fury in him that he didn't understand.

Why should he care what happened to a landwalker?

Drakōn shook his head. She wasn't just any landwalker; she was a goddess. Perhaps he had done this Dagonian a favor by knocking him unconscious.

"What happened to my husband?" a voice cried out

as a female came into view.

Drakōn was surprised at her boldness until he saw the anguish in her face. She obviously loved the Dagonian.

"Did that human do this to him?" she asked as she brushed her hands over her husband's body, searching for injuries.

Drakōn shook his head. "No. I did."

Her eyes flew open wide. "Wha…?" Her voice dropped off as she bowed her head. "Why?" she said softly. It looked like she finally remembered her place. Though this show of submission was to be expected, he didn't like it. Not after he'd spent so much time with Sara and Gretchen—women who were strong, intelligent, and showed no fear in voicing their minds.

"I saved his life." Drakōn spoke the truth, but he didn't enlighten her that he would have been the one to deal the deathblow. Being sworn to protect Tana, he would have killed to fulfill his duty. Instead, he had chosen to show mercy.

The woman nodded, accepting his answer. Drakōn had no doubt she thought the human would have killed her husband. Dagonians had an irrational fear of the land-walkers. If they really understood how physically helpless they were, there would probably be a lot more human deaths at the hands of his kind. Fear of the humans kept the humans safe—for the most part.

Drakōn passed her husband to her, and she swam, pulling him toward their home. Before she got to her door, he said, "You might want to think about moving

Raging

away from here. They may come back."

Her eyes widened in fear as she nodded. "Thank you for saving him."

Drakōn nodded in return. "He loves you," he said, surprising her with his words. Hades, he surprised himself. He'd never been one to express his feelings. Why he felt compelled to right now, he didn't know. "He fought with a ferociousness that is only seen from a man protecting the woman he loves."

Her lip trembled, and Drakōn could taste her tears as they leaked into the sea. She nodded and gave him a weak smile. "Thank you for telling me. Sometimes, I wonder…"

"He does love you."

She nodded with a light in her eyes that hadn't been there before.

Drakōn turned away and swam back to the boat, just in time to see it being pulled toward shore. He surfaced just enough for his eyes to take in the view of the boat. Tana stood at the stern. The wind whipped her hair around her head like orange flames against the blue sky. Her eyes searched the water as if trying to get a glimpse of the mysteries below the surface. Drakōn scowled at the overwhelming emotion showing clearly on her face—curiosity. If she weren't careful, it would mean the death of her. That was if a goddess *could* die.

Tana stiffened as her eyes widened. They seemed to pierce the waves and lock on him. Drakōn immediately slipped beneath the surface. She couldn't have seen him at that distance. Not with the churning sea surrounding him. No, there was no way. Still, doubt clouded his mind.

He needed to stick close to this woman. She had no idea the peril she had put herself in. But in order to do that, he needed help—someone who knew humans well, someone who knew how to navigate their world. Someone he could trust.

Gretchen stepped onto the dock with a baby sleeping in her arms and Kyros at her back. With her husband towering over her at more than six and a half feet and Gretchen barely reaching five foot, she seemed tiny. Despite her height, Drakōn learned very quickly not to underestimate her—especially since her father was back in her life. Thane, the demigod son of death, had taken to teaching his daughter a few things. And, from what Drakōn had heard, Gretchen was a natural. He didn't know exactly what that meant, but death powers had to be formidable.

Drakōn wasn't sure if he was supposed to sit or stand at her approach. To be safe, he decided to stand.

"Hello, Gretchen," he said with a tight smile.

"Hello, Drakōn." She smiled, wrapping her arm around his side and squeezing his waist. He stiffened in shock at her unexpected hug. He looked up at Kyros and noticed the scowl on his face. It looked like Drakōn wasn't the only one having difficulty with human greetings.

"So, you need my help," Gretchen said bluntly. Drakōn had to force himself not to deny her statement.

Raging

Dagonian males never liked to admit they needed help. It was a shameful thing—especially asking a woman. But the truth was, he really did need her.

"I'm sure Drakōn could handle the situation just fine, love," Kyros said diplomatically. "But the prophecy was given to you, after all. I'm sure he thought you might want to help."

Gretchen raised her eyebrows and turned to her husband, obviously surprised at his words. Understanding lit her face as she relaxed and returned her gaze to Drakōn. "Right. I'd really appreciate it if you would let me help, Drakōn. I hate being left out." She blinked her eyes innocently as she looked up to him.

"Well," Drakōn said, "since you put it that way, I'm sure I could find things for you to do to help me."

Gretchen looked as if she were holding back a smile. Drakōn sincerely hoped she didn't crack. This situation was difficult enough to deal with without her laughing in his face.

"Is there some place we can go to talk?" she asked.

Drakōn and Kyros both looked at the water at the end of the dock. Because he and Kyros were both Dagonians and Gretchen and her son, Donavan, were Mer, that seemed to be the ideal place to go.

"On land," Gretchen said. "I really don't want to wake Donavan."

Drakōn shook his head. "I've only been here a couple of days. I haven't really settled myself in with the humans yet."

Holly Kelly

"Okay," she said. "Why don't I start helping now? Let me go get us a couple of hotel rooms."

Minutes later, they stepped up to what looked like a palace overlooking the sea. Palm trees rose like canopies above the walkway leading to the building. Kyros leaned toward him and whispered, "You have to admit, humans are great architects."

"Yeah," Drakōn said, agreeing reluctantly.

"Make sure the rooms are on the ground floor, love," Kyros said to Gretchen.

"Good thinking," Drakōn said and gestured above. "I'd not want to be caught up too high if a battle were to ensue."

Kyros nodded. "Exactly."

Gretchen smiled. "A battle? Seriously?" She shook her head as she passed the baby to Kyros and then stepped up to the counter. The hotel clerk looked from Kyros to Drakōn and swallowed. Gretchen smiled and gained his attention—helping the human relax. She gave the man the specifics of what they wanted—two rooms with one king-sized bed in each room, one with a crib, and both rooms on the ground floor. The man agreed and told her the total amount they owed. Gretchen gave him a plastic rectangular card. When the man gave the card back, Drakōn wondered if he was refusing to rent them the rooms. He was about to ask Kyros about it when the man behind the desk gave her his own plastic cards and explained which rooms they were in.

As they stepped away, Drakōn leaned over to Kyros

Raging

and said, "How much do I need to pay? Do the humans take gold?"

"No. You *can* get human money in exchange for your gold, but there's a process to it. One positive thing, you'll find your gold will go a long way here—apparently, it's a rare element among the humans."

"I was pretty well off back home." Drakōn raised an eyebrow.

"Well, then you'll be filthy rich here."

"Hmm." Drakōn's mood lightened. Rich was good no matter what world you lived in. Living on land might not be so bad.

"I'll have Gretchen talk to Triton. He can get the exchange done much more quickly than we can. Until then," Kyros pulled out a folded leather pouch and removed a card much like the one Gretchen used, "you can use this to pay for anything you need."

"I appreciate it." Drakōn shifted, uncomfortable at having to use another man's money. "I'll pay you back."

"I know you will."

Drakōn nodded.

Gretchen stepped toward Kyros and said, "I'll take this little guy." Kyros gingerly transferred Donavan back into her arms, careful not jostle him awake. "Why don't you go and get our bags?" she said to Kyros. "I'll see if I can lay this little monster down without him waking up."

Kyros smiled and brushed a kiss across her lips. "Sure thing, baby."

Drakōn looked away at the show of affection. He

still wasn't used to the way humans interacted with loved ones—always hugging and kissing regardless of the fact that they were in public. Kyros didn't seem to mind. In fact, he initiated the show of affection just as often, if not more, than Gretchen did.

Drakōn wondered for a brief moment if Tana was as brazen about public shows of affection. The thought of her mouth on his and her arms around him—despite surrounding onlookers—filled his mind and brought a smile to his face. When he realized what he was doing, he clenched his jaw and shoved the errant thought away. Tana was an annoyance and a problem he was forced to deal with. Any thought of more was a waste. She might be beautiful with the body of a goddess—Hades, she *was* a goddess—but she was also rude, irresponsible, and a danger to the world. She was the last woman he should be having fantasies about.

"Do you have any changes of clothing?" Gretchen asked, pulling him from his thoughts as she led him toward the elevator.

"No," he answered. "Just what I'm wearing now."

"Hmm. We'll need to go shopping."

Drakōn cringed at the thought. His one experience shopping for human clothes was one he'd rather forget.

"What?" she asked, smiling. "You don't like to shop?"

"I'd rather be infested with rhizocephala."

"What in the heck is that?"

"Believe me, you don't want to know."

"Alright, you and Kyros are about the same size. How

Raging

about you two stay here and watch Donavan while I go shopping for you?"

Drakōn didn't know which prospect seemed more terrifying—going shopping at a human store or caring for a baby. "Um, can't you take the baby with you?"

"Uh, no," Gretchen answered. "That would be a nightmare. He'd do much better here where he can crawl around and play."

"Crawl?"

"It's what babies do before they learn to walk. They crawl on their hands and knees."

"Like an animal?"

"No," she said firmly. "Like a baby." Less than a minute after Kyros came back with their bags, Gretchen was out the door.

Drakōn looked on the floor where Gretchen had laid the baby on a blanket and said, "Tell me you've done this before."

"Yeah, lots of times," Kyros said, frowning. "I'd say it's as easy as spearing a jellyfish, but it's not."

Drakōn was afraid to even breathe. What if he woke the child up?

"He is cute, though. Don't you think?" Kyros asked.

Drakōn looked on in shock at his friend and then shook his head. "Yeah, sure. If you say so."

Chapter 7

The smell of burning flesh permeated the air. Hades smiled, satisfied. As the king of the Underworld, killing came easy to him—like breathing. He looked around at the carnage he'd created. Smoldering bodies heaped over the landscape, nearly unrecognizable—save for the black skulls and raised bones silhouetted in the smoky air. Charred flesh crunched under his feet as he walked.

Hunting down the escaped criminals had been simple, but he had yet to figure out why Skadi had freed them, or where under Olympus she was. Goddesses did not just disappear from existence. Even in the unlikely event that she had been killed, she would have shown up in the Underworld. Not only that, he was missing a prisoner—his daughter. He wasn't too concerned over finding her. Soon enough, she would lose control. When that happened, he would have no trouble tracking her down. His heart sank as he contemplated what he must do. Sooner or later, she would have to die—and there was nothing he could do about it.

"Hello, brother," a deep, familiar voice spoke from behind. "Looks like I missed the excitement."

Raging

"Yes, you did." He turned to face Zeus. "To what do I owe the pleasure?"

"Not one for catching up on the good old days, are you, Hades?"

"Ha!" Hades shook his head. "We never had any good old days."

"True. But we are brothers, and brothers should always be there for each other."

Hades wanted to scoff at Zeus' words. The king of the gods had only shown interest in his siblings when he needed something from them, but whenever he or Poseidon needed a favor from their king, their pleas—more often than not—landed on deaf ears. Still, Hades kept his mouth shut. Calling Zeus out on his faults was never a wise thing to do.

"Ares is missing," Zeus said. "He cannot be found on earth or on Olympus. There is only one other place he could be."

Hades frowned at the assumption. Zeus thought his son was dead.

"I need you to return him to me," Zeus said.

"I can assure you, he's not in the Underworld. I would have been notified immediately."

Electricity crackled as the wind began to swirl the ash around them. "Why do you lie?" Zeus' voice growled with power. Hades stepped back at the sudden anger.

"Why would I?" He halted his retreat, not wanting his brother to see his fear.

"You've always been jealous of my power. Perhaps

this is a way for you to strike a blow at me."

"I am perfectly content with what I have, and I haven't seen your son in decades. I have more important concerns."

"Not anymore. My son is your greatest concern. You will bring back Ares to me or face destruction." Light blinded Hades' eyes as a powerful bolt struck him full in the chest. Hades barely had time to brace himself against it, clenching his teeth at the energy that exploded against him. As he leaned into the bolt, the energy pushed him back as his feet carved wedges through the burnt bodies and rocky ground. As stunned as he was from the attack, he was even more stunned at the power behind it. Zeus never used to be this powerful. Somehow, his powers were gaining strength. Hades had no chance of meeting this attack with equal force—as he once would have.

Thankfully, Zeus ceased his assault. Hades dropped to his knees, gasping.

Zeus stepped forward to stand above him. He said, "You will bring me my son. Or I will wreak destruction against you and all you love. And I won't just destroy you—I'll annihilate you so that there will be nothing left to send to Tartarus. Do you understand?"

Hades looked into his brother's face, and for a brief moment, he saw the impossible—the power of many gods and goddesses swirled in his eyes.

Hades looked down to hide his surprise. "Yes, I understand."

"Good. Then we have an understanding," Zeus said

Raging

and disappeared.

Hades stumbled to his feet and looked toward the thunderclouds above. He now had a new mission—find out what secrets his brother hid, and hopefully learn how to stop him before Zeus made good on his threat.

CHAPTER 8

Drakōn stepped through the gate at the local pool with a scowl on his face. He was about to do the most humiliating thing he'd ever done in his life. He would rather be skinned alive and have his body strung up to feed the sharks than take swimming lessons from a woman. The only consolation in this was that his sacrifice would save the world.

A pretty, blonde girl who looked to be about sixteen glanced his way at his approach. She sized him up from top to bottom, smiling as her eyes lingered on his chest and abs. He narrowed his eyes, furious. Where under Olympus was this child's father?

"Hello," she said sweetly.

"Can you tell Tana I'm here?"

"Tana?" she said, frowning. "Oh no, she called and said she wasn't going to be in today."

"What?" he bellowed. "I made arrangements to meet her at this exact time. Where is she?"

"Um…" She backed away, apparently unnerved. "I can't tell you."

"What is her cell number? I need to speak to her now," he said with fury ringing in his voice.

Raging

"Um, I can't tell you that either."

He took an intimidating step toward her and growled, "You will tell me, or I will..." His voice trailed off as he thought of what he'd be willing to do. Actually, he could do nothing to these humans. Still, he narrowed his eyes further and glared daggers into the girl's eyes.

She began to tremble as her eyes darted around, probably looking for someone to rescue her from his intimidating stare. "Listen, I...I'll tell you where she is, but don't tell anyone I did. Tana would fire me for sure."

He nodded, and she proceeded to give him everything he asked. Minutes later, he stood at the dock near Tana's boat. She rushed around the deck.

"Listen, I don't care what your personal problems are," she shouted to someone below deck. "I just need my boat fixed, and I need it done yesterday." Her phone rang and she put it to her ear. "Yes. I need to know what kind of protection I can get for a manned submersible. No. Not lethal. I—" She hesitated, listening to whoever was on the other side of the phone call. Drakōn didn't like the sound of this conversation. The whole chaotic situation gave him a sour stomach.

"Tana," he shouted as he stepped onto the deck. "What under Olympus are you doing?"

Her eyes snapped up and widened in surprise. "I..." she began. "What? You're Drake, right?"

"Drakōn."

"Whatever. What are you doing on my boat? Who told you where to find me?"

"You missed our appointment."

"Listen, Drake, I don't know what kind of people you are used to dealing with, but I don't like your tone. And you showing up here is completely unacceptable! Now you just get your sorry butt off my boat before I call the police and have you arrested."

"You're the one who broke her word, but I would be the one arrested? What kind of messed-up society is this?"

"Wait a minute! I didn't break my word. I left Vanessa there to give you your lesson."

"Our agreement was for you to teach me. You said that you weren't cheap, and I agreed to your fee. Now if you are not a woman of your word, then I will accept that. But do not accuse *me* of any wrongdoing." His voice rose, as did his anger.

She swallowed and shifted her stance. Taking a deep breath, she spoke. "Listen, I'm sorry. You showing up here just caught me off guard. I didn't mean to accuse you of anything. But I am not going to be able to teach you. I have a lot going on right now. I really don't have time."

Drakōn frowned and took a quick glance at the supplies on deck. She had something big planned, and he feared it had to do with the Dagonians she had sighted. In fact, he was sure of it.

There was shouting coming from her phone. "Excuse me for a minute," she said and raised it to her ear once again. "What? I know. But…I can't wait two weeks. I

Raging

need it now!" She frowned, clearly disappointed. "No, I know. Okay, but can you give me your word it will be here in two weeks? Alright. I'll be waiting." She lowered her phone and swore under her breath. "Well, Drake. It looks like my schedule just cleared up."

"Do we still have time for a lesson today?" He didn't want her backing out again. He had a job to do, and the sooner it was underway, the better. Keeping this woman safe would be a lot easier if he didn't have to slink around in the shadows to watch her.

"Yeah, sure." She turned toward the boat. "Rodney!"

The man responded with a grunt from below deck.

"I'm taking off. Let me know when you have the engine fixed."

Another grunt.

She turned back to Drakōn. "I'll meet you at the pool in fifteen minutes."

He nodded, turned his back, and returned to his car.

Standing at the pool's edge, Drakōn held onto the railing of the steps.

"It's alright," Tana said in a soothing voice as she stood below him in waist-deep water. "You don't need to rush it."

"I'm not afraid," he said as he stood, unwilling to move. He shouldn't be afraid. Sara said he'd be able to remain human in the sea, and this was not seawater. Even without god powers, he'd remain human in this pool. But still, he'd never been in the water with legs before. He didn't want to make a fool of himself.

"It's alright to be afraid. Many people have a fear of water. Just don't let it stop you."

A fear of water? Drakōn had never heard anything so ludicrous in his entire life. He feared water like a human feared air. He wanted to shout at her that he was not afraid. But instead, he decided it would be best to show her.

The first step into the pool brought immediate comfort as he could feel the power he drew from the water. Why had he hesitated? There was nothing to fear here.

Instead of taking the last few steps down, Drakōn dove in. He felt elated being in the water once again. Breathing air, walking on land, it was all so limiting. Without thinking, he opened his mouth to take in a refreshing breath and felt an immediate and excruciating burn in his nose and painful spasm in his lungs. He'd breathed seawater, brackish water, even fresh water, but nothing compared to what he experienced at this moment. Thrashing around, he fought his way to the surface.

Arms came around him and pulled him up so that his face broke the surface. He coughed and sputtered as he attempted to clear his windpipe of the foul liquid.

"Of all the idiotic… I can't believe you…" He could hear parts of Tana's rant between his coughs.

"Hades," he shouted when he finally found his voice. "What do you humans put in your water? Acid?"

Raging

"Humans?" she said, her voice rising in confusion.

He stilled, and then another cough shook his chest. Hades, he spoke carelessly. "I meant it was inhuman what you put in your water."

"Oh," she said and relaxed, apparently relieved. "It's called chlorine, and it kills germs and prevents disease. And you're *not* supposed to breathe it in." She stared him down with her hand propped on her hip.

"Hmph," he answered.

She shook her head as she took him by the arm and pulled him toward the side of the pool. "For a second there, I thought you'd lied about not being able to swim. But now I know better. You obviously have no idea what you're doing."

She frowned as she sized him up. "So, first lesson—how to put your face in the water without drowning."

He didn't make the same mistake twice. He held his breath from then on. Swimming in this pool was much more tolerable if he kept all orifices free from the chlorinated fluid.

After teaching him to submerge, Tana taught an extremely ineffective way for him to propel himself through the water—by kicking his human legs. Getting around the pool was excruciatingly slow. Arms were just not made to be the major source of propulsion, but his legs were even worse. He felt awkward, clumsy, and like a total idiot. Still, Tana praised him, calling him a natural. A natural swimmer? He certainly hoped so.

Soon enough, she allowed him to swim alone. Tana

Holly Kelly

swam alongside him as he used a technique called the breaststroke. He decided it was easier to watch her with his head out of the water, though, so he didn't bother submerging it like she'd showed him. Besides, he couldn't see a thing with his eyes closed, but he wasn't about to subject his eyes to the same burn his nose and chest had gone through.

"Hmm," Tana said as she stroked alongside him. "Now you have me confused again. This can't possibly be your first swimming lesson."

"I have a lot of excellent swimmers in my family," he replied.

"So what made you afraid of the water?"

He raised his eyebrow. How under Olympus was he to answer that question? Instead, he asked her a question. "Why are most people afraid of the water?"

"So you had a bad experience?"

"Yeah." *Bad, good, and everything in between.* "How long ago did you learn to swim?" he asked her.

"My mom taught me," she said. "She and my dad owned this swimming pool and a diving company. That is until they passed away."

"They died together?"

"You're really blunt, aren't you?" They reached the edge of the pool, and instead of turning around, she held on and floated to a stop.

"I'm sorry if my question offended you," he said. He wondered about her memories. He knew full well that her real father and mother never owned a pool. Most likely, the memories she had were those of another.

She shook her head. "No, it's alright. They died in a car crash a few months ago. I left grad school to come back and run things. It was a good choice. I'm happy doing it."

Drakōn bet that if he did some digging, he'd find Zeus had a hand in her pseudo parent's deaths. But that would be pointless to find out. He was only here to protect her, not play detective.

Tana pushed up on the side of the pool and lifted her body out of the water. He tried not to stare, but he found everything about her beautiful, especially the way she moved—with grace and confidence. He followed her lead, pushed himself up, and stepped onto the hot pavement.

She sighed. "Okay, your first lesson went amazingly well. I don't know that you need a second lesson."

"Actually," Drakōn said. "I was hoping to learn to scuba dive. I heard you're the one to learn from."

She smiled and shook her head. "From your first swimming lesson to scuba lessons? Even you're not that good."

"I beg to differ." He smiled and took a step toward her.

Tana smirked, lifted a hand, and pressed it against his chest. The moment she touched him, her smile disappeared as she jerked her hand away and looked down. A warm glow brightened her face. *Was she blushing?* Drakōn had to fight back a smile. Hades, but she was appealing, and her touch—though brief—set his blood on fire. From her expression, he knew she liked touching him. She just didn't *want* to like it. He felt a smug satisfaction in that revelation.

She blinked and raised her eyes to his face. "Okay, scuba lessons. Um… tomorrow," she said, tripping over her words. Gathering her damp hair, she pulled it over her shoulder. Then she nodded as if everything was settled and turned to walk away.

"Tana," Drakōn said.

She turned around. "What?"

"When and where?"

"When and where, what?"

He couldn't help but chuckle. "What time will you teach me, and where do you want to meet?"

"Oh, um, early. How about six o'clock again. Tomorrow morning, right here at the pool."

"We're going to scuba dive in the pool?"

She nodded. "It's the best place to start."

He flashed a crooked smile at her. "I'll see you tomorrow then."

"Okay," she stammered as she turned and bumped into a garbage can.

Drakōn shook his head. She went from an ornery barracuda—snapping and baring teeth—to timid and awkward. She may be a land-walker, but gods, he was beginning to like her. He scowled at that realization.

Chapter 9

Malia shook her head as Tana cut through the admittance line to the pool and stepped behind the counter. "I can't believe it," Malia said. She followed Tana into her office and shut the door.

"What?" Tana asked as she slumped into a chair.

Malia sat on the edge of her desk. "I saw you outside. I can't believe he's your type. Seriously? A tall, dark, bad boy with enough muscles to give Chris Hemsworth an inferiority complex?"

"I don't know what you're talking about." Tana shrugged and pulled out yesterday's receipts.

"Right. You are totally attracted to him! Now it makes sense."

"What makes sense?"

"Why you never date. You don't come across a man that hot very often. It looks like your bar is set past the stratosphere."

"He's just a customer."

"Yeah, and the Atlantic Ocean is just a puddle. A word to the wise—I've dated men like him. It rarely turns out well."

"We're not dating."

"Not yet. But I saw the way he looked at you. He's just as hot for you as you are for him."

Tana dropped a file folder and papers fluttered, spreading out across the floor. "You think so?" She looked into her friend's frowning face.

Malia slipped off the desk, dropped to her knees, and started scooping the papers up. "I know so. So, does he know you're still a virgin?"

"Of course he does. That's the first thing I tell all my students."

"Smart mouth," Malia said, holding back a smile. "A man like that can eat you up and still have room for dessert."

"I'll be careful."

"It's not *your* behavior I'm worried about."

"Listen, I know I haven't had much experience with men, but I'm a big girl. I can take care of myself."

Malia sighed. "Yeah. I know. By the way, what's the rush to get Old Faithful fixed?"

"I've got dives to make, and customers I'm losing."

"You're not thinking about going back to take more pictures of those creatures, are you?"

"No," she answered. Technically, she wasn't lying. She wasn't *thinking* about doing it; she'd already made up her mind. She absolutely was going back.

"Good. That place is dangerous with a capital D."

"Yeah, I know. I was foolish to go diving there without any protection."

Raging

"Even with protection, it's suicide. I got a peek at that thing climbing onto the deck. It was a total monster. I thought for sure we were both dead."

"Yeah, good thing something scared it off." Tana still wondered what that thing was. It was one big reason she had to go back. Something protected her. And she just had to find out what it was.

Malia glanced up at the clock. "I'd better get out there. I've got to get Laurence for his break."

"I'll see you in a few. Oh, and can you close up tonight? I've got some errands to run."

"Sure thing, boss."

Tana smiled. Malia knew she hated being called that—which was probably why she persisted in doing it. "Thanks, peon," Tana answered.

"A peon with a bachelor's degree."

"In philosophy." Tana laughed.

"Yeah, I use my degree to philosophize my stupidity," she said as she stepped out the door.

Tana chuckled as she shook her head. She really didn't know what she'd do without Malia. Tana locked the door, opened her laptop, and pulled up her website. She had photos to post.

Reaching into her bag, she searched for her camera. She found her cell phone, her sunglasses, the paperback novel she'd been reading, junk mail, but…no camera! Turning her purse upside down, she dumped the contents onto her desk. "No, no, you have to be here," she said as she frantically searched.

Holly Kelly

How could she have lost it? Seriously, she was sure she had put it in her purse. Where in the world did it go? Stuffing everything back in her bag, she retraced her steps in her mind. She had taken it out at home and looked at the images again, and then she was sure she put it back in her bag. Yes! She absolutely did. She had every intention of posting the pictures today at work and didn't want to forget her camera.

She had it at the house, she had it on her boat, and then she brought it here into the office. Only she and Malia knew what was on that camera—and Malia certainly hadn't taken it. Could it have been the mechanic? Perhaps. She would have to have a talk with the man and see if he had sticky fingers. If so, she'd personally break each digit.

"You stole her camera?" Gretchen sat cross-legged on the hotel bed and examined the expensive-looking piece of equipment. Kyros sat against her back with his arms wrapped around her, looking over her shoulder.

"That part was easy," Drakōn answered as he paced the floor. "What I can't figure out is how to see the images she took on it."

"Oh, no," Gretchen said as she dropped the camera on the bed and rushed over to the baby sitting on the carpet. She picked him up. "Donavan, we don't eat stuff off the floor." She shoved her finger in the child's mouth and pulled out an unrecognizable black lump.

Drakōn whispered to Kyros, "Is there something

Raging

wrong with that child?"

Kyros shook his head and whispered back, "She said that's normal behavior, but I'm not so sure."

Gretchen kissed the baby and sat him down on the blanket she'd spread across the floor. The child had a dozen colorful toys to play with, but he insisted on crawling around the room and putting everything he could find into his mouth. Gretchen turned to Kyros. "Can you please call the desk and tell them they need to actually vacuum this floor when they come to clean?" She turned her attention back to Drakōn. "Okay, so where were we? Oh, right, you want to see the pictures on the camera." She picked it up, pressed a few random buttons, and the screen lit up. A few swipes and an image came into view.

"Hmm," Gretchen said. "I think she caught something here. Looks like it could be a mermaid."

"No," Kyros said. "That's a Dagonian, sweetheart."

"It's not very clear," Drakōn said, sighing in relief. "In fact, you can barely make it out. No one would believe it if she claimed it was anything supernatural."

Gretchen scrolled through images that were more ambiguous and then froze at an image that came up on the screen.

"Great gods of Olympus," Kyros said.

"She saw this." Gretchen gaped at the image in front of her.

"If she were human…" Kyros said.

"Yeah," Drakōn said. "We'd have to kill her." Drakōn's expression darkened. "Her friend, Malia, saw this too."

"What? You are not killing anyone," Gretchen said.

"Tana is safe, but Malia…" Drakōn's voice trailed off.

"No," Gretchen shouted. "No, no, no! You are not doing anything to that innocent woman."

"Sweetheart, you don't understand," Kyros began.

"Oh, I understand perfectly." Gretchen jumped to her feet and pointed first at her husband, and then at Drakōn. "You will not go near that woman."

"Listen, Gretchen," Drakōn said. "I don't relish the thought of killing her. But keeping ourselves hidden from the humans is of paramount importance. It's the only thing that keeps us safe from them. I will not have innocent Dagonian blood on my hands. If the humans knew we existed, our whole society could be in danger—men, women, and children could perish. If she talks—?"

"She won't," Gretchen interrupted. "I'll take care of it."

"What can you do?" Drakōn asked.

"A mermaid has ways of influencing the mind, or have you forgotten?" She propped her hand on her hip.

"No, I haven't," Drakōn said, remembering all too clearly what he'd done under the influence of a siren's song—the lives he had taken. It still weighed heavily on his conscience.

"By this evening, Tana's friend will remember nothing. I promise."

"If you fail," Drakōn said. "I'll have no choice but to act."

"I won't fail."

CHAPTER 10

Tana sank into her chair and dropped her head into her hands. Weariness engulfed her. She'd searched everywhere—at the wharf, in her house, in her car, in her boat, here at the pool. The camera was gone.

"Tana?" A small voice came from the doorway.

Tana raised her head. Vanessa stood, shifting her weight from one foot to the other as she twirled a lock of hair around her finger. "I'm sorry to interrupt, but we were wondering if we could leave for the day."

Tana looked up at the clock. "Malia hasn't sent you home yet?"

"No, I haven't seen her since closing time."

"Is everything locked down for the night?" Tana pushed away from her desk and stood.

"Yeah, we finished ten minutes ago."

Tana pursed her lips and sighed. "Okay, tell everyone to go home." Worry tightened her chest. It wasn't like Malia to shirk her duties.

Vanessa turned to leave. "Wait," Tana said. "Make sure you girls are walked out by the guys."

Vanessa turned back and frowned. "Isn't that a bit

sexist?"

"Yeah," Tana answered. "Do it anyway."

Vanessa shrugged. "Sure thing."

As soon as the girl left, Tana unlocked a desk drawer, pulled out her pistol, and stuffed it into the waistband of her shorts—against the small of her back.

She really wished she could just text Malia. But she'd been working, dressed in her swimsuit—with no good place to keep a phone.

When she stepped out into the pool area, everything looked quiet. Malia was nowhere in sight. There weren't too many places to hide. In fact, the only place she could be—if she were still here—would be in or around the utility shed.

A breeze chilled her, raising goose bumps over her body. As she stepped closer, she heard something—a voice. It was too faint to make out the words, but her heart pounded in response as she paused. Images swirled in her head as her knees slammed against the pavement and her hands slapped the ground to stop her fall.

Images raced through her mind—raging fire, a wall of ice, a handsome farm boy leaning against an oak tree. With these images came emotions just as jumbled and confusing—an anger so hot Tana wanted nothing more than to bury her fist into someone's chest and crush their beating heart. Despair soon followed—despair so deep that she felt as if she would drown in it. Yet, woven into these horrifying emotions, there were flashes of love, laughter, happiness…

Raging

Looking up, she could see the pool with its glassy surface beckoning her. She had to get to the water.

The water was safe.

As she inched her way to the edge, her desperation grew. She didn't know why, but she was afraid that if she didn't reach the water in time, she would spontaneously combust. Finally, she reached the edge. Without a moment of hesitation, she plunged into the pool.

The cool water enveloped her, but the images raged on more powerful than before. The song seemed to increase in volume beneath the surface.

Curling up into a ball, she sank to the bottom of the pool while fire continued to rage in her mind. She cried in agony for the images to stop.

And then they did, when the song ceased.

Tana opened her eyes. The water glowed as if fire lit it from above. Fear once again struck her. Her lungs began to burn as she refused to surface. She simply couldn't. Whatever fire raged above her, it was a thousand times more terrifying than her fear of drowning, a thousand times more painful than the burn in her chest.

A shadowed silhouette flashed across the water's surface a moment before it splashed into the pool. A large shape swam toward her. As it got closer, she could see its face—Drake. He wrapped his arm around her waist and pulled her up.

No! She couldn't go there. Fire raged above.

She fought him—striking him, kicking him, and trying with everything she had to get away from him and back to the bottom of the pool. As she screamed out in terror, bubbles burst from her mouth and then she took a breath. Mind-blowing panic seized her as water filled her lungs. Seconds later, blackness flooded her vision.

"Tana!" She heard Drake's voice clearly as water poured from her mouth. "Tana, please, come back to me."

"What's happening?" another panicked voice, Malia's voice, asked. "Tana, oh please no!"

"Do we need to do CPR?" Another deep voice spoke.

"No," Drake answered. "She's breathing now and her heart is beating fine. She just needs to wake up."

"Tana." At the sound of that soft, hesitant voice, fear once again rose. Her eyes flew open as she searched for the face that belonged with that terrible voice. There were four people surrounding her—Drake, another large man, Malia, and a beautiful young woman. She sneered at the stunning woman. "Get away from me." She scrambled to her feet—her legs giving way before she could stand. Drake caught her before she could fall. She raised her hand and pointed to the woman's stunned face. "Keep her away from me!"

Malia narrowed her eyes and grabbed the menacing woman by the arm. "You. You and I need to talk."

Drake's arms came around her. "It's okay, Tana. You're safe now."

She buried her face in his chest and sobbed. "Where's the fire?"

"Fire?" Drakōn said.

Raging

She gripped his back, driving her fingernails into his skin. "I saw it. The sky was orange, lit with fire." Her whole body trembled as she clung to him.

"There's no fire, Tana. It's the sunset. It's brilliant tonight. That's the only thing coloring the sky—nothing else."

"Are you sure?"

"Yes." He lifted her chin and she looked up. Water droplets trailed down over his face, and his eyes were filled with concern. His strong arms surrounded her, and she finally felt relief. This man was safe. She didn't know how she knew; she just knew that as long as he was with her, she would be okay.

She shook her head, coughing. No. She couldn't possibly know that. The near drowning must have soaked her brain. She pressed her hands against his chest and pushed herself away from him. "I'm sorry. You probably think I'm crazy."

"Not at all."

She searched his face to find any sign that he was attempting to pacify her. He seemed completely sincere.

"Now you're not going to develop a fear of water, are you?" he asked with a smirk.

"A fear of—no, I can assure you, I'm not." *There are much worse things to fear.* She didn't know where that errant thought came from, but she had every confidence in its truth. "Wait a minute!" she said. "You saved me?"

He nodded. "Yes."

"But…" she coughed, "you just had your first

swimming lesson."

"Yeah, and what better incentive to practice what I've learned than a beautiful woman needing to be rescued?"

Tana swallowed and then sighed. "Hmm." There was more to Drake than what showed on the surface.

"Listen, I just…" She pushed away from his chest. "I just want to go home."

"Are you sure you should be alone?" he asked.

She shook her head and barked a laugh. "Are you volunteering?"

He stood above her; concern etched his brow. It didn't look like he was coming on to her. Did she even want him to?

Probably.

"You had a near drowning. You probably still have water in your lungs. You shouldn't be alone for the next twenty-four hours."

"Are you trying to tell me my job, hot shot? Oh, that reminds me." She reached around and felt for her gun at her back. "It's gone."

"What's gone?"

"My gun."

"What do you need a gun for?"

She shrugged, coughing once more. She didn't want to let him know she'd been spooked.

"Tana." He frowned down at her.

"I was just being careful. It wasn't like Malia to go missing at closing time." Tana looked toward her office. Light spilled out the door. "Speaking of, I have to find out

Raging

who that woman is and what she's doing here."

Tana stopped in the doorway. Drake bumped into her back and clutched her shoulders to steady her.

Malia sat alone at her desk, staring at the wall.

"Malia?"

At hearing her name, she seemed to snap out of a trance. "Oh, hey Tana."

"Where's that woman?"

"Woman?" She looked confused for a moment. "Oh, she's gone." She waved her hand dismissively toward the door.

"She is?" Tana asked. "Well, who was she?"

"Oh, uh. Nobody. She just heard the commotion and came to check things out. I sent her away."

"You're serious?"

"Oh, did you want to talk to her?"

She opened her mouth to answer yes, but shut it before the words were out. If she were being honest with herself, the last thing she wanted to do was face that woman. Something just wasn't right about her. "No, it's okay." Tana coughed. Her throat burned as air breezed out of her lungs. She tasted chlorine in her mouth. "Listen, I'm going on home. Can you finish locking up?"

"Sure, no problem," Malia answered as she rose. "See you tomorrow."

Tana hesitated a moment before answering. "Okay, I'll see you then."

Thoughts churned, muddled in Tana's mind. Something was off with Malia. She'd nearly drowned and her best friend acted like this was just another day. Why didn't she fuss over her, offer to take her to the hospital, insist on—her coughing interrupted her thoughts.

"Come on, Tana," Drake said. "I'll take you home."

Tana shook her head. "I can get home by myself."

"You really shouldn't be alone."

"So you want to come home with me?"

Drake raised an eyebrow and said, "Do you want me to ask Malia?"

Tana shook her head. "No, that's okay." She stopped and spun around. "I..." she began when another cough seized her.

"You're not okay, Tana."

Once the coughing stopped, she said, "I don't want to go to the hospital."

"Then you need someone with you."

She frowned, once again fighting the urge to cough. She cleared her throat. "Do you promise me you won't try anything?"

He gave her a blank look. "I don't understand."

"You need me to spell it out for you?" *Is this guy for real?*

"You lost me again," he said.

"Okay, let me simplify things for you."

"That I understood. " His eyes narrowed. "You're insulting me."

"I..." She dropped her shoulders, sighed, and coughed softly. "I'm sorry. I know you're trying to help. I didn't mean to imply you're unintelligent. I've just had a

Raging

really bad day, and I'm afraid I'm a bit irritable."

He took a step toward her as his glare relaxed. "That's understandable. I truly mean you no harm. I'm just…worried about you."

"That makes one," she said as she thought of Malia's complete lack of concern. She shook her head. "I'm sorry. Okay, um, I have a couch. You're welcome to sleep there."

He pressed his brows together. "And you'll be sleeping in another room?"

She frowned at him. "Yes."

"How am I supposed to watch you when we are in separate rooms? Perhaps I *should* take you to the hospital."

She huffed and looked back toward the main gate of the pool. She did nearly drown, didn't she? Perhaps she should go get checked out. But seriously, she really didn't want to. "Okay, you can sleep on the floor in my room, but if you try anything—touch me, grope me, or anything of the sort, I'll castrate you—do you understand me?

He once again looked confused, but still he answered, "Yes. Your virtue is safe with me."

"Virtue, huh?" Her gaze brushed over his body, waking butterflies in her stomach. Finally, she looked him in the eye. "Yeah, it had better be."

Chapter 11

Tana swung on a rope swing, dangling down from a high limb of an old willow tree. As she peered through the branches, she could see her childhood home. She had many love-and-laughter filled memories there. Her parents were older when they had her, but their advanced age didn't slow them down much.

"Hey Tana!" a voice called from around the side of the house.

"I'm back here," she responded, her voice high and sweet—a child's voice.

A young girl stepped from around the side of the house and into the backyard. "So, did you ask?"

"Ask?" Tana said, confused.

"Yeah, ask if we can go treasure hunting."

"Oh, I completely forgot," she said as she jumped off the swing. "I'll go ask my mom." Her feet pounded through the grass as she ran to the house.

As she scrambled into the quaint kitchen, she skidded to a stop. Rage burned in her blood at the sight in front of her. A man stood before her—handsome, dark, and smelling of campfire.

"You." Her voice, though still that of a child, took on a sinister tone as she glared at him.

"Hello, my dear," he answered with a smile. "Is there something you needed?"

Raging

Her whole body shook, enraged. She didn't know where they'd met or how she knew this man, but she hated him with every fiber of her being. The man glanced down at the table. Her eyes followed his and there, prominently against the dark oak, lay a carving knife. Her eyes shot back to his face. He smirked as if daring her to use the knife against him.

Snarling, she leapt forward and snatched it with her tiny hand. Without a thought, she raced to the man, raised the knife, and hacked—screaming as she sank the blade into his stomach. A spray of blood misted over her face. She closed her eyes and shrieked as she continued her assault. The knife was clenched in her blood-slick hand as she thrust the blade again and again into the man's body.

"Tana!" a deep voice shouted. "Stop!"

Tana froze.

Letting go of the knife, she wiped the blood from her eyes. Finally able to open them, she gasped at the sight before her—Drake stood with the knife protruding from his shredded chest. He looked at her in shock and disbelief. "Why?" he said in a raspy voice. His eyes rolled back white as he slumped, lifeless, in a pool of blood.

"Drake?" she said as she stood, her legs trembling beneath her as tears burned in her eyes. "Drake...oh..."

"Wake up, Tana," he snapped, his eyes suddenly open.

She gaped at him, unable to believe that he could still be alive.

Her eyes flew open as she awoke. When she blinked at the sudden darkness, tears flowed as her breath hitched. Something extremely heavy pressed her hard against the ground, so hard it made it difficult to take in a breath, and her arms were pinned above her head.

"Tana." Drake's voice was heavy with concern.

"Gods, Tana. You're awake." Relief accompanied him, relaxing his grip. "You're not going to attack me again, are you, sweetheart?"

"Attack you?" she asked as the image from her dream burned into her mind. Could she have really attacked Drake?

He sighed. "Yeah, you must have been sleepwalking."

"Sleepwalking?" Tana scrambled to her feet.

"Um, yeah."

"I didn't hurt you, did I?"

"Just a few…" he grunted, "scratches."

She swore as she reached out, making her way to the wall to feel for the light switch. As soon as she found the nub, she switched it on. She squinted at the light, but the image before her was clear. Drake sat holding a bloody knife in his hand. No. Not a knife. Her letter opener. Blood soaked his torn shirt.

Tana's stomach threatened to heave just before someone once again turned off the light.

Tana fell in a dead faint. If Drakōn hadn't just pulled a small dagger from his chest, he might have made it to her in time to keep her from hitting the floor. At least the floor was soft, plush carpet. Looking at the small knife, he debated what to do with it. Obviously, Tana hadn't known what she was doing. She was lucky to be alive. Drakōn didn't normally let people stab him without fatal repercussions. But even in the midst of her homicidal rage, he knew she didn't realize what she was doing. She

Raging

was caught up in a night terror.

Tearing off his bloodied shirt, he looked at the wounds he sustained. Most were superficial, but one went deep between a rib, nicking his lung and bringing sharp pains as he breathed. As a god, he should be able to heal himself.

No time like the present to find out.

Closing his eyes, he willed his torn flesh to knit back together. He could feel power surface from within and directed it to his wounds. He was rewarded with flashes of heat over each injury as they healed. He growled as the pain heightened and then faded. Opening his eyes, he looked down. His skin looked completely unblemished—no blood, no injury. Not even the hint of a scar remained.

Tana moaned as she began to move. She'd wake soon. Quickly, he stuffed his bloodied shirt and the knife under her bed. He'd have to discard them in a more proper manner later. As soon as the bloodied items were out of sight, he pulled Tana into his arms, lay back on his makeshift bed, and covered them both with his blanket.

Hades. He forgot to turn off the light.

Glaring at the switch, he willed it to flip. And it did, right before Tana sat up.

"Drake!" She screamed and turned onto her knees. Her hands reached out, but were hesitant to touch his bare skin. "Are you…are you okay?"

Drakōn blinked. "Huh? What's wrong, Tana?" He put his acting skills into play, but then, the way she couldn't seem to focus on him, he wondered how much she could actually see. A sea-god's night vision was very sharp, but it looked like hers wasn't.

"I didn't...I didn't hurt you, did I?" Her voice hitched as she asked the question. She was clearly worried about him.

"*You* hurt *me?*" he huffed. "I don't think so."

"I...I could have sworn."

He pulled her down by his side. "It was just a dream," he assured her. "Now, come on. It's late. Go back to sleep."

He could feel her tremble as she nodded. After a few minutes, she began to relax, so Drakōn did too. And then she stiffened.

"What am I doing on the floor with you?" She sat up.

Drakōn mirrored her movement.

"How did I get down here?" she asked.

"Perhaps you were sleepwalking?"

He knew the moment he said it, it was the wrong thing to say. Shock and remembrance caused her to gasp. "Sleepwalking? Are you sure——?"

"Tana," he interrupted. "As long as you're unwilling to go back to sleep..." He paused to gain her attention.

She turned and opened her mouth to speak. Before she could get out a word, he pulled her close and covered her mouth with his. The woman amazed him with her reaction. She simultaneously fell apart and came alive in his arms. Her body went all soft and compliant as her hands weaved in his hair. She lay back and wrapped her leg around his hip. He'd never kissed a human before, and never dreamed he'd actually enjoy it, but Hades, she

Raging

caused him to burn for her.

Her hand wandered over his chest as her mouth tore from his to nibble down his neck, sucking along the way. "Tana, sweetheart. You keep this up, and I'm not going to be able to stop."

She stilled at his words. "Really?"

Her naivety shocked him. It wasn't unusual for an unattached Dagonian female to be so naive, but for a human woman in her twenties…it was extremely unusual. Or so he'd heard. "Well, I *could* stop, but it would be extremely difficult, not to mention painful."

Her brows scrunched together as she frowned. And then she did something completely unexpected. She slapped him.

Drakōn was more shocked than hurt. "What was that for?"

"I warned you not to touch me."

Completely dumbfounded, it took him a moment to collect his thoughts. "If I'm not mistaken, you kissed me back."

"That doesn't count, I was still half asleep."

"Looked to me like you were wide awake."

"Hmm. Well, just don't do it again." She looked over to the bed and then back to him. Was she really considering sleeping on the floor with him after she slapped him? This woman was so confusing.

"Go on back to bed."

"Fine." She huffed as she stood up and crawled under her covers, tossing and turning dramatically before settling down. Fifteen minutes later, her breathing was still shallow. She was obviously awake. A light breeze from the window stirred the air in the room and a salty scent washed over Drakōn's face—tears. Hades. Tana was crying.

Throwing the blanket off him, he sat up, contemplating what to do. He hadn't had much experience with emotional females, but he felt compelled to do something. But then, he didn't want to get slapped again.

"Come near me, and I'll slap you again," she said, echoing his thoughts.

Drakōn threw himself back down on his makeshift bed and attempted to get some sleep.

Chapter 12

Zeus stepped through the gilded archway leading into a wide chamber. The low hum of voices filled the air. Hundreds of television screens played news from all around the world—death, destruction, scandals…every depravity played out in HDTV.

"Husband!" Hera stood up from the sofa. A mess of pillows and blankets covered the cushions and spilled onto the floor. The goddess stumbled toward him, her matted hair framing a gaunt face with wild, bloodshot eyes.

Perhaps he'd been a bit too neglectful.

Patting her hair down, she said, "Why didn't you tell me you were coming? I would have prepared."

Zeus scrunched up his nose at the odor coming off her. "I'm not staying long. I just wanted to ask if you had seen Ares lately?"

Confusion crossed Hera's face. "Ares?"

"Yes, your second-born son, the one with brown hair and blue eyes. God of war. My second in command… Any of this ring a bell?"

Hera swallowed as her eyes dropped. "Of course, I

know who my own son is. I was just wondering why you thought he would come here. He hasn't visited me in a millennia."

"I've tried everywhere I could think of."

"He's gone?"

Zeus frowned. "What gave you that idea?"

"But you just—"

Zeus let his hand fly, striking his pitiful wife across the cheek. She flew, falling into the pile of bedding. "Of course he's gone, you stupid woman!"

Covering her head, she sobbed into a pillow. "Forgive me, husband."

Zeus shook his head. "I should just let the siphons drain you completely and put you out of your misery. They're wasted on you anyway—goddess of marriage and family. It's pointless!"

Hera raised her tearful eyes to the television screens. "So much sorrow, so much hatred. Why do you make me watch this? Do you hate me so much?"

"Your firstborn son was supposed to be mine!" Zeus snarled. "Instead, you bore Hephaestus—son of no one."

"He's my son," Hera said, raising her chin.

Zeus clamped his fist around her throat and lifted her off the floor. "I'm through with you, woman, and until you tell me where you are hiding Hephaestus, you will remain here in your prison. And if you don't know where Ares is, our meeting is done." Hera clawed at his hands as her lips stained blue. Zeus' anger burned hot, and then he felt it—a burst of flames coming from deep

Raging

inside and erupting out. Fire danced in his vision as he dropped Hera. She collapsed in a fit of coughs. Her eyes rose to him, widening at the sight of him surrounded by flames.

Panic rose in Zeus at the power he struggled to suppress. He was a god! The power was there to do his bidding, not the other way around. Drawing on the power of the Skadi, the ice goddess, he pushed hard against Tana's power. He'd had no idea her power could be so overwhelming. He'd never felt this way before—this out of control.

Screeches of pain stung his ears as he looked up to see Hera on fire as she ran for the door, but collapsing before she could reach it. There was a time when the sight of his wife's flesh burning away would have upset him. But now what concerned him more was his lack of control. Besides, Hera still had some power; she couldn't be killed. But it had to hurt like Hades.

Hades…the one man who might know where his son was. And if Ares were in the Underworld, Hades would find out that there were worse things than death for a god.

Zeus transported himself to the Underworld and away from Hera, leaving her to burn out and eventually regenerate. That should take some time. Perhaps he'd leave her trapped in that charred hellhole. She deserved worse. But the televisions, he'd bring those back. A grin spread across his face. He couldn't have his wife ignore her duties—ones she was powerless to fulfill.

Chapter 13

Morning light glowed through Tana's closed eyelids. She opened one eye to see if Drake was still asleep on her floor. *Yep.*

He lay on his back with one arm flung over his eyes. With his shirt missing, he was quite a sight to observe. All tanned muscle, with not a stray hair to be seen. Not even under his arms and on his legs. *Hmm.* This guy was either a body builder or a swimmer. What other men shaved their legs? With his build, he could be either. Or both. He legitimately seemed to be inexperienced in the water, but if he really were, how did he learn to swim so darned fast? Something wasn't adding up.

She really didn't know much about this man. Yet, he'd weaseled his way into her house. Even worse, into her bedroom! For all she knew, he could be a murderer.

She needed to call Malia. She'd be over in five minutes if Tana asked her to. In fact, she should also invite Malia's older brother over. Tana looked at the muscle-bound stranger sleeping on her floor. Perhaps she should invite both of Malia's brothers to come over.

Tiptoeing over Drake, she slipped out the door and

Raging

closed it quietly behind her. The sounds of a steel drum band played softly from somewhere in the house. Oh no! How long had it been ringing?

Scrambling to find her purse, she pulled it out and swiped the screen.

"It's about time you answered," a deep voice with a warm Texas accent greeted her.

"Karl! It's nice to hear from you again."

"Nice to hear y'all too," he answered.

"So are you back in the Keys?"

"Yep, and I have a hankering for adventure if you know what I mean."

"I know exactly what you mean. How about I meet you at the pier at eight?"

"Sounds good, sugar."

Tana smiled. "It's a date." She swiped the phone to disconnect and spun to find Drake standing there next to her.

"Who was that?" he asked. He seemed relaxed, but the tightness around his eyes let her know he was upset about something. Could he be jealous?

"Um, it was a client. I'm going to do some diving today."

"Aren't you supposed to teach me how to dive this morning?"

"Oh…" Tana glanced at the clock. It was 6:49. "Looks like you already missed your class."

Drake narrowed his eyes. "Because I was up half the night listening to you snore."

Tana's jaw dropped. "I do not snore!"

Drake raised an eyebrow. "Perhaps there's still water in your lungs."

"Nope. I feel fine. And I do not snore!" She turned, opened the fridge, and grabbed some orange juice. "Listen, I appreciate you watching over me last night, but I can't miss this dive. This client is big, and—"

"Isn't your boat out of commission?" he interrupted.

"Oh, shoot!" she said, and then murmured under her breath, "Stupid merman."

"What did you say?"

Tana shook her head. "Nothing. Look, I'm going to have to find someone to borrow a boat from. I can't afford to pass up this kind of money."

"How much money could this man have?"

"Well, he pays me $3,500 for a week of dives."

"That's all?"

"Are you trying to insult me? I'm sorry if thirty-five hundred seems like pocket change to you, but for me, it's more than enough to pay the bills and then some." Tana narrowed her eyes and looked Drake over. He didn't look or act like a rich boy. Actually, a man with that much muscle and testosterone could never be called a boy. But he certainly scoffed at her pay.

"No, not at all. It's just—"

"So how much are *you* worth?" she asked, not caring that her question was personal. After all, he started it when he insulted her pay.

"Isn't that a personal question?"

Raging

"You don't know?"

"Of course I know how much I'm worth."

"That's not what I... Oh, never mind. So spill it."

"I...don't know if I feel comfortable—"

"You started it when you insulted me."

"I did not."

"Yes, you did! You practically laughed at how much I'm paid."

"Okay, forget it. I'll tell you. I don't know how much it is in American dollars," he frowned at her, obviously uncomfortable answering her question, "but I own approximately..."

"Yes?" She urged him to continue.

"Ten times my weight in gold."

Tana's knees went weak. She sank down in her kitchen chair. "As insanely tall as you are and as much muscle as you have, you'd have to weigh..." Her brain was too stunned to do the math.

"Well, if the bathroom scale is right," he said, "I weigh about two-hundred sixty pounds."

She pulled out her phone and punched in a few numbers. "Gold is currently trading at just over a thousand dollars an ounce. At ten times two-hundred sixty, you'd be worth... forty-three million dollars!" She jumped out of her seat. "Good grief! What are you doing here, standing in my kitchen? Why...? You...? She began to pace the kitchen floor. "It doesn't make sense. Why in the world did you come to me to teach you how to swim? With that much money, you could have private lessons from Michael Phelps!"

Her blood ran cold at her next thought. "Or…" She turned on him and glared. "You are a big, fat liar!" She marched toward him and slapped her hands against his chest. "How could I be so gullible?"

"I knew I shouldn't have told you." He shook his head.

"Yeah, you shouldn't have lied," she growled. "And I have an appointment to make."

"I didn't lie."

"Oh really? Can you prove it?"

"Yes."

"How are you going to prove it?"

"You're going to take me on a dive."

"Oh really. So you think we'll strike forty-three million dollars in gold on your first dive? No one's that lucky."

"Don't be ridiculous. I don't keep all my gold in the same place. I have a stash not too far from here. It's only a fraction of all I own, but it still should be worth about…" He looked to be doing the math in his head. "Eighteen thousand dollars."

"Right. Even if you have that much gold, how do I know you have any more than that? For all I know, you have a net worth of eighteen thousand dollars, which in this day and age, is not much."

"You can have it."

"What?"

"You can keep it all. Consider it your pay for taking

me diving."

"I can't accept that for one dive."

"Alright. How about you agree to take me diving whenever I want for the next two weeks. But you'll have to leave your millionaire friend behind."

"Oh, no!" She stepped toward him and jabbed him in the chest with her pointer finger. "I am not going anywhere alone with you. I don't even know you. For all I know, you're a rapist, a murderer, and a liar."

"I can guarantee I'm not a rapist or liar."

She raised her eyebrow. "You didn't deny the murder part."

He didn't say anything, simply frowned at her. Oh good grief, if that wasn't a red flag, she didn't know what was.

"You can bring Malia," he said, "and Eric, and Natalie, and the rest of your staff, if you want. Just not the rich guy, Karl."

"Hmm. I still don't have a boat."

"I can get us a boat until yours is fixed," he said confidently.

She sighed and frowned. "If you can get us a boat, we'll go, with whomever *I* choose to bring along."

"Agreed, but no Karl."

She couldn't hold back her smirk. "No Karl."

Chapter 14

Drakōn dialed up Kyros. He sure hoped his friend knew how to get him a boat. If not, he was… what was that saying? Oh yes, up a creek without a paddle.

"Hey, Drake," Kyros answered, chuckling.

"Oh, not you too."

"What? I think the name sounds good on you."

"Yeah, well, forget my name. I need your help getting a boat."

"So I heard."

"What's that supposed to mean? How did you—?"

"Someone wants to talk to you."

Drakōn heard rustling in the background. "I hear you're in need of a boat."

"Andre? What are you doing in The Keys?"

"Like I said…"

Drakōn shook his head and mumbled, "Oracles."

"I brought out the Olympus," Andre said. "She should be perfect for all your needs."

"I'm sure the boat is fine. We'll meet you at the dock at nine."

"Sounds good to me. I'm waiting."

Raging

"Aren't you going to ask me which dock?"

"I'm already there, son of Proteus."

"Hey, how did you—never mind."

Minutes later, Drakōn stepped onto the dock—a familiar boat was tied to a slip.

"Well, well…" Andre's voice boomed as he stepped onto the deck and shook his head. "I can scarcely believe it. There's a god on my boat."

"I've been on this vessel before."

"Yes, but I didn't realize you were a god. Even oracles aren't given all the answers all the time. Most often, we are as much in the dark as everyone else."

Drakōn shook his head. "You knew I'd need a boat."

"Yes, well, that was Sara's doing. She's keeping an eye on you from a distance."

"She'd be more help up close."

"Oh, no. You know it doesn't work that way. She can't see things she's personally involved in. Something about the universe never allowing a person, or god, to know their own fate."

"Right. So, what's so important about me diving for gold that one of the Fates would make sure I had a boat?"

Andre shook his head. "I have no idea."

"Some oracle you are."

"I only know it's important to the progression of things."

"Right." Drakōn thought about how his relationship had progressed with Tana. He'd kissed her, and she kissed him back. And the most troubling thing about that was he wanted to kiss her again.

"So who am I taking out on the water? I'm assuming you aren't going alone."

"I'm taking a woman who thinks she's a human."

"So what is she?"

"The daughter of Hades and Eos."

"Eos had a child with the king of the Underworld?"

"Apparently."

"Wait! She's the one."

"What?"

"The one who may destroy the world."

"So I've heard."

"So why don't you kill her, sea-god?"

Drakōn's anger boiled at the suggestion. He concentrated on calming himself down. After all, he'd suggested that very thing to Sara. "We can't kill her. She's one of the four needed to free the forgotten king."

"Ah, such a powerful goddess would be needed to bypass the protections laid out."

"Protections?" Drakōn's voice rose. "What protections?"

"The false king wanted to make sure the true king could never be released. Zeus laid down protections to keep anyone from getting close to his brother. So," Andre continued. "What do you need from me today?"

"I just need you to drive your boat above the black hole."

"Black hole? I'm guessing you aren't talking about outer space black holes."

Raging

"No, but this one is deadly as well. It's an underwater cave that can be a deathtrap to the Dagonian who doesn't know its secrets."

"Why would you want to go there?"

"Because it's close by, and I have gold hidden in it."

"What does a sea-god need with gold?"

"I'll be giving it to Tana."

"You are giving this woman gold? Are you paying her to help us free the forgotten king?"

"No." He shook his head. "She doesn't even know about him; she doesn't know about any of the gods."

Andre looked confused, and Drakōn didn't blame him. What he was doing made no sense. Why *was* he giving this woman his gold?

"Ah!" Andre said as if he'd had an epiphany, and then he narrowed his eyes at Drakōn. "You're falling for the goddess."

"What? That's ludicrous!"

Andre raised an eyebrow. "Is it?"

Drakōn couldn't answer. In truth, he didn't know how to answer. He only knew that if it were up to him, he'd be skinned and flayed for shark bait before he'd fall in love with a land-walker. Doubt sneered at him as he wondered if he truly had any say in the matter.

Tana stepped onto the dock with Vin and Kai on either side of her. Normally she felt protected by Malia's brothers. They were both well over six feet tall and very fit, but Drake…well, he stood close to seven feet tall and looked like he could bench press her car. Seeing him step out onto the deck of a nearby Mainship trawler, she was struck again by how massive this man was—and he claimed to own ten times his weight in gold.

Gorgeous and insane were not a good combination. But if he weren't crazy, she'd be nearly twenty thousand dollars richer by the end of the day.

"Hello." Drake stepped up to Vin—the older and friendlier of the brothers. Vin smiled and put out his hand.

"Hello, Mr.…?" Vin began.

"Sumer, but you can call me Drakōn."

"I don't think so, Mr. Sumer," Vin said, smiling. "You can call me Mr. Saunders."

"Okay, Mr. Saunders." Drake turned to Kai. "And what do I call you?"

"You can call me Mr. Saunders too."

"That won't be confusing at all," Drake said with a smirk. Tana did her best to suppress a smile.

"So," Kai said. "This is your vessel?"

"No, this vessel belongs to a friend of mine." He turned to the boat. "Andre!"

A grey-haired man with bright eyes stepped out of the cabin. "Yes? Oh, these are the passengers?"

"This is Tana, and then we have Mr. Saunders and Mr. Saunders."

Andre put out his hand to her, and she took it in her grasp. His warm smile faded as he continued to hold her hand. His grip increased until he began to squeeze so

Raging

hard, it became painful. Just before she could pull her hand away, he dropped it.

Worry etched his eyes as he swallowed. "Sorry, miss." He looked as if he wanted to say more, but instead, he abruptly turned away and stepped back toward the cabin. As he walked by Drake, Andre mumbled something. It sounded like, *"You weren't kidding,"* but Tana couldn't be sure.

"Alright," Drake said. "Let's get underway."

Two hours later, Tana awoke to the sound of hushed voices.

"I tell you, I know what I saw." Vin's voice rose and caught her complete attention.

"I believe you," Drake said.

"Well, that's you and Kai," he said, frowning. "Everyone else laughs at me when I try to talk about it."

"That's because they're ignorant," Drake said.

Vin turned to his brother and smiled, jabbing his thumb in Drake's direction. "This man knows what he's talking about."

Tana adjusted the pillow under her head and turned her back on the three of them. Why did she bring Malia's brothers in the first place? They were supposed to be there to intimidate Drake. Instead, here they were, talking like best friends.

"I'll tell you what *I've* seen," Drake said, his voice low.

Tana sensed he was about to say something interesting, so she listened closer.

"I was on a dive in the Atlantic. I was down deeper than I ever had been before."

"How deep were you?" Kai asked.

He paused, and Tana suddenly wished she could see his face. Then he spoke low, matter-of-factly. "Deep."

"Well, I saw something I'd only ever heard of in legends. After swimming in darkness for a good distance, I saw a light flicker across a mile-long crevice below me. At first, I thought I was seeing a large school of bioluminescent fish, but then the light rose and began to move toward me. The first thing I could make out was its large jaws and sharp, spiny teeth. The canine teeth were longer than my body, and then I could see its two big, bulbous eyes, glowing red and looking right at me.

"Truly, I thought I was dead. But, instead of chomping down on me, it turned away—its whole body emerging from the trench. It looked like the body an eel, but it was at least a mile long—and it glowed in a kaleidoscope of color—and then darted away, disappearing in seconds. The concussion from the wake of its departure was enough to tell me he was real, and not a figment of my imagination."

"You're a liar," Tana said, no longer able to pretend she was sleeping. What he'd said was impossible.

Kai shook his head and glared at her. "That's what everyone says when I tell them what *I* saw!"

"Are you telling me you've never seen anything unusual in your dives?" Drake asked her, raising his eyebrows as if challenging her. As if he knew.

Raging

"Tana," Kai said. "Malia said you showed her a picture of a mermaid, and then she said you both saw a merman. How can you call Drakōn a liar?"

"You're on a first-name basis now?" she asked.

"We've bonded over sea-monster tales," Vin said, stepping forward.

Tana huffed. "What I saw was different."

"Oh, right," Kai said, "because you saw it. So you can pick and choose what you believe from your friends, but we have to believe you unconditionally."

"No, I know he's a liar because I just gave Drake his first swimming lesson last week. How could he have gone on a deep dive?"

"That wasn't my first swimming lesson," Drake said sheepishly. "I've been swimming my whole life."

"I knew it! Why did you lie?"

"I just wanted to get close to you."

"You could have just said hi."

"Are you kidding?" Kai said. "Both Vin and I have tried to flirt with the elusive Tana. We barely survived."

"You're joking," she said, chuckling dryly.

"Nope. We crashed and burned."

"Seriously?" she asked.

They both nodded at her.

"I didn't know."

"Yeah, we figured that out. You've got some serious walls up, chick. We're lucky we have Malia as a sister. Otherwise, we'd be taking our lives in our hands getting close to you."

Tana didn't know what to say; the stunning revelation had rendered her speechless.

"We're coming up on the coordinates," Andre called from the bridge.

Tana breathed a sigh of relief as their attention was diverted.

Drake stepped up to her. "Ready to collect some gold?"

"I'll believe it when I see it."

"Ha, yeah, ever the doubter."

"So, I take it you know how to use scuba gear?" Tana asked.

"I prefer to free dive."

"How deep is this gold you hope to bring up?"

"About six hundred feet."

"You're not seriously going to free dive that deep."

"Yes, I am. I just need to attach the crane to the box, and the boat can do the work of bringing it to the surface."

"You're crazy! Only a few people in the world are capable of reaching those depths."

"Where I'm from—a six-hundred-foot dive is nothing."

"Yeah, right. Listen, if you die on this dive, do I still get the gold?"

He cracked a smile and stepped toward her, his lips hovering just above hers. Her heart took off in a sprint.

"So all you care about is my gold?" he asked.

"Yes." She licked her lips. His warmth and masculine

Raging

scent drove her crazy. *Oh, please, just kiss me!*

"If you say so." He smiled and lowered his mouth. As soon as their lips touched, her whole body filled with heat and she hungered for more. As if sensing her desire, he pulled her to him, pressing her body to his. His mouth moved with hers, and she felt drenched in desire as she clawed her fingers into the contours of his shoulders.

"Wow," Vin said, shattering the spell. "The ice queen melts."

Drake growled as he pulled away. Tana trembled at the sudden emptiness she felt in his absence. The scowl on his face told her he was just as frustrated with being interrupted as she was.

"Looks like you two need a room," Kai said.

Drake's scowl went from dark to murderous. In a blink, Tana was once again afraid. How could she have let her guard down with this stranger? There was something seriously wrong with the man.

"I would never dishonor her like that," he snapped.

"Hey..." Kai put up his hands. "I didn't mean anything by it. I mean, if she had resisted you at all, my brother and I would have been all over you. But, from what we saw, she was just as into you as you were her. We were just wishing you'd take your saliva-swapping session somewhere where we didn't have to watch."

"Seriously," Vin said, frowning.

Drake wouldn't dishonor her? Was he really so angry at the suggestion he would bring her dishonor by having sex with her? Where did this man come from, the eighteenth century?

"I'm sorry," Drake said, his anger fading. "You're right. I shouldn't have kissed her so publicly. Can you forgive me?"

"Um," Kai said, shifting his weight. "Yeah, sure."

Drake turned and stepped over to the crane that held a cable with a steel hook. "Okay, it shouldn't take long for me to hook this onto the box."

"Box?" Tana asked. "Oh right, the gold." She'd forgotten completely why they were there.

Drake held the hook in his hand and climbed over the railing. He turned and looked at Andre. "After I finish my descent, watch for me to pull on the cord with three quick jerks. You can pull it up then."

"How are you going to get up?" Tana asked. "Do you have an inflatable bag?"

"Don't need one." He shrugged.

Tana blew out a breath. "You know, I once considered free diving to see how deep I could go down."

"You did?" Drake asked, his eye wide.

"Yeah, and then I decided I didn't have a death wish."

He chuckled. "I don't have a death wish. I know exactly what I'm doing, and what I'm capable of."

"Yeah? I'll be sure to include that in your eulogy."

His shook his head as he chuckled at her lame excuse for a joke. "Goodbye, sweetheart." With that said, he dove into the water.

The line whirred as he descended. The wheel with the metal cable continued to spin.

Raging

"Is there a way to know how deep he is?" Tana said, looking at her watch.

"He's about a hundred feet," Andre said.

"Already?" she asked.

"How do you know?" Vin asked.

"By how much cable is gone," Andre said. "It shouldn't take him much longer."

Minutes later, the spinning stopped. And then they waited.

"What's taking so long?" she asked, her eyes glued to her watch. "He's been submerged for over five minutes."

"He's fine," Andre said, obviously not bothered by the length of the dive.

Another five minutes, and he still hadn't pulled on the cable.

"Maybe he couldn't get the cable hooked, and he's on his way up."

Tana shook her head. "No, he'd pull it anyway. It's not like we can leave the cable hanging."

As she paced the deck, her nervousness grew. "Something's wrong." She looked at the small waves cresting and lapping, looking for bubbles. Seeing none, she came to a quick decision. Turning to Andre, she said, "I'm going down."

"Scuba diving at those depths is not safe. I'm sure he's fine. You just need to be patient."

Rushing over to her gear, she shouted, "He's not fine, and free diving at those depths is even less safe. I should have never let him go; he's obviously crazy. I shouldn't have pushed him." Pulling on her suit and gear, she rushed through all her checks. "Call the Coast Guard; I'll bring him up as fast as I can." *Oh, please don't let him be dead!*

She splashed down in the water and descended quickly. Normally, she'd follow bubbles to locate divers below, but there were none. Of course, with a free dive, Drake would be essentially holding his breath. Still, this was much longer than a normal free diver could handle.

She just needed to stay on track and dive straight down. The deeper she dove, the darker it got until there was little light left. Pulling out her flashlight, she pointed the beam downward. Did Drake bring a flashlight? He'd be blind at six hundred feet down.

Movement caught her eye to the left. She turned the flashlight on it.

Nothing.

Panning the light around, she tried to find what she was sure she'd seen. In a flash, she saw the flicker of a fin as it moved out of sight. Something about that fin looked familiar, but she couldn't put her finger on it—possibly a shark? If it were a shark, it likely wouldn't see her as food. Of course, curiosity could drive him to take a nibble at her, and a nibble from a shark could be fatal—especially at this depth.

Tana looked around and caught sight of it again—a tailfin. And then a human face—inches from her own. She screamed, bubbles rising as she expelled her air much too fast. And then darkness descended.

Chapter 15

Drakōn raced to the surface with Tana unconscious in his arms. "She can't die," he mumbled, hoping beyond hope it was true.

She thrashed around, the movement causing his heart to stop. Looking down at her face, he found her looking back at him—her eyes wide in fear. Was she afraid of him, or was she afraid of the fact she woke up under the water's surface?

He wanted to speak, to tell her she was going to be all right, but he couldn't. She thought he was human, and humans couldn't talk under water. Of course, humans didn't have fins under water either, and he was pumping his fin back and forth as hard as he could as he propelled them toward the surface. They moved faster than any human could. Hopefully, she was disoriented enough not to notice.

Finally, they broke through the surface and he took a deep breath of air. Tana tore off her mouthpiece and face mask, taking in a few deep breaths of air herself. He'd changed to his legs—hopefully before anyone could see the shadow of his tailfin—and now he was treading water at her side.

Tana continued to gasp and looked down at her watch. "Twenty minutes," she shouted between breaths. "You were down there for twenty minutes!"

He shook his head. "Impossible," he said, assuming a twenty-minute dive wasn't possible for a human. He actually had no idea how long humans could hold their breath. Tana swam to the ladder of the boat and climbed aboard as Drakōn followed.

Pulling off her fins, she stood, turned back, and jabbed him in the chest. "I was watching the time. I know exactly how long you were down there."

"Your watch has to be wrong."

"It's not wrong!"

"So what you're saying is that it's more likely I held my breath for twenty minutes than the possibility that your watch malfunctioned?"

"I…" She heaved a sigh. "Well, when you put it that way. But seriously, I thought…"

Drakōn looked at her and shrugged.

"You're right." She plopped down on a bench. "The world record for a person holding his breath underwater is twenty-two minutes, and that's in a pool with no movement and relaxation techniques to slow body processes. There's no way you could do it while actively diving."

She turned to him and jabbed him once again. "But still, you stayed down there a heck of a long time!"

"I know," he said, relieved she believed him. "I'm sorry, but I was trying to find the gold. It appears someone

Raging

else found it first. It's gone."

"Why am I not surprised?" She shook her head. "I'll get you the gold I promised. I give you my word."

"No," she said, scowling at him. "Forget it. There's no way I'm putting your life on the line while you go off on another fantasy treasure dive."

"Fantasy? You think the gold doesn't exist?"

She looked him in the eye and sighed.

He shook his head. "Believe what you want. I don't know why I've been trying to please you. You think I'm a liar, and just for that, I should simply leave you to your fate." Even as he said it, he knew he could not do that. Without him, her life would be worth nothing. But still, her continually calling him a liar struck a nerve in him. Since when did he allow anyone to question his honor?

Tana stood, stepped up to him, and narrowed her eyes. "Leave me to my fate? You're insane."

"I'm not the one who is insane. You can't even read a simple clock, you can't make a dive without needing to be rescued, and you see imagined fires in the sky that cause you to hide at the bottom of a pool. You would drown yourself to escape a stinking sunset!" His voice rose until he was shouting at her. What had he ever seen in this woman?

Moisture sprang to her eyes as a stricken look passed over her countenance.

The tears were like a slap to the face. What was he doing? When had he ever been so cruel? Well, truthfully, he had been cruel plenty of times, but not to a woman whose only crime was to not believe the unbelievable. "I'm sorry—" he began.

"Forget it," she snapped and stood, blinking back the tears and avoiding his gaze. "Just take me back to shore."

"Tana—"

"No." She put her hand up and pushed past him. "Just stop." He swallowed back a lump in his throat as she climbed below deck.

"And I was just beginning to like you," Kai said. "That was pretty low, you know."

Drakōn looked up and frowned. "Yeah, I know."

"Listen, I still think you're a good guy, so you need to make things right with Tana. You're the first man I've ever seen her open up to—and a woman that beautiful is not lacking for offers. Don't blow your chance by being stupid."

"Hey, Andre!" Tana shouted from below deck. Seconds later, she raced up the stairs with a harpoon in her hand. "I'd like you to take a little detour."

"Are you threatening me?" he asked, eyeing the harpoon.

She lowered it and said, "No, of course not. This harpoon isn't for you."

Drakōn stepped into the cabin; his heart sank as his concern grew.

"I want you to take me to these coordinates," she said as she dashed down some numbers on a piece of paper.

Andre pursed his lips and nodded. "Okay. Are you looking to take a dive there?"

Raging

"Looking for gold?" Drakōn said hopefully.

"Nope. I'm looking for proof that I'm not crazy."

"Tana," Drakōn said as he looked at the numbers that meant nothing to him. Still, he knew exactly where she was headed. "That's a dangerous spot to go to."

"How do you know?" she asked.

"I'm familiar with it. You dive in that spot and you likely won't be coming back."

"Hey, whoa!" Vin said. "What do you mean she won't come back? Tana, listen to the man."

She shook her head as she pulled on her flippers. "I have been down there several times. It's perfectly safe."

"Now who's lying?" Drakōn asked.

"I'll be fine."

"Then I'll come with you."

"No! You'll just get in my way. I'll be back in less than twenty minutes."

Drakōn frowned as Tana pierced him with her gaze. "I don't like this."

"You don't have to like it."

An hour later, they approached the spot. Drakōn's muscles tensed as his nostrils flared at the scent coming off the sea—he could smell the Dagonians in the water below.

Tana already had her gear on. As soon as they stopped, she splashed into the waves. And then she was gone.

"By gods," he mumbled to himself as he pulled his shirt over his head. *I should just let them kill her. It's not like*

Holly Kelly

she wasn't warned. She barely survived last time. This time, it will take a miracle to save her. Drakōn kicked off his sandals and pulled down his pants.

"She won't like you coming," Vin said.

"I don't care. She really doesn't know what she's getting herself into."

"You're not going to use a tank?" Kai asked.

"Nope, it'll just slow me down," he said and dove into the water. Seconds after his descent, his legs slapped together and morphed into a fin. The sun shone brightly, blue rays crisscrossing through the water. He couldn't see Tana, but he could smell her, and he could smell the fear she'd tried to hide on the deck. If only she'd listen to her instincts. She knew this was dangerous. Bubbles fluttered like tiny jellyfish in the distance.

Drakōn dove down. He needed to keep an eye on her without being spotted. With a flick of his tail, he was off, racing towards her. In moments, her black silhouette came into view, just above him.

Swimming forward, she held her harpoon out front as her head turned from side to side. She kept close to the coral, doing her best to keep out of sight. She was doing a lousy job. First from the left, and then from the right—two Dagonians came into view, coming up behind her. One was smaller, but still a full-grown male, but the second was large, with muscles bulging. Drakōn had to take out the larger one first.

He shot through the water. The Dagonian turned around—sensing his approach—and Drakōn came face

Raging

to face with a livid creature. The male's face relaxed when he saw him. "Gods!" he whispered harshly. "What are you—stupid? You're lucky I didn't kill you."

"You, kill me?" Drakōn smirked. "Not likely."

The Dagonians eyes widened. "Hey, I recognize you." His eyes narrowed in suspicion. "Shouldn't you be in prison?"

"Shouldn't you be asleep?" Drakōn answered just before he struck multiple times—hitting the nerves in the Dagonian's neck, arm, and wrist. Three strikes and he was out—as in unconscious. Too many impulses overwhelmed the nervous system and caused it to shut down.

Drakōn dragged the limp body over to the coral and shoved him into a hollow. Hopefully, he would revive before a predator found him. He had no idea who this man was, but Drakōn wasn't surprised at being recognized. He had gained quite the reputation over the centuries.

The second Dagonian was much easier to handle. Drakōn stuffed him in with his friend. Now to find Tana.

Drakōn snaked his way through the coral. The scent of Dagonians was unusually sharp in the water. Either there were a lot of them, or they were highly agitated. He certainly hoped it wasn't both.

Angry voices shouted in the distance. As he drew near, the volume increased, but with so many of them, it was hard to make out what they were saying. He picked up speed as his heart began to race. The voices should be getting louder, but by the gods, they weren't. In fact, they were diminishing. Why were they—?

Drakōn broke through to a clearing, and his heart stopped. A portal shimmered just ahead—a wide one. This one was large enough to transport a crowd, and it looked like the crowd had already exited through it.

"You almost missed it, friend," a Dagonian smiled at him as he floated just outside the gateway. "This is not something to miss."

"So," Drakōn said, hesitant, "you knew the human was coming?"

"We didn't *know*, but we were hoping she would. She's been here before. The Destroyer thought it was worth all the preparations for even a slight chance she would make an appearance."

Drakōn felt the blood drain from his face. "Skylla? You have a demigod with you?"

The Dagonian chuckled. "Yeah, I can't believe it either. This should be quite a show. After you…" He gestured to the portal. "I've got to enter last."

Drakōn swam through and found himself in the middle of a nightmare. He'd been to this place once before—the day of his daughter's trial, the day he narrowly missed being executed himself. A stone dome encircled the entire group. The Dagonian who had greeted him came through and sealed the portal. Now there was no way in, and no way out. *Perfect. Now how was he supposed to save Tana?* Guilt pressed down on him. He drove her to do this. If only he hadn't been such an idiot,

Raging

she wouldn't be in such danger.

Drakōn swam forward, his tail stirring the strong scent of old blood, the weak scent of new blood, and the smell of fear and excitement. Of all the places Tana could have been taken, this was by far the worst. Drakōn swam in further and the water brightened. He approached the edge of a bubble. The center had been drained of water—and Tana sat in the middle, covered in mud. The strap from her facemask hung around her neck and blood trickled down her temple. She looked desperately around her, obviously terrified at the scene surrounding her.

Drakōn's blood boiled.

"By the gods…" A deep voice spoke in his ear. Drakōn looked over. The Dagonian who had closed the portal floated nearby. "That's the human? But she looks so…"

"Innocent?" Drakōn said.

"Well…" He sighed. "Yeah."

Drakōn looked over to Tana. She trembled as her eyes darted from face to face. Drakōn's anger rose along with his power. He could feel it simmering below the surface of his body. Still, he didn't know how to use it. For all he knew, if he unleashed his power, he could kill everyone in this hellhole—including Tana.

No, his god powers would not save her today, but maybe he could convince the Dagonians to let her live. Or perhaps…

His heart lightened when realized he had another

option. He could summon the god of war. Xanthus would be able to handle this situation with no problem.

Xanthus?

Drakōn waited for his reply. He got no response.

"Dagonians, allies, fellow brothers of the sea…" Drakōn looked up to see who was speaking. A large creature stepped up next to Tana. Her eyes widened as her jaw dropped. She appeared too terrified to scream. Drakōn didn't blame her. The demigod didn't look human, and he looked nothing like a Dagonian. His upper body appeared human in shape, but his color was a mixture of red and orange splotches. The most striking thing about him—his lower body wasn't a fin or human legs; his appendages were shaped like those of a crab.

The Destroyer narrowed his yellow eyes as he looked Tana over and stomped forward—his sharp legs piercing the stone floor. "I'd been informed of an intruder—a land-walker—and I simply couldn't pass this opportunity by. The humans have polluted our seas, killed our friends and loved ones, and they have never once shown the slightest remorse for what they have done. And here is one of them!" The shouts from the crowd were deafening. When they finally quieted, he continued. "This woman has come into our home, armed with a weapon she intended to use against us. She came here to murder us! To slaughter our families! Man, woman, or child… it does not matter to her. She would kill your loved ones in their sleep. She is a human! And as you well know, all humans are heartless."

Raging

He turned and grabbed Tana by the hair, lifting her onto her feet. She cried out in pain. Closing her eyes, she covered her ears. She appeared to be mumbling to herself. Perhaps she was offering up a prayer. Drakōn wanted to leap forward, but he dared not. At least not yet.

"What do you think I should do with her?" Skylla asked.

"Kill her!" the crowd shouted.

Drakōn clenched his fist, determination in his blood. He looked to the one Dagonian who might be the key to their escape. "Do you want to save her?"

"Save a human?" He looked back at Drakōn, confusion on his face. "Why?"

"That's no human," Drakōn said. "She's the daughter of Hades. She just doesn't know it yet."

The Dagonian looked at Drakōn, his eyes widening. "Do you speak the truth?"

"I swear on the sea."

"Gods, if Hades finds out we've harmed her, he'll kill us all."

"Will you help me save her?"

Drakōn narrowed his eyes and clenched his fists as the crowd once again shouted at the Destroyer's continued taunts.

"No," the Dagonian answered. "But I'll help you save us. If that means saving her, then so be it."

"That's all I ask," Drakōn said. "When I give you a signal, open the portal."

"Okay, but—"

Drakōn didn't wait to hear what else he had to say; he couldn't afford to wait. The Destroyer had drawn his sword. Drakōn swam forward and pushed his way into the center of the court. His body hit the dry floor. His tail slammed against the ground as he looked up.

"Drake?" Tana said, her eyes wide in confusion. "You're one of them?" Tears welled from her eyes as she backed away.

"Drakōn, I did not ask you to join me." Skylla stepped toward him.

Drakōn allowed his legs to change. Gasps and murmurs surrounded him as he stood on his feet.

The Destroyer narrowed his eyes. "So, you are more than what you seem, Dagonian."

"You noticed, huh?" Drakōn said, glancing down at his feet.

"Not just the wretched legs," he said as he approached and stopped just in front of Drakōn, closing his eyes. "I feel power."

Drakōn knew exactly what he was talking about—he could feel power himself. "Yeah," Drakōn said. "I've been through a few life-changing events."

"So," the Destroyer said opening his eyes. "Have you come to take part in the fun?"

"Drake?" Tana's shaky voice called out to him. "Please…" She didn't finish the words, but her eyes begged for his help.

"Sounds like the human knows you," the Destroyer said and gestured toward Tana.

Raging

"She's no human," Drakōn said low enough to avoid the ears of the crowd.

The Destroyer's appendages pounded the ground as he stepped over to Tana and leaned in, examining her. "She looks like a human." He closed his eyes and sniffed. "She smells like a human." He opened his eyes and moved in closer. Tana leaned away from him—terror in her eyes. "She feels like a human." He lifted his leg, the sharp point hovering just above her head. Drakōn tensed. Surely, he wouldn't kill her until he knew who and what she was. He realized how wrong he was a heartbeat later. The Destroyer stomped the point down into her skull—driving it into her head. "And she dies like a human," he said dismissively as he pulled his leg from her. Blood poured from her wound as she collapsed and convulsed on the ground.

"No!" Drakōn shouted as he rushed over. Pulling Tana to his chest, he murmured. "Oh gods, Tana. No." He crushed her to him, her breath coming out in gasps. Her eyes were rolled back in her head. She was dying in his arms, and he could do nothing to change it. As he pressed his lips against her temple, a tear leaked from his eye. "I'm sorry... I'm so sorry." Finally, her breathing slowed to a stop and her clenched muscles relaxed, her body going limp in his arms. He could hear the last stuttered beats of her heart, and then silence.

She was dead.

Chapter 16

Drakōn froze, unwilling to accept what his eyes were telling him. Tana was dead. He'd failed to protect her. His heart shattered just as he realized what this woman meant to him. He cared about her. Hades, as much as he'd been trying to deny it, he'd been falling for her. And now, she was gone.

His fists clenched and he could feel his eyes burn as he raised them to the Destroyer. Gathering Tana up in his arms, he carried her to the water's edge and lay her down gently.

Drakōn's eyes were burning as he turned back to confront her murderer. He roared, driven forward by rage as he ran. Skylla turned to meet him, his sword raised. Drakōn was unarmed, but that didn't faze him one bit. He ducked under the demigod's blade as it flew toward his head. He leaped and tackled him. They both flew, hitting the ground in a tangle of limbs and appendages. Skylla's legs wrapped around him, like iron bars pinning Drakōn to his chest.

The demigod laughed. "Do you think to destroy the Destroyer? You may be powerful, but you don't know how to use that power, do you? If you had, your lover

Raging

wouldn't have died."

Drakōn snarled at him.

"I know you cared for her. I could smell it on you. Why else would I kill her immediately? It's a disappointment that I didn't torture her first. But I couldn't chance you intervening with her execution."

"You son of a—"

"Careful what you say to the son of Phorcys. My father might take offense."

"If he's not offended by having you for a son, I doubt anything would faze him."

"You were never one to back down, were you, Drakōn?" he asked as he drove his blade into Drakōn's back.

At the sudden pain, Drakōn hissed, "Coward."

"Oh, you think it's cowardly to stab an unarmed man in the back?" he asked as he pulled the knife from Drakōn's body and smiled at the blood staining the blade. "I can feel your power. Smell it in your blood. You are far from helpless."

Darkness filtered in at the edge of Drakōn's vision. Skylla sneered, excitement building in his expression as the crowded roared. White mist mingled with the darkness in Drakōn's vision as strange words whispered in his ear. Drakōn growled as he clamped his hand over the Destroyer's and peeled away his grip.

A strange silence descended on the crowd. Drakōn pushed with all he had, widening the distance between himself and his opponent. Pulling his feet up, he pressed them against Skylla's chest. He shouted as he pushed with his feet.

Claws raked like knives over Drakōn's back, and then the Destroyer hit the wall of water and flailed like a turned-over crab attempting to right itself.

Drakōn regained his feet and stood in stunned surprise. He felt wetness as he touched the open wounds burning his ribs and came away with blood on his hands. In seconds, he could feel the searing pain of healing.

His heart stopped when he heard the whispered moan of a woman. He turned to see Tana push herself up off the floor.

Skylla flipped onto his feet and froze, staring at the impossible sight. "You," he said as his eyes widened, locked on Tana. "You should be dead."

Tana trembled as she sat—her hands braced to hold herself up. "I… please, I just want to go home." A strange mist surrounded her, circling her. Drakōn could see the face of a woman in the mist just before it passed over him, blowing across his skin as it fled.

Several things clicked into place at once. Tana was powerful—so powerful that even death could not hold her. And from the looks of it, her death seemed to have released the siphon that had been draining her powers. Drakōn thought of his conversation with Sara.

"The power she was born with is immense."
"What power is that?"
"Wind and flame."

"Drake?" The fear in her voice pulled him out of his

Raging

shock. Tana crawled onto her knees. She looked at him in horror as she stood and backed away—towards Skylla. It wasn't the Destroyer she was afraid of—it was herself. "You need to get out of here. I feel... I dreamed about this." She shook her head, trembling so hard she could barely stand.

Yellow flames sprouted from her chest and spread to her arms. Her eyes searched her body and then her surroundings as her desperation grew.

Skylla roared as he stepped toward her. "You think I'm afraid of you? Let's see how powerful you are without your head."

Drakōn scrambled toward her as the Destroyer's blade sliced through the smoky air. His heart stopped the moment he realized he would be too late.

The sword sliced through with no resistance. Skylla's chest heaved as he held his blade up—his eyes widening. The sword's blade was broken. No, not broken. Melted.

"What... are you?" Skylla dropped his weapon, his anger replaced by awe.

Tana shook her head and collapsed to the ground as she sobbed—flames dancing over her skin, burning her wetsuit. "Drake, you need to get back in the water. I—"

An explosion blasted Drakōn's ears as light blinded him and seared him with heat. The sound of a hundred screaming voices surrounded him. Skylla shrieked as his flesh burned. Within moments, all that remained of the notorious demigod was a hollowed-out shell and a blackened skeleton.

Holly Kelly

Drakōn sank to the ground and raised his arms—as if that would protect him from the inferno. Yet… he could no longer feel it. Raising his head, he could see fire emanating from Tana like a supernova. He could see Tana herself—a blindingly white silhouette against blue pulsing flames. She was curled up in a ball, rocking back and forth as she knelt against the floor. But what shocked him most—his hand. It shimmered, transparent. His eyes trailed down his arm and to his body. He looked to be made up entirely of water.

Tana sobbed as the fire continued to rage. Stepping towards her, Drakōn hesitantly reached out to touch her. The flames retreated from his hand, and he pressed his watery palm against her bare flesh. Emboldened, he dropped to his knees at her side and wrapped his arms around her. Cool water flowed from him—no, not from him, it *was* him. He surrounded her, swirling and flowing. Covering Tana, he doused the fire. When the heat of the flames cooled, he pulled himself back. Moments later, his flesh returned to normal.

Tana looked up. "What are you?"

"I'm…" He looked down on his hands. "…a sea-god."

She shook her head, doubt clouding her eyes. "That's impossible." She looked around, her eyes landing on the burned shell of the demigod a few feet away, and then on the surrounding water held back from their bubble. Drakōn was sickened when he looked at the arena. Dagonians surrounded them—their bloated, blistered

Raging

bodies floating lifelessly in the water.

"All of this is impossible," she said. "I...I dreamed about something like this, but it can't be real." She struggled to stand on trembling legs. "I..."

Drakōn caught her just before she fell unconscious to the ground. "Gods of Olympus, Tana." He shook his head in awe. "What am I going to do with you?" he asked as he lifted her into his arms. He looked down on her angelic face and felt an intense relief that she was alive. She should be dead.

As he looked up at the destruction around him, he knew he should feel anger at what she'd done. She'd killed dozens of Dagonians. But he couldn't muster even a flicker of fury. They'd attacked her unprovoked. They'd meant to kill her. They deserved their fate.

A glimmer among the bodies caught his attention—the portal. That Dagonian must have opened it. Drakōn could escape with Tana through it, but he didn't know what he'd find on the other side. Perhaps an army had assembled. But if he didn't use the portal, how would they get out? Tana wasn't a Dagonian; she didn't have gills. After what he saw, she probably wouldn't drown, but it would likely be extremely unpleasant for her if he swam her out of here. The surface lay about a mile above.

If only he could...

Actually, he should be able to transport them anywhere he wanted. He was a god after all. And after what he heard about Sara's first attempts at translocation, it didn't seem too difficult. But where should he take

Holly Kelly

Tana? She was a clear danger to those around her. Except for perhaps Gretchen. She was a demigod of the Underworld, and she was fireproof! Yes, who better to help him?

Closing his eyes, he pictured Gretchen's face, and then he felt it. A tug. Without being able to explain it, he could feel her. She was somewhere on land. Grasping the tenuous thread of contact, he pulled. Light flashed from the other side of this closed eyelids—so bright, he was grateful his eyes were closed.

The first thing he noticed was a breeze blowing across his face, and then he could hear shouts of fright. It sounded like humans. Opening his eyes, he found himself standing on a crowded sidewalk.

"Drakōn, you idiot," Kyros' voice rumbled behind him. Humans surrounded him—their eyes wide in shock as they looked and pointed at him. Gretchen stood at his side, holding the handle of a stroller as she shook her head. She opened her mouth and began to sing softly.

Drakōn's fists clenched as he attempted to hold on to his thoughts. He remembered clearly how it felt to be under a mermaid's spell. Resisting was excruciatingly painful. But this was different. It was still difficult—like being tethered to a whale and dragged through the sea, but somehow, he held on with only a twinge of pain in his head. Finally, he relaxed as Gretchen's voice quieted.

"I'm impressed," Kyros said as he clapped Drakōn on the back.

Drakōn turned to his friend in shock. "Likewise.

Raging

How—?"

"Triton," Kyros said.

"Ah…" Drakōn said. "So you're immune?"

"Yes, but you weren't. Yet, you resisted."

"Yeah." He looked around at the humans who had resumed going about their day as if nothing had happened. In fact, they didn't even look at him, despite the fact that Drakōn was holding an unconscious woman wearing a melted wetsuit that barely covered her. People should be, at the most, shocked and in awe, or at the least, curious.

"We need to get out of here," Gretchen said as she pushed Donovan and his stroller in between two buildings. Drakōn and Kyros followed. "It looks like you've figured out how to beam us out of here, and since I can't, I would appreciate it if you would—" she said.

"Um," Drakōn interrupted. "I'm not really an expert on it yet."

"You can do it," she said. "Sara says it's easy."

"For her. She's a goddess."

"And you're a god."

"You know?" he said, and then relaxed. "Oh, right, Sara told you."

"Yes," Gretchen said. "Now just think about the hotel room, and do what you did before, but try to take us with you."

"Okay." He sighed and then closed his eyes.

"Oh, and Drakōn?" she said, interrupting. "If you mess up and harm my child, I'll kill you." Her glare was enough to stun a whale.

He shook his head. "Okay, here goes nothing."

Light once again flashed. He opened his eyes, and they all stood in his hotel room.

Kyros stepped towards him, his eyes locked on Tana. "Why is she unconscious? And Hades..." He reached his hand toward her but hesitated to touch her. "What happened?"

"She killed Skylla."

Kyros' eyes widened as he blew out a breath.

"And dozens of Dagonians," Drakōn added.

"They came up on land?" Kyros asked.

Drakōn shook his head as he leaned down to lay her on the bed.

Kyros pulled him back. "I wouldn't do that. The heat coming off her is intense. Don't you feel it?"

Drakōn looked down, confused. "No. She feels fine to me."

"You lay her on that bed, and she might catch the bedding on fire."

Gretchen stepped forward. "Why don't we put her in the tub? Some cool water might help bring her around."

"You think it's a good idea to wake her?" Kyros asked.

"We can't help her unless we can talk to her. She's not hurt, is she?"

Drakōn shook his head. "No."

"But how can you be sure?" Gretchen asked. "I mean, there has to be a reason she's not awake."

"She was dead."

Raging

"What do you mean—she was dead?" Kyros asked.

"Skylla drove one of his legs through her brain, and then her heart stopped beating. I don't know how much more dead she could be."

"Okay, wait a minute," Gretchen said. "Let's get her in the tub and you can give us the whole story from the beginning."

※ ※

"If you are lying, I'll kill you," Kai shouted through Kyros' phone as Drakōn held it away from his ear.

"*We'll* kill him," Vin's voice shouted in the background.

"No," Drakōn said. "I'm not lying. Tana is fine, just a little disoriented from being struck by a fishing boat. The captain felt horrible and brought us to shore so she could get checked out. The doctor in the ER said she'll be fine, just a slight concussion. She needs to rest; otherwise, I'd have you talk to her right now."

"Okay, well, tell her we'll be in to visit as soon as the doctor okays it."

"I will. And sorry for worrying you." Drakōn ended the call.

"Hmm, sounds like she has some good friends," Kyros said as he sat on the bed at Drakōn's side.

"Yeah, Kai and Vin are great."

Kyros wiped the sweat from his forehead and fanned his hand at the steam. "Opening the windows didn't do any good."

"Yeah," Drakōn said. "I'm aware of that."

"Is the water still boiling?" Kyros asked.

Holly Kelly

"It's gone from a rolling boil to a low simmer," he said as he stepped into the room and sank on down in a chair. "I can't believe Gretchen left." Drakōn shook his head. "I thought she hated being left out."

"Yeah, worrying about her baby burning in a fiery inferno caused her to rethink things—especially after what happened on the island with her mother. Gretchen might be fireproof, but Donovan definitely isn't."

Drakōn kept his eyes on the bathroom. He should go back in there. He really wished he could see through the haze.

Kyros sighed. "You care about her, don't you?"

"Yes. No. I don't know what I feel. She's a danger to everyone around her. You see what's happening with her, right?"

"Yeah."

"Well, that's nothing compared to what happened in the Goussin. She had no control over her power. She boiled everyone in the dome to death within seconds. The only thing left of Skylla was a burnt-out shell. She would have burned me too. What am I supposed to do with her?"

"I would have a hard time controlling myself in that place too. Anyone would have. But you stopped her. You were able to douse her fire with your…whatever power you call it."

"Yes, but I can't be with her every second of the day."

Kyros shook his head. "No, you can't."

Drakōn trembled with worry. He thought protecting

Raging

her from Hades and everyone else would be the biggest part of his job, but he was wrong. The biggest part was protecting others from Tana. "If only I could talk to Sara."

"You should definitely summon her," Kyros said.

"I tried. She won't involve herself anymore."

"What in Hades is that supposed to mean? This isn't important enough for her?"

Drakōn shook his head. "She said the closer she is to us, the less clearly she can see things."

Kyros sighed as he sank down in a chair. "Oh, right."

"I just—" Drakōn's eyes wandered toward the bathroom. "Wait a minute. There's no more steam." He rushed inside, and his heart dropped. Tana was gone, the water still as glass with a hint of steam rising off the surface. Drakōn's eyes wandered to the window. Running forward, he searched outside. He looked at the opening. She'd removed the screen. He slammed his fist against the wall, smashing the tile. "She's gone."

Chapter 17

Tana stumbled as she made her way across the hotel complex. She needed to get home. The world had suddenly become a crazy place. Had she dropped down a rabbit hole? Giant crab creatures didn't exist, mermen didn't exist—okay, she was ready to believe that one and expose it to the world. But she wasn't ready to accept all this other crap!

She had to have been dreaming. Seriously, that had to be it!

"Hello, my dear." A voice spoke to her from behind. She spun around and came face to face with the man who'd plagued her nightmares—the one who'd filled her with rage and broke her heart with betrayal. But she couldn't remember who he was or what he'd done to deserve such animosity from her.

He stood—a black mist swirling around him as sadness filled his eyes. "I'm sorry, Tana, but it's time."

"Who are you?" she asked, taking a step back.

"Don't try to plead ignorance. You know who I am. And you know why we're here."

"We?"

"Erebos and I." He gestured to the black mist swirling

Raging

around him. "If only you'd remained in your prison. You wouldn't have to face punishment. Now it's time you pay for your crimes in the Underworld."

Her blood ran cold. "Listen, I don't know you, but I do know I don't have any crimes to pay for. I don't have so much as an unpaid parking ticket." She tried to block out the images of the floating corpses from the nightmare she'd just woken from. It was a nightmare, wasn't it? "You just get away from me, or I'll be the one calling the cops."

He stepped towards her and paused, his eyes narrowing as they bored into hers, and then they flew wide open as he stepped back. "You're not lying."

"And you're crazy," she said as she backed away.

He raised an eyebrow and said, "Oh really? I'm not the one wearing a... What is that thing?"

She looked down and felt the blood drain from her face. Her wetsuit hung off her, melted. It cut into her skin—hardened to a shell. Curious, she reached down and pulled at it. A piece of her suit snapped off her shoulder.

"It's not decent for a daughter of Hades to be seen like this."

"A daughter of Hades?" She slowly stepped back.

The man stepped forward and towered above her. "Who stole your memories?"

"My memories?" she asked, suddenly angry. "You are seriously insane."

Wasn't he? She barely had time to put her hands up as

the mist filled her vision and enveloped her. Her stomach took a lurch, and she could feel something. It was inside her head. And then it was gone.

The mist withdrew and once again swirled around Hades. "Zeus," he breathed. He took another step forward, forcing her to step back. She could feel the mist as it brushed over her once again and made her skin crawl.

"What does my brother want from you?"

At his glare, a spark lit in her. She clenched her fist. *No one tries to intimidate me!* "I don't care who you think you are—Hades, Zeus, or the Easter Bunny. You get away from me!"

The scent of burnt rosewood surrounded her as the heat inside her built once again. Orange light flickered across the windows of the hotel building.

"Losing control again, are you?" The words were teasing, but there was true pain in his eyes.

"Tana!" a familiar voice shouted from a distance. Not a moment later, Drake pushed her behind his back. Refusing to let him shut her out completely, Tana stepped out from behind him.

The man who called himself Hades narrowed his eyes. "And who have we here?"

"The name's Drakōn."

"Demigod? No," he said, answering his own question. "You have too much power. Who are your parents, stranger?"

"Like I'm going to tell you."

Raging

"Hmm," he said, glancing at Tana and then returning his gaze to Drake. "Why are you protecting this criminal?"

"What crime has she committed?"

Hades narrowed his eyes. "Mass murder."

Tana's legs nearly buckled as the accusation hit her—harder than it should. Could he be right? She shook her head in denial. No. It wasn't possible. She'd never intentionally kill anyone.

"How did she kill them?" Drake asked. "Did she plan her attack and unleash her power when they least expected it? Was she cruel? Did she revel in their suffering?"

Hades didn't bother to answer; he just glared.

"I'll take that as a *no*," Drake snapped. "Did she even mean to kill them, or was it your negligence that caused the deaths? Could you perhaps be passing off your own guilt and placing the blame onto your daughter? A parent is supposed to teach and guide their child in their god powers. Did she defy you? Or were you just unwilling to be bothered by her?"

Hades eyes glowed like flames. Tana trembled at the sight. She lowered her head and grabbed Drake's arm, attempting to pull him back. That man really was a god, and not just any god. He was Hades—the most terrifying of them all. And Drake was provoking him. But still, *she* couldn't possibly be…what? His daughter? Was she a goddess?

Hades expression twisted in anger as he raised his hand. Tana could feel power rise as the black mist gathered and flew toward him. Without thinking, she stepped in front of Drake. Pain drove into her—stealing her breath and overpowering her senses as her knees buckled underneath her. As quickly as the pain hit, the attack ceased. She collapsed in a heap on the ground, her breath heaving. The most curious sound filled her ears—rushing water and muffled shouts. Looking up, she gasped.

Hades floated in the center of a mass of dirty water. It morphed and flowed like a giant, clear bubble. He swung his arms, kicking his legs as he shouted—bubbles flowing from his mouth as he raged. Suddenly, the water stilled. It looked frozen, like ice—with Hades and the black mist locked inside. Drake stumbled from behind it.

The sight mesmerized her. The hint of a memory hit her with a power that took her breath away.

Ice.

Cold.

Despair.

Drake yanked her back to reality as he nearly pulled her arm from its socket. She found herself sprinting behind Drake. "That's not going to hold them for long," he said. "We need to get to the water."

"The water?" she repeated, dazed.

"Yes, we'll be safest there."

They reached the shore in moments and trudged through the pounding surf.

"Was I dreaming, or are you really a sea…thing? Creature…?"

Raging

"God," he supplied.

"God. Right. Oh…good grief. You were right. I'm utterly and completely nuts."

"No. You're not crazy." He pulled her down, and her face submerged. Not ready for it, she inhaled and shot back up, coughing and sputtering. He surfaced next to her.

"I'm not." She coughed more.

He shook his head, his eyes filled with understanding. "No, you're not crazy."

She shook her head. "No, that's not what I meant. I'm not a sea-god. I can't breathe underwater."

He pursed his lips and sighed. "I can help. I'm getting better at this."

"At what?"

"Controlling the water." He tugged her again, apparently wanting her to submerge. "Come on. Trust me."

She shook her head. "But I don't trust you."

He frowned at her.

An explosion rocked the shore. They turned around to see the ice prison holding Hades had shattered, replaced by a fiery inferno that mushroomed like an atom bomb. Half the building was blown to rubble in the blast, and the other half stood defiantly—the levels and rooms open like a horrific, charred dollhouse.

"We don't have time to argue," Drake shouted. "Let's go." He pulled her down. Reluctantly, she followed, but her face never submerged—even after the surface of the water rose above her. She remained in a bubble of air—and that wasn't a good thing. She could see clearly, but only a few inches around her face. It felt like the whole ocean was closing in as Drake pulled her down deeper and deeper. She'd never been claustrophobic before, but this was a whole new experience.

"Drake. Drake! Get me out of here!" she shouted as she clawed at the air bubble—trying to push it away. The air expanded and Drake's face appeared. Tana threw her arms around him and buried her face in his shoulder—holding on for dear life.

"Oh, gods, Tana," he breathed as he brushed his hand over her head. "You're terrified. I don't understand. What's wrong?"

"I feel trapped."

He expanded the bubble to give her more room.

She took a quick glance and once again buried her face in his chest. "That doesn't help."

"I…gods," Drake said. "I don't know what to do. We can't go back. Hades is waiting for you. And I may be a god, but he's much more powerful."

"Wait a minute," he said as he pulled away from her to look her in the eye. "I think I know someone who can help." He closed his eyes and mumbled indecipherable words under his breath.

Tana could feel a change—a burst of power and then a muffled voice.

"Well, this is something you don't see every day," a deep voice resonated. Tana couldn't see who had

Raging

arrived—just a shadow of a figure through the water, but she could hear their voices.

"King Triton," Drake said, stopping her heart. First Hades, and then Triton? What was this? This was impossible—that was what it was!

"Majesty," Drake continued. "I need your help. Sara charged me with protecting this woman, but Hades wants her dead, and he's waiting on shore for her."

"What do you want *me* to do? I'm not about to wage war against the king of the Underworld."

"I'm not asking you to wage war. I'm asking you to allow her sanctuary in our realm. I can think of no place safer than here in the sea."

"You can't mean…?"

"Yes, I want you to change her. You were able to turn your wife into a mermaid. I need you to do the same for Tana."

"Tana? Hades' daughter?" he asked, his voice low.

"You've heard of her?"

"Yes." His voice hardened. "I thought Hades had imprisoned her. You said Sara told you to protect her?"

"Yes, Tana's one of the four."

One of the four? What does that mean?

"Tana, daughter of Hades, one of the four?"

"Yes."

"Makes sense, but she's a dangerous one. Were you aware she burned an entire village to death? Men, women, and children—several hundred innocent humans—all incinerated in minutes."

Holly Kelly

Tana slapped her hands over her ears. *I didn't kill anyone. I couldn't have!* She pressed her hands against her skull and buried her face in Drake's chest as she attempted to banish the images that threatened to surface in her mind. He tightened his hold on her.

"I'm convinced it wasn't intentional," Drake said. "Sara said that she does not have the ability to control her power. Please, Majesty. Who will she burn here?" Drake was obviously leaving out the fact she'd already burned those mermen.

"Transform her into a mermaid," Drake continued. "So I can protect her, and then you will be able to protect the world from her."

"She'll have to surface eventually, Drakōn," Triton said. "She'll need to in order to free the king."

I'm supposed to free a king?

"I know," Drake answered. "But she doesn't even remember who she is. Let me talk to her. Prepare her for what is coming. But, I beg you, let me do this here—where she feels safe."

"She doesn't look like she feels safe now."

"She's claustrophobic in this air bubble. Normally, she loves swimming in the sea. She told me it's the only place she feels safe."

"A daughter of the Underworld and the skies feels safe in the sea? Interesting."

"Please, if you do this, I will take responsibility for her."

"Do you swear on the River Styx?"

Raging

"I swear."

Triton paused. "Okay, I'll grant it. But if she harms anyone in my realm, I will take my retribution out on you."

"Agreed."

Why was Drake doing this? He was risking a lot for someone he barely knew. Tana's thoughts flew from her mind when her whole body began to tingle. Her legs slapped together as the most curious feeling washed over her. The bubble of air covering her face disappeared—replaced with a rush of water. And then the scene in front of her became crystal clear.

A merman floated in front of her—a trident in his hand. He was young and handsome, with blond hair, bright blue eyes, and a scowl pressing a crease in his forehead. This had to be King Triton. He looked nothing like the Triton she'd seen in fairy tale pictures.

He swam forward. "Tana," he said as he looked her over. His scowl loosened, and he shook his head. "You do look harmless. But looks can be deceiving."

"She doesn't understand Atlantian," Drake said.

Atlantian?

"She understands," Triton said.

Tana's lungs burned as she resisted breathing in the seawater.

"You can breathe now, child." Horror crossed over her face when she considered the possibility. Triton leaned forward, inches from her. She'd blinked, and then the sea-god was flying away from her.

"Hades, what's *wrong* with you?" Triton shouted.

"You were going to kiss her," Drake growled angrily. In the meantime, Tana's lungs burned so badly that she thought they'd burst.

"Are you kidding me? My wife would slice me to ribbons. I was simply going to help Tana breathe, but if you'd rather do it, be my guest. Personally, I would do it *before* she passes out."

Drake swam forward. With just a hint of hesitation, he pressed his lips against hers and blew water into her mouth. It breezed into her before coming out behind her ears. It was the strangest thing she'd ever felt, and it caused immediate relief. Hesitantly, she pulled away and took her own breath of water. Soon, she was comfortable enough with the process to breathe deeply. This was ten times easier than breathing in a mouthpiece. A smile broke out on her face as she looked around at the colorful fish and coral surrounding her. It appeared much more vibrant and clear than she'd ever seen through a mask.

Triton shook his head and blew out a breath. "You're right. She seems very comfortable in the water."

"I've spent my life in the water," she said. "Of course I'm comfortable."

"Your life in the water, huh?" Triton said.

Tana nodded and then looked herself over. She looked like an honest-to-goodness mermaid. Her tailfin was the most brilliant blue, and her breasts were covered with what appeared to be a bikini top made of luminous fabric that sparkled as if embedded with diamonds. She

Raging

pulled at the blue fabric, surprised to find her natural skin under the scales. "So I don't have real scales?"

Triton smiled. "No. You're not a fish. Your form is that of a mermaid."

"Wow. This is..." She couldn't find the right word. Amazing? Incredible? Impossible? "Insane."

"Yeah." He chuckled. "I may have to agree with you on that."

"Thank you, just the same," she said. "And this," she gestured to the blue fin, "is beautiful."

"I'll tell my daughter, Iris, that you said so."

Tana looked up. "What? Your daughter made this?"

Triton nodded.

"Tell her thank you for me," Tana said.

"I will," Triton said. He then looked from her to Drake. "Good luck, Dagonian. Keep her safe. By the way, do you need help getting Tana to your home?"

Drake shook his head. "Nope, I've got it covered."

"Okay, well, I've got to go." A scowl settled on Triton's face. "Nicole has me spelunking. I appreciate you getting me out of those surface caves. A sea-god is not built to handle being surrounded by millions of tons of rock and dirt."

"Yeah, I understand. So does your wife have you looking for an entrance to where the king is being held?" Drake asked.

Triton shrugged. "I'm not sure what we're looking for. Hopefully, we'll know when we find it."

Chapter 18

Drakōn transported himself and Tana to the mouth of a cave outside his underwater home. The landscape looked just as he remembered it—filled with jagged, coral spires hundreds of feet high. The towers twisted and bent, casting gnarled shadows over the silt blanketing the base of the features. This coral reef repelled most fish and larger predators. No one knew why, but even Dagonians were unsettled by this rare species of coral—which was why Drakōn chose this area to build his home. He appreciated being alone; the coral didn't bother him at all. In fact, he felt at home here.

"What is this place?" Her eyes widened as she craned her head to see the top of the mountainous stalks.

"This is a coral forest."

"That's coral?"

"Yeah, in Atlantian, it's called kondyioss."

"What does kondyioss mean?"

Drakōn shrugged. "It's an ancient word meaning danger."

"Is it dangerous?"

"No, it just feels dangerous. It's actually very safe in

Raging

here."

"So, where's your house?" Tana asked.

"It's not far." He pointed to the opening through a tangle of coral to the south. "Just through there."

"Seriously?" She turned to him and frowned. "What are you afraid of? Why would you build a house inside the coral?"

"It's not inside the coral; it's in a clearing on the other side. And I built it there to discourage visitors."

"You've put up some serious walls."

"Walls are pretty ineffective underwater."

"I was speaking figuratively." She smirked.

"I'm not the only one with walls." He brushed his hand over the side of her face as he cracked a smile. He took her hand. "I want you to wait here."

"Wait. Why?"

"I want to make sure my home is still empty."

"And if it's not?" She frowned.

"I'll simply evict whoever has taken up residence there."

"Oh," she said. "It's not dangerous, is it?"

He shrugged. "For them, perhaps. Just stay here and I'll be right back."

"What if you aren't?"

"I will."

Tana scowled at him. She didn't look convinced.

"Seriously," he said. "I'll only be a few minutes."

"Alright." She sighed. "Hurry up then."

Drakōn swam through the coral, keeping low—but

not too low. He didn't want to stir up silt. When his manor came into view, he could see that everything appeared intact. There were no broken windows or doors ajar. Circling the house, he found absolutely nothing out of place.

And that was what worried him.

He'd been gone for two years. The place should show signs of being abandoned, but it didn't. There were no barnacles, no coral pods, nothing. It looked pristine. Someone was taking care of his home—probably living in it. He peered through the window, but it was too dark to see if anyone lurked inside.

Goose bumps rose on his skin. Drakōn pulled out his dagger.

Eyes were on him. He could feel them.

With the handle tight in his grip and the blade tucked against his forearm, he kept his eyes down but used all his other senses to pinpoint where the threat may be.

And there it was—at his back. The reflection of a figure passed over the glass pane. It looked to be a female. For a moment, he thought perhaps Tana had followed him but dismissed it seeing that the figure had dark hair and a dark tail—a strange color choice for a female. Even stranger, she seemed to be attempting to sneak up on a male with a knife in hand.

Drakōn sheathed his blade, knowing it would only complicate things. The woman raised her knife and sliced down. Drakōn turned, lifted his arms—one crossed over the other—and caught her wrist as it came down.

Raging

Snaking around, he grabbed her hand and continued the downward momentum until the blade was redirected to the woman's own stomach. He stopped just before the blade thrust into her. The point pressed against her skin.

With fading twilight filtering through the coral canopy, and her unbound hair floating over her face, he couldn't see who she was, but he did catch the gleam of a glaring eye.

"Who are you?" he growled, tightening his grip on her wrist and pulling her toward him.

"The mistress of this house," she snapped. Drakōn was impressed with her courage, but she was also foolish to antagonize him when she was completely at his mercy.

"I don't think so," he said. "This is my house."

Surprise flickered in her eye. The next word she spoke caused his heart to stop.

"Father?" She brushed her hair away, and the familiarity of her face struck him.

He let go and backed away, stunned. "Selene?"

Before he could process the fact that he was face to face with the daughter he'd only met once, she was gone—leaving a cloud of silt swirling in her wake. Without a moment of hesitation, Drakōn was on her trail.

She was fast, she was agile, and she was headed in Tana's direction. His heart pounded at the thought. At least he'd disarmed her. Of course, if Tana felt threatened, Drakōn didn't know what her reaction would be. Fire may not be able to ignite under the water, but he didn't discount the possibility that she could heat it up to lethal temperatures. He'd never prayed to the gods, but right now, he felt compelled to. He desperately needed both of these women to stay safe.

Before he could utter a word of prayer, a squeaking cry in the distance warned him something was wrong. "Drake," Tana shouted—her voice distressed.

Finally, he reached them. Selene floated unconscious, blood trailing from her nose. "I'm so sorry," Tana said, worry etched in her face. "She surprised me."

Drakōn swam in and pulled Selene toward him to inspect the damage. "What did you do?"

"I punched her. She came out of nowhere, tearing around the coral. It was a knee-jerk reaction. And it's all your fault."

"My fault?" he turned, surprised.

"Yeah, you freaked me out with all your talk of danger."

Drakōn couldn't see any real damage. Selene began to moan but didn't open her eyes. "She'll be alright. Let's get her into the house."

"Do know who she is?" Tana asked.

"Yeah," he said as he swam toward his home with Selene in his arms. "She's my daughter."

"Your daughter?" Tana said, rushing to keep up. "How can she be your daughter? She's a grown woman."

Drakōn barked a laugh. "Yeah, I'm older than I look."

Tana put her hand on the front door of the house to stop him before he opened it. "How old are you?"

Raging

He pursed his lips as he regarded her. After several long minutes, he said, "You really don't want to know." Pulling her hand off the door, he shoved his way inside.

He could feel her at his back when she said, "Yes, I really do."

"My age is not important. What is important is the fact my daughter is unconscious."

Tana swam around to face him. "Do you think she'll be okay?"

"I'm sure she will."

"Do you think she'll hate me?"

Drakōn shrugged. "I have no idea. I've never gotten the chance to get to know her."

"Wait," Tana said, once again heading him off. "You don't know your own daughter?"

He stopped and growled, "It's a long story. Come on, let's go in."

He took in his surroundings. The house looked just as well cared for on the inside as it had on the outside. In fact, it looked better than when he'd lived in it. It appeared that Selene had redecorated. Sculptures of sea creatures adorned the hall—large ones towering above and small ones placed on the tables next to stunning bouquets of colorful, rare coral and anemones.

"Wow," Tana said. "I've never imagined underwater homes looking like this. It's incredible."

"Yeah," Drakōn said. "From the looks of it, my daughter has made herself at home. I wonder what her mother thinks of her living here?"

"She doesn't know," Selene mumbled.

"Gods, Selene," Drakōn breathed. "Are you okay?"

She shook her head and pressed her hand against her forehead. "Who is the woman with the powerful jab?"

"Um, that would be me," Tana said. "I'm really sorry. You came out of nowhere, and I panicked."

"I understand," Selene said. "Really, I do."

"Why did you flee?" Drakōn asked.

"I...well, you were in prison because of me, and my mother warned me if you ever got out, you'd come after me. I just never expected you to escape."

"I never thought I would either."

"Wait," Tana said as she turned to Drakōn. "You were in prison? You're a criminal?"

"I'm the criminal, not my dad," Selene said. "And I just have one request."

"What is it, child?"

She sighed and straightened her shoulders. "Kill me quickly."

"What?" Drakōn said, stunned.

"Please," Selene begged. "I know it was cowardly to flee, but I really..." Her voice dropped away.

"What?" Tana asked.

"Don't want to die." Selene hardened her voice.

Drakōn threw up his hands. "Hades! I'm not going to kill you. What kind of lies did your mother fill your head with?"

"I...she didn't fill me with lies. I've learned enough about you on my own to know how brutal you are. I

Raging

mean, that one fugitive, the one you went after in the Bering Sea—you brought him back in pieces. In pieces! You had his head raised on the point of your spear."

Drakōn shook his head, sickened that his daughter knew the things he'd done. He glanced over to Tana, wondering what she thought of him now.

He wished he hadn't looked. She looked like she'd seen a ghost.

"Listen, he was a hardened criminal. I was told to bring him back dead or alive. Dead was… much easier."

"But why did you cut him in pieces?" Selene asked.

"Because he deserved it!" Drakōn shouted, and then immediately regretted his outburst. Both Tana and his daughter backed away, obviously frightened by him. Perhaps they should be afraid of someone like him. But, truth be told, he'd die before he harmed either one of them.

Drakōn swallowed and sighed. "He was a monster who preyed on children. When I found him, he had a young girl with him. And I'll not say more, other than I don't regret what I did."

"So…" Selene's eyes softened. "You're a hero?"

"Oh, gods. No," he growled. "I'm no hero."

He shifted, uncomfortable with the direction the conversation had gone. He cleared his throat. "Listen, you're welcome to stay as long as you like. You are my daughter, after all." An uncomfortable lump filled his throat.

"Really? I can stay?"

"Of course."

She looked down, obviously uncomfortable. "Thank you. I'm sorry for misjudging you," Selene said with a hint of a smile. "We aren't so different after all." Her smile faded. "I'm sorry you ended up in prison because of me. Speaking of Panthon, how did you get out of there?"

"That's a long story." Drakōn said. Turning to Tana, he reached out his hand. She hesitated a moment before taking it.

"I've got time," Selene said.

Tana swam through Drake's house. Drake and Selene needed privacy, so she left them to get acquainted. Besides, she wasn't about to pass up the chance to explore an underwater home. And she needed to clear her mind and think about something else for a while. Swimming around this house was the perfect remedy.

The scene around Tana floored her. This mansion came straight out of a fantasy novel. There were glowing patches of coral across the hallway floor with smooth marble shining beneath. The rooms were large and surreal, with the strangest furniture she'd ever seen—made completely out of shells, coral, and stone.

The next room looked to have orange jellyfish tentacles hanging from the ceiling—partitioning off parts of the space. She had to take a closer look at it.

Hesitantly, she entered. Reaching out, she was about to touch the tentacle curtain when a thought crossed her

Raging

mind. What if it stung her? But who in their right mind would put poisonous curtains all around their home? She sighed in relief when her finger brushed up against it. It wasn't made of tentacles, but something more like fabric—but smoother, silkier. Pulling it back, she found a hidden bookcase. Actually, it looked more like a hollowed-out cave with shelves. Leather spines of books lined up in rows, strapped inside with gold-colored rope.

For a moment, she wondered how a merman would open a book and relax under the water. But then, movement from the corner of her eye caught her attention.

Balloons?

It looked like a giant bouquet of translucent balloons hovering just above the floor in the corner of the room. Swimming forward, she inspected it closer. The balloons seemed to be suspended without strings. Actually no, there was a string, but only one—attached to the lowest balloon.

"What in the world is this?" she mumbled to herself. "Man, I wish I had my camera."

The shadow of a stingray caught her attention as it passed by the window on the far side of the room, darkening it for a second. In that moment, everything lit up with colorful light. As soon as the stingray passed, the light once again poured in from the window.

"Holy crap," she breathed. Swimming over to the window, she pressed her hand against the glass. It seemed like normal glass. Outside, there was a clearing of silt, with hills of coral as a backdrop. Fish swam in formation above the coral, almost like an underwater flock of birds.

Tana shook her head. "I have to be dreaming."

"That's what I thought when I stepped out on land." Drake's voice came from behind.

Tana jerked around in surprise. "You startled me." She gasped.

"Sorry." He swam into the room with a smile on his face, not looking the least bit apologetic.

"Where's your daughter?" Tana asked.

"She was expecting visitors. She went to go head them off and keep them away. She said she'd be back by the week's end."

"You mean the weekend?"

Drake smiled. "Right."

Tana nodded, trying to wrap her head around the strangeness of this place. She truly couldn't have felt more out of her element if she'd been kidnapped by aliens and taken to another planet.

"What's wrong?" Drake reached out and took her hand, concern creasing his forehead.

Tana shook her head. "Nothing…I mean…" She sighed. "This is just a lot to take in."

"I really do know how you feel."

She searched his face. He was serious. "You felt like this when you went up on land?"

"I felt like a fish out of water," he said.

Tana chuckled. "Very funny."

He gave a weak smile and shrugged. "You'll get used

to it. It took me a while, but eventually, I did. Sometimes, I'd even forget I was out of the water."

"I can't imagine ever forgetting that I'm in the ocean. Not when I'm down here seeing this." She gestured around the room, her eyes landing on the balloon contraption. "I mean, what is that? I can't even begin to figure what it's for."

Drake chuckled. "That's a…*acumvene*."

"That sounds like a word I should know, but I can't quite understand what it is."

He shook his head. "Triton gave you the ability to understand Atlantian, but I guess your mind is having difficulty finding a frame of reference. It's something like…hmm. Sort of like a recliner."

He swam into the center of the balloons and flipped onto his back. Cushioned in the balls, he lay back, relaxed. "Join me and try it." He raised an eyebrow.

She took a breath and said, "Okay, here goes." When she swam into the middle of the balloons—or rather, the *acumvene*—they pressed against her, cushioning her body and obscuring her view. Drake's tailfin scratched her skin as she swam beside him. Using his body as a guide, she grabbed hold of his arms to pull her up. When her head popped out of the top, she stopped swimming and relaxed. His arms came around her in a gentle embrace. She felt cradled on every side with his body heat warming her.

She looked him in the eye, and then glanced down at his body pressed against hers, his arms cradling her.

"You had ulterior motives," she said, smirking.

Drake shrugged and brushed her floating hair out of her eyes. "I can't say I don't like having you in my arms."

She shook her head. "I have to admit, this is really comfortable."

"And I must admit, I'm enjoying it more than usual."

Tana chuckled and then gave a yawn. Fatigue tugged at her as her eyes drooped. Closing her eyes, she sighed, relishing the feeling of Drake's arms around her. Flashes of images flew across her vision—images of dead, cooked corpses. Tana jerked as her eyes flew open.

"Whoa," Drake said, his voice deep and soft. "What's the matter?"

"Um, it's just…I've been avoiding thinking about what happened. I…I keep seeing things. Things that are impossible and horrifying." She sighed. "So who am I? I have a feeling you know exactly who I am."

Drake blew out a breath. "Yes, I do."

There was silence as she waited for him to elaborate. "You are the daughter of Hades and Eos."

"I'm sorry, but I'm a bit rusty when it comes to Greek mythology. Hades is the god of the Underworld, but who is Eos? The name sounds familiar."

"She is the goddess of sunrise."

Tana shook her head. The memories of her parents were still there, but they seemed to be fading—like the details of a dream. It felt as if her identity was slipping away, with nothing but flashes of horror and regret to replace it.

Raging

"Did I know her?"

"I don't know. I wasn't given a lot of details about your past. I was simply charged with protecting you, and…"

"What?"

Drake was silent. It sounded like he didn't want to tell her.

"I'm supposed to protect others from you."

"I don't understand. I…" Her voice fell away as she considered what she remembered. "I'm dangerous. Those mermen—"

"Dagonians."

"Right. Dagonians." Tana tensed as she allowed some of the memories to trickle forward. "I killed them all."

"You were protecting yourself."

"No, I…was out of control. I couldn't stop it." Tana shook her head. "I…"

"What?"

"I'm afraid."

"You don't need to be afraid." Drake squeezed her tighter. "I'll protect you."

"How can you protect me from myself?"

He tightened his hold and pressed a kiss against her head.

After several minutes, she spoke. "There's one question you haven't answered yet."

"What question?"

"How old are you? Really."

He chuckled. "I'm not sure of my exact age. But I've been around for over five hundred years."

"Wow," she breathed. "You look good for an old man."

His chest rumbled as he chuckled. "Thanks."

Chapter 19

Hades paced across the sand—the water lapping at his feet. What had happened to Tana? She didn't have even a spark of familiarity in her face. Someone had freed her and then erased her memories. And then, where did the sea-god go? Why under Olympus was he protecting her?

He felt a surge of immense power at his back. Hades turned to find a goddess watching him. Her white hair billowed in the sea breeze, her green eyes penetrating as she regarded him. She seemed familiar, but he couldn't place where they'd met before—which was impossible. His memory should be infallible.

"Uncle," she said.

"Do I know you?" he asked.

"No, you don't, but you knew my grandfather."

"And who is your grandfather?"

She cracked a smile. "If I tell you, you'll think I'm crazy or a traitor to the king of the gods."

Hades perked up. A traitor to Zeus? Perhaps this little goddess knew something of the mystery. "*Are* you a traitor?"

"No, I'm not. Zeus is the one who's a traitor."

"You *are* mad." He scowled at her, wishing her words were true.

"No, I'm a goddess with her memories intact."

"You never answered my question; who is your grandfather?" He took an intimidating step forward.

A hint of a smile pulled at her lips. "My grandfather is Petros, your older brother."

The familiarity of that name struck him like a blow to the chest. Hades searched his mind. He knew that name. He was certain he did. So why couldn't he remember?

"Search out your past, Majesty. Look for the places where the seams don't match up. There you will find the answers you seek—about Zeus, Petros, and yourself. You will not see me again until your memories are restored."

Hades could see she intended to leave. There was no way he'd let her until she answered every single one of his questions—and he had a million. He didn't hesitate to throw up a block to prevent her from transporting.

The goddess smiled—a knowing glint in her eyes—just before she disappeared.

"By Olympus," he growled angrily. First, he was struck down by Zeus, then a sea-god, and now he couldn't even cast a simple block against this little goddess. Could he be losing his touch?

Look for the places where the seams don't match up. What under Olympus did that mean? She sounded like one of the Moirai. In fact, she looked like one too. Hades swore under his breath. He absolutely hated when the Fates got involved in events.

Raging

Look for the places where the seams don't match up. The words rose unbidden in his mind, as if somewhere deep inside, he knew they were important. Okay, if they were so deadly important, he would solve this puzzle. It wasn't as if he had anything else to do—except for finding Ares, who it seemed had disappeared from existence, and finding a daughter who was buried under a mile of seawater. Oh yeah, and if he didn't do either of those things, both his life and the lives of countless others might be in jeopardy. He definitely didn't have time for this.

Look for the places where the seams don't match up. "I heard you the first time!" he shouted to himself. In a swirling, fiery vortex, he transported himself to the depths of hell.

The moment Hades saw Persephone dancing, his heart lightened. Stepping behind a pillar to shield himself from her view, he watched her glide and twirl—dancing in the garden to the tune of the tortured souls she had imprisoned. The ghostly shades howled behind prison bars covering the mouth of a nearby cave.

At the close of her dance, she folded down in on herself, like a beautiful flower wilting at the approach of fire. Lying back on the ground, she flung her arms and legs out and laughed. She was so much happier now that she was no longer forced to return to the human world. And Hades rejoiced in her happiness.

Stepping out from his hiding place, he strode forward. His wife glanced over at him, her smile widening as she sat up. "You weren't watching me, were you?"

"Watching you lie in the grass? I'm afraid I was."

She smiled suspiciously and looked him over. He could read her like a book. She suspected he had been watching her dance, but she didn't want to admit to it, just in case he wasn't lying. He adored seeing his wife happy and loved everything about her—especially her eyes. They sparkled with such life. At this moment, she never looked more beautiful.

Look for the places where the seams don't match up.

His mood immediately darkened. Why couldn't he simply live happily with his bride in the Underworld? Why did trouble seem to seek him out at every turn?

"What is it, darling?" Persephone asked, tugging on his arm.

"We need to talk."

She nodded, her brows pinched together.

"Is this about Tana? Listen, I know you are torn up about what you have to do, but your hands are tied. You can't save her, you know."

He shook his head, "No. I can't." The image of Tana's protector crossed his mind. Hades could still feel the immense power that had erupted from him. "But perhaps there's someone who can."

"Who?"

"A sea-god. What better way to quench a flame but in the depths of the sea?"

"Tana, live in the sea?"

"There's no place safer for her, don't you think?"

Persephone smiled. "No, there isn't. Could you just

Raging

let her go unpunished?"

"Yes," he answered with hope in his heart. "As long as she agreed to never leave the ocean depths. I think that is the perfect solution—a prison where she can live in freedom and happiness."

"I'm so happy you found a solution. Now is that what you wanted to talk to me about? I feel there's more than what you've told me."

"Yes, I have a question—a seam that doesn't match up."

"A what?"

"Never mind, dear. I just have one thing to ask you."

"Okay, fire away."

"How did you and I meet?"

"We met…" Persephone's voice drifted off as she looked down. She narrowed her eyes and pursed her lips. "I…" The color drained from her face. "I've no idea."

"I don't either. All I know is that we did meet, we married, and we've lived a happy life."

"How could we forget such a thing?"

Hades shook his head. "I don't know, but I do know I was visited by a Fate today."

"A Fate? The three usually travel together."

"This woman was not one of the three. I've never seen her before."

"Then how do you know you can trust her?"

"I don't know; I just…do. What she said feels right."

"And what did she say?"

"She told me I have a brother named Petros."

Persephone scoffed. "That's impossible. How could you forget a brother? However, the name…"

"Sounds familiar?"

"Yes."

"This Fate said in order to restore my memories, I needed to find the seams that don't match. The first thing I thought about was you. You are my past, my present, and my future. So I decided I would go through every memory I have of you and see if there was anything unusual in my memories. It didn't take me long to figure out there was a problem."

"So how do we remember?" Persephone asked.

"We'll go through our memories, one by one, and see what else may be missing. Perhaps we can find a pattern."

Persephone sat down in the midst of her lilies and nodded. "Okay. Let's get started."

Chapter 20

Tana awoke, annoyed. It felt like a fly had chosen her nose as a landing strip. Swatting at it, she opened her eyes. A gaping mouth opened and closed in front of her—framed with bulging eyes.

"Eek!" she screamed as she jerked her head back and hit something hard. "Get it away; get it away," she shrieked as she swatted at the water.

"Ouch! Gods, Tana," Drake shouted just behind her. He had his arms around her. "What under the sea is wrong?"

To her relief, the fish swam away. It looked much smaller when it wasn't trying to eat her face. "It's a fish," she gasped, still trembling as she tried to catch her breath of water. "Oh my gosh, it's just a fish."

"Yeah, I'm familiar with that type of creature. Why were you screaming at it?"

"I didn't scream, I just...well, it was nibbling on my nose!"

Drake chuckled. "I know it's annoying, but gods, it was only a small, foraging fish. Now, if you'd woken up face to face with a shark, then I'd be worried."

Tana attempted to turn and face him. Once she had

him in her sights, she'd give him a piece of her mind. Drake loosened his grip and allowed her to turn.

"Listen," she said, "I've never slept in the ocean before. And waking up with a fish sucking on my face was a bit disturbing."

Drake didn't respond, but the smirk on his face didn't waver.

She frowned at him. "Weren't you ever freaked out by a…you know, a land animal?"

His smile vanished replaced by a scowl. *Ah ha!* He had been. "What was it?"

He shook his head and attempted to swim out of the recliner thingy. "It was nothing."

"Oh no, you don't." She pulled him back. "What was it?"

"I'm sorry for laughing at you."

Tana broke into a smile and chuckled. When he turned to glare, she subdued her amusement. "Drake," she said, drawing out his name. "What was kind of animal was it?"

He looked away and sighed. "A cat."

Holding back her smile became increasingly difficult. "A house cat?" She covered her mouth just as she lost her battle and laughed out loud. "I'm sorry. I know it's not funny."

Drake cracked a grin and said, "Actually, I'm told it was pretty funny."

"You didn't hurt the poor thing, did you?"

"The cat was fine, but I got a few bruises when I tried

Raging

to get away from the animal. I fell trying to climb the steps of Xanthus' house. In my defense, I had no idea whether the creature was poisonous or how sharp its teeth were."

Tana shook her head. "Alright, how about we agree to keep this between us? I won't tell anyone you were terrified of a kitty cat."

Drake frowned at her. "And I won't tell anyone you were freaked out by a little herring. Speaking of herring, where is that little nibble?" He squeezed out and darted across the room. "There you are."

"Nibble? You aren't going to—" Before she could finish her sentence, he snatched the tiny fish out of the water and popped it into his mouth.

"You just ate a live fish."

"Mm, yes, I did."

"That's disgusting."

He shrugged. "To each his own."

Tana slipped out and swam into the middle of the room. She continued, snaking around Drake and enjoying the feel of swimming with a tailfin. She'd never felt so free. It was like she could fly. "How about we go for a morning swim? I'd love to be able to do some exploring."

"I don't see why not. So what do you want to explore, the coral forest?"

"I want to explore the ocean."

Drake shook his head and smiled. "The ocean is a big place."

"I know that." Tana frowned. "How about an

underwater city?"

"That's not a good idea."

"Why?"

"I'm a wanted man," he answered. "If I'm caught, I go back to prison."

"But, you're also a god. Can they really put a god in prison?"

"Huh, good point."

"So, let's go. Really! An underwater civilization would be such a fascinating place to visit."

Drake looked at her and frowned. "I suppose you could pass for a Dagonian. Okay, if this is going to work, you'll need to stay beside me. Don't make eye contact with anyone. And don't, under any circumstances, talk to anyone."

"You can't be serious."

"I'm dead serious," he said without a hint of humor. "Dagonian women are subservient to the men. They're barely above property in value. I'm not saying it's right, but that's the way it is down here."

"Your daughter didn't seem very submissive."

"Yes, but don't forget, her behavior led her to be sentenced to prison. It's only because I accepted her punishment that she was able to go free."

Tana's chest trembled with nervousness. Could she pull off subservient? Possibly. "I'll do my best."

Drake sighed. "Just remember to keep your eyes down in the presence of another male, and keep your mouth shut."

Raging

"Alright, I think I can handle that."

"Okay," Drake pursed his lips and sighed. "I'll bet you'd like to see something modern as opposed to ancient. How about we visit Corin? I spent the better part of the last several decades there training with Xanthus."

"Xanthus?"

"His wife sent me to protect you."

"She did? Why would she do that?"

"That's a long story." He took her hand. "I'll tell you everything you want to know. Later."

From his expression, he seemed to ask her to trust him. Did she trust him? She kept telling him she didn't, but truth be told, she was beginning to. "Alright. Let's go visit the city. That is something I can't wait to see."

Drake cracked a smile. "Okay." He wrapped his arms around her as she closed her eyes.

CHAPTER 21

Tana noticed a change at once. The water was noticeably cooler and less oppressing.

"Open your eyes," Drake said into her ear. She lifted her lids and looked up. A gasp escaped her lips.

In the distance, an immense city stood with tall, twisting spires. The buildings must have been made of some kind of luminescent material because the whole metropolis shined like a group of lit-up Christmas trees the size of skyscrapers. What was most strange, though, was that the entire place was surrounded in a tangled canopy of...coral? Rock? She couldn't tell which, but it was not unlike the coral forest hiding Drake's house. Tana pointed up to it. "Is that to keep the city hidden?"

"Yes, from sea monsters, mostly."

"Sea monsters? What kind of sea monsters are we talking about?"

Drake shrugged. "Krakens, leviathans, keteas, charybdis, and hydras, to name a few."

"A few! That sounds like a heck of a lot of monsters."

"Yeah, but I didn't name the most feared creature."

Tana's skin crawled, wondering what the most feared creature in the sea was. "What is it?"

Raging

"Humans," Drake said gravely.

Tana sighed, somewhat relieved. "Seriously?"

"Absolutely. They've killed thousands and polluted the sea so much that many places are unlivable."

Tana frowned, her head hung low. "I guess I can understand that."

"Alright, come on. I didn't bring you here to give you a guilt trip. Let's go see the city."

Moments later, they passed through the towering gate that led to a paved city street. There were several mermaids—or rather, Dagonian women, swimming into buildings with large windows. Were they stores? They had strange things in the windows. Some, Tana recognized—boxes, tailfins, and jewelry, but others looked strange. Like what in the world would someone do with the skull of a giant fish on the end of a staff?

"What?" Drake whispered out of the corner of his mouth.

"Huh?" Tana asked, puzzled at his question.

"You look confused."

"What's up with the fish skull?"

Drake smiled. "Oh."

"Oh, what?"

"Shh. Not so loudly." He couldn't help the smile. "I'll tell you later."

"Seriously?" she whispered.

He chuckled. "Yeah."

They swam on for several minutes, with more buildings, but less large windows. The buildings deeper in the heart of the city looked more like places to live. Tana looked up and found a few Dagonians swimming above. She looked over to Drake and found him frowning. "What's wrong?"

He shook his head, his frown remaining in place. "I don't know."

As they came around a corner, a colorful, towering feature came into view. It was filled with twisting tunnels and openings. And then there were colorful, sculpted fish swinging on the end of wires, and what looked to be balls and colorful disks scattered on the ground. "Is this a playground?"

"Very good."

Tana was excited to have guessed it right, but then she wondered at Drake's somber tone.

"What's wrong?"

"It's mid-afternoon."

"Yeah."

"Where are the children?"

Tana looked around, trying to catch a glimpse of anyone. The place seemed deserted. "Um, maybe everyone is busy doing other things."

Drake shook his head. "This is one of the largest cities in the sea. The streets are usually filled with people. My biggest worry taking you here was that I might lose you in the crowd. There is something seriously wrong."

"Why don't you ask someone where everyone is?"

"I haven't seen anyone to ask."

"What are you talking about? I've seen several along

the way."

Drake looked around. "What? Where?"

Tana looked across the playground. A woman came out of a nearby building, looked around, and then swam on to her right. "Over there." She pointed.

"That's a woman."

"Um, yeah."

"I can't ask her. I'd probably give her a heart attack, just by speaking to her."

"Well, why don't I ask her?"

Drake's eyes continued to wander, searching the area. He sighed and said, "Okay, but stay within sight of me."

Tana nodded. "Alright, I'll be right back." She swam forward, rushing to catch the woman before she disappeared.

"Excuse me," she called out.

The woman swished to stop and turned. "Yes?"

"Hello." Tana gave a weak smile. "I just arrived in the city, and I couldn't help noticing that all the men have gone."

"You haven't heard?"

Tana shook her head.

"They've gone to battle the humans."

Tana's heart took a pounding leap against her chest. "What?"

"I know. It's impossible, but it's true. There has been another attack. The humans have poisoned Atlantis." She frowned, heartbreak in her eyes. "The entire city is dead." Her voice broke on the word dead.

"No," Tana breathed.

The woman nodded gravely. "It's true. Poseidon himself has only just given the order to go to war. All able-bodied creatures in the sea have been commanded to kill all humans on sight. They've even been given permission to breach the shore."

The sea lit up so bright that Tana couldn't see a thing. Her hands flew up to cover her face as strong arms locked around her waist. When she could see again, she was no longer on the same street. She was in Drake's arms in front of an enormous underwater castle, and she was surrounded by a crowd of Dagonians. Triton himself was there also. Was this his castle?

"Drake?" she said as she looked up at his face.

"We need to find out what's going on," he said.

"Drakōn, have you heard the news?" A handsome man swam toward them.

"Straton." Drake reached out, and they locked their hands onto each other's forearms—obviously in greeting. "I just heard."

"He's done it." Another man shook his head. "I can't believe he's ordered this."

"Majesty," another said to Triton, "you need to take your rightful place as king. You must stop this madness."

"Petros is the rightful king."

"Petros can't stop this. You can."

"Only a few remember. I don't have enough power to take the throne from Zeus, or order my father to back

Raging

down from his command."

Tana was filled with confusion as she turned to Drake. "What are they talking about?"

"I'm not sure," he whispered.

"Are we to simply hang back and watch them kill innocent humans?" another asked.

A beautiful woman with white hair swam toward them, followed closely by another with dark hair—Tana recognized her immediately. She was the woman at the pool—the one she didn't trust.

"Tana." The woman with white hair spoke. "I'm so glad to see you safe."

"Do I know you?" Tana asked, confused by the woman who looked at her as if they were old friends.

"Not yet, but you will." She looked from Tana to Drake. "I knew you two would get along," she said as she smiled weakly.

"Princess," another said, and the woman with white hair looked back. "What do we do?"

Princess? "Is she—?"

"King Triton's daughter, Sara," Drake supplied.

"Wow," Tana said.

"That's not the half of it," he mumbled.

"Let's all go inside," Sara said. "I'll give you my message, but I can't stay long—for obvious reasons."

The castle was more spectacular inside than on the outside. The place was immense, with columns, tapestries, and more glowing walls—not to mention a giant sea squid.

The group entered and gravitated into a circular crowd. Tana thought King Triton would take charge, but the white-haired mermaid spoke.

"First of all, I want to introduce everyone to Tana. She's the daughter of Hades and Eos, and she's one of the missing four."

Tana's heart stopped when all eyes turned toward her. It was bad enough being a spectator in this freaky fantasy, but now she was the center of attention—a place she always avoided. Everyone nodded, some smiling.

"What about the Dagonian attack?" Straton asked. "Did the humans really poison all of Atlantis? I heard there were no survivors."

Sara shook her head. "It wasn't the humans. There was a pocket of carbonic acid under the city. It released because of the shifting of the sea floor due to underwater earthquakes."

"But they're blaming the humans," Kyros said.

"It's easier to blame them," Triton said. "And it doesn't help that this event looks eerily similar to what happened in the South Pacific—when it really was the humans."

"We can stop the Dagonian attack," Sara said. "This is not the big worry. What happened in Atlantis will be nothing compared to what will happen if we don't stop Zeus." Sara turned to Tana. "Tana, I know that Drakōn was going to fill you in on everything, but I'm afraid we've run out of time to do it tactfully."

Sara approached. "May I?"

Raging

Tana nodded. Triton's daughter pressed her hands to the sides of Tana's head and spoke. "You already know that you are the daughter of Hades and Eos—although, I sense you doubt it. Actually, you doubt all this. But doubt it or not, you are the daughter of the king of the Underworld and the goddess of sunrise. Your mother, fearful that your father would steal you away from her, hid you from him when you were young and made a deal with the Moirai. They decreed that your father would not be allowed to personally intercede in your life and would have no direct power over you. To secure this deal, your mother gave up a portion of her power—her immortality.

"Your mother thought to protect you and keep you safe, but she only succeeded in cursing you and allowing herself to be subject to harm. As you came into your powers, your father was not allowed to help you or guide you, and your mother, unable to guard herself, perished.

"I know how much you've suffered because of this. And I know you have a lot of anger and resentment towards Hades. But know this—his hands were tied. He was powerless to come to your aid."

"But why didn't he tell me?" Tana cried.

"He didn't want to taint the memory you had of your mother."

"I...I remember her." Tana's heart stopped. If she'd been standing on land, she would have collapsed. "I killed her. I burned her to death."

"It's not your fault," Sara said.

"That's what my mother told me. She said she was sorry, that she failed me."

"She accepted the blame," Sara said. "She knew what she had done."

"No. It was my father."

"He couldn't help you, Tana," Sara said gently.

"He put me in a prison of ice."

"Only to spare you from a worse fate."

"A worse fate?" Tana shook her head. "A worse fate *he* would have inflicted on me. How can I just cast aside a thousand years of resentment? I've wanted nothing more than to see him suffer. To see my father writhe in agony."

She turned her glaring eyes on Sara and shouted, "Why did you give me my memories back? How could you be so cruel?"

"I'm sorry. To move forward, you have to remember your past."

"If that's the deal, I don't want to move forward!" she screamed as she clutched her hair in her hands and squeezed her head. If only she could squeeze the memories out. If only… "I don't want this. Any of this."

Drake reached out to touch her shoulder. She slapped his hand away and turned on him. "Don't touch me! You stay away from me. I don't want anything more from you." She turned and looked on the faces filled with pity. "I don't want anything from any of you." With that, she swam to the door, pushed it open, and raced toward the surface.

CHAPTER 22

Drakōn clenched his fists, wishing beyond anything he'd ever desired that the last few minutes had never occurred. Tana was suffering. She was angry. And she blamed him.

"Drakōn." Sara inched her way toward him. "I'm really sorry. I had to do it."

"She hates me."

Sara shook her head. "She doesn't hate you. She loves you."

His eyes shot up in surprise.

"She's just in too much pain to realize it."

"She doesn't love me."

"Yes, she does."

"No. Right now, she can't. Sara, I know you're the goddess of fate, but I know. I know exactly how she feels. The betrayal, the anger, and the blame. There's no room in her heart for love. I saw it in her eyes. She wants vengeance, plain and simple."

"You may be right," Sara said. "But vengeance can't bring her what she needs. She needs to find her heart again. And only you can help her, and there's not much time. She's running away. And she running right into—"

"A war zone," Drakōn said, the horror rising in his voice.

Without another word, he shot out the door, hot on Tana's scent. He had to get to her before she found herself in the middle of a nightmare.

Within minutes, he caught a glimpse of her. How should he approach her? She wanted nothing to do with him. If he didn't tread carefully, he might lose her forever. But if he didn't stop her, she could find herself in the center of a battle with no control. She was already tortured with guilt. Truly, that was where her anger and loathing found its fuel. She needed someone other than herself to blame.

He followed her until she'd nearly reached the surface. "Tana," he called.

She stopped and whipped around. "Get back, Drakōn." The coldness of her voice broke his heart.

"I'm sorry, Tana. The last thing I wanted was to hurt you."

"Well, you failed miserably." She turned back and resumed swimming.

He swam alongside her. "Where are you going?"

"I'm going home."

He nodded. "It's a long way from here—about four thousand miles."

The rhythmic stroke of her tailfin stuttered. He'd gained her attention. Still, she moved on.

"Swimming at this pace," he continued, "even without sleep and time to eat, it would still take you

Raging

several weeks."

She continued on, but her pace slowed.

"Tana." He tentatively reached out to her, expecting her to slap his hand away again.

She didn't.

Instead, she stopped. Her shoulders slumped over as her head dropped. He took a dangerous gamble and pulled her into his arms. Instead of fighting him, she sank into his chest and began to cry.

He held her and absorbed her pain for several long minutes before her sobbing abated and her breathing slowed, hitching every few seconds. Finally, she calmed and her watery breaths passed smoothly. It was only then that he dared speak.

"Do you feel better now?" he whispered in her ear.

She nodded. "I don't know what to do, Drake."

Drakōn sighed, relieved down to his soul at hearing the nickname he once hated. "You don't have to do anything, love. You can stay with me—forever if you like."

"I don't think I know how to forgive."

Drakōn shook his head. "You don't have to. You can hold onto your anger for as long as you need, but speaking from experience, the person you hurt the most from not forgiving is yourself."

"Who did *you* have to forgive?"

Drakōn shook his head. "Huh, I have a long list. I was abandoned by both parents, physically and emotionally abused by my foster parents, betrayed by the woman I thought I'd loved, and sent to prison to die for a crime I didn't commit."

Tana shook her head and gave a half-hearted smile. "That's all terrible. But you don't even come close." Her eyes closed as pain washed over her features. "Do you know what it feels like to be frozen in an icy prison for a thousand years? Do you know what it feels like to be responsible for the deaths of everyone you've loved?"

Drake sighed. "No."

"I hate my father with every fiber of my being. But that's not the worst of it. I hate myself more."

"You did nothing wrong—"

"Don't," Tana snapped as her eyes hardened. "I did *everything* wrong. I grew up with a loving mother, who doted over me. But what did I do to repay her? I threw a fit when she wouldn't let me go to a stupid party." Tana's fists clenched. "That was the first time…the first time my powers showed themselves. Once the flames began, I didn't even try to stop them. I was too shocked and afraid to know what was going on. I ran to my mother for help. She tried to escape me, but the flames caught on her skirt."

Drakōn's heart broke for Tana, for what she'd gone through.

"I tried to get a blanket to douse the fire, but that too caught fire in my hands. I watched my mother burn to death in front of my eyes. And the whole time, she screamed, 'Tana, it's not your fault. It's not your fault…' So whose fault was it?"

Drakōn could see the hardness, the hate in Tana.

Raging

His heart broke when he realized who she hated most. Herself.

"Eventually, I found a way to move past that. I did everything I could to put it behind me. And I found a new place to live—alone. Safe from harming others. But then Gabriel found me."

"Gabriel?"

"A man from the nearby village. I loved him."

Drakōn felt a flare of jealousy. But she said loved—as in the past.

"He wooed me for over a year before I let my walls down enough to admit I loved him in return. I was so happy. It had been a long time since the tragedy. I'd even convinced myself that what happened with my mother was a freak accident. Gabriel asked me to marry him, and I accepted. I couldn't wait to be his wife. But then…"

Drakōn waited for her to finish, but truly, he feared to hear what happened. Actually, he knew. Still, she needed to accept it. She needed to move on. "What happened, Tana?" he asked, gently.

"Some girls from the village taunted me." She paused and then whispered, "I killed them. I killed them all, and in killing them, I also killed the man I loved." She raised her eyes, regret stealing the light from them.

Then a spark lit up her eyes with hope. She turned to Drakōn. "Wait a minute. You're a powerful god, right?"

"Relatively speaking," he answered.

She looked at him, doubt flickering in her eyes. "I know what I want. I know how to make everything well again."

Drakōn narrowed his eyes, suspicious at her change. "What are you talking about?"

Her eyes searched his face before resting on his eyes. "I want you to kill me."

"What?" Drakōn pulled back.

"If you kill me," Tana said, "I won't be able to hurt anyone ever again."

"But," he said. "You're already safe from hurting others."

Her brows pinched down in confusion. "No, I'm not."

"And how, pray tell, do you think you can combust submerged in water?"

"But…I killed all those Dagonians."

"You weren't submerged."

Tana frowned as she seemed to consider his words. Her face relaxed. "What about the forgotten king? Triton said I had to go save him. I'd have to leave the water to do it."

"I'll just have to come with you."

"You'd have to stay with me every moment."

"Of course I would."

Tana shook her head. "I…I just can't. I'm not a hero. I'm a villain."

"I've seen my share of villains; you're not one of them."

"I've killed hundreds of people. I'm a mass murderer."

"You're not. Your mother was right. It was not your

Raging

fault. You are just as much a victim in all this as the others."

"I'm a long way from believing that."

"I'm a patient man. And you're a smart woman. You'll figure it out eventually."

The roar of an engine passed overhead. Tana looked up, her attention turned at the strange sight. "They're running that boat *way* too fast. They're going to overheat the engine."

At that moment, several Dagonians swam into view. Their expressions were intent as they raced to catch the boat.

Tana felt the currents of the water as they swept past her. "Oh no—" she gasped.

Drakōn swore. "Stay here," he ordered as he took off after them.

※ ※

Tana froze in place in the wake of Drake's quick exit. Stay here? That was crazy! Those Dagonians were going to kill someone—someone like Malia. She couldn't sit here and do nothing!

Tana took off, swimming as fast as she could. She could feel heat building in her chest. If she were on the surface, she'd be on fire right now. But Drake was right. Underwater, there was no opportunity for her to ignite.

She could feel the concussion on the water as the boat's engine blew. "Wow, talk about déjà vu." Was this what it looked like from below on the day she was attacked?

Holly Kelly

Finally, she could see the boat—a small yacht from the looks of it. The Dagonians were ramming it, pushing it, and several were climbing up the side. The boat was being tossed around like a toy. What was happening on deck?

Tana surfaced. She searched for the humans and found them—a man, woman, and two teenage girls. They were in the cabin, the mother clinging to the daughters, and the father wielding a fire extinguisher in his hands like a weapon. The terror she saw in their faces sickened her.

Tana raced in closer. A Dagonian noticed her approach and said, "Woman, are you an idiot? You need to get out of here. This is no place for a female."

"This is exactly my place," she shouted back. "What are you monsters doing? That's an innocent family."

"They're humans!" he shouted, stopping to glare at her.

"And what's wrong with being human?" Tana challenged.

"You're insane," the Dagonian said. "When we're through here, the council will hear of your treasonous words."

Out of the corner of her eye, she saw one of the Dagonians had reached the deck. She sighed in relief when he turned. It was Drake.

His fin changed to legs as he stood and turned to address the Dagonians. "If you want to get to this family…" He raised his hands. The water rushed like

Raging

giant waves rising from the side of the boat and crashing, sweeping the Dagonians back into the water. "You'll have to go through me."

"Who are you?" a Dagonian challenged.

"I am Drakōn, the son of Proteus."

"I've never heard of you or your father," the Dagonian said, seemingly unfazed.

Drake narrowed his eyes, and then something amazing happened. His fingers turned transparent—like water. The change spread, working its way up his arms. The Dagonians gasped and backed away in fear.

Tana's heart sank. The father of the family didn't know Drake was trying to help him. Fighting the fear and desperation he obviously felt, the man crept up behind Drake and raised the fire extinguisher.

"Drake," Tana shouted. "Watch out!"

Before he could turn, the man slammed the metal canister down on Drake's head. Tana could feel the crack in her bones. Drake dropped to the deck.

The Dagonians laughed. "Son of nobody, brought down by a lowly human."

The heat in Tana's chest rose as her fear and anger mingled. She looked at the crowd, livid that they could laugh at Drake, who only wanted to protect the innocent. They would have killed them. They might still kill these people. And what had the humans done to deserve it? Nothing!

"Tana," Drake shouted as he rose from the floor and looked up to her.

Holly Kelly

Up?

Tana looked around and realized she was no longer in the water; she floated several feet above the surface. Looking around, she could see orange flames had sprung from her. Her legs had returned and kicked out below her. Then she looked to one side and saw the most incredible thing—a wing, completely made of fire. It stretched out longer than the length of her entire body. She turned and on the other side, spread another wing—just as magnificent. They flapped slowly, the wind generated by them holding her easily aloft.

The Dagonians gawked at her from below. And then she could feel the heat building. The fire threatened to explode from inside. "Drake," she shouted.

"Yeah," he yelled back. "I've got it." He lifted his arms, bringing a curtain of water from beneath the ship and covering it in a shimmering dome. And then light filled her vision as she combusted.

The Dagonians who were above the surface burned in that instance. The others fled—it seemed out of reach of the heat. Tana shouted, her voice booming louder than the explosion. "You threaten the humans, you deal with us!"

The flames continued to burn for several moments before dying down. Once the fire diminished, Tana floated down to the water again. With her energy spent, she felt as weak as a newborn kitten. She sank beneath the surface. Darkness descended down on her as she closed her eyes.

Raging

Drakōn lowered the barrier and turned to the family. "Go back to shore, and stay far away from the sea. There will be more of them, and they *will* kill you." Hopefully, they understood English.

The father staggered to his feet, his eyes wide and his face as pale as seafoam. "What...are you?"

"A friend," Drakōn said. Without another word, he dove into the sea, desperate to find Tana. He couldn't get over how much power she'd used. The flames had reached miles away. And the wings? That was something new.

She truly was a powerful goddess, and by Tartarus, she was beautiful in her winged glory.

There she was! Drakōn spotted her tailfin first, and then she came into full view. She was a mermaid once again. When he pulled her into his arms, she came easily, her body limp, unconscious. He could feel her power—diminished almost to nothing.

He and Tana would be little help to the others. And the humans...they were probably being slaughtered. Well, if he wanted to know how the humans were faring in this war, there was one man he was sure would be in the thick of things.

Xanthus? Drakōn waited a few minutes, wondering if his friend heard him.

I'm pretty busy, Dagonian, Xanthus finally answered. *We could use your help, though.*

I wish I could. Tana saved a family on a boat from attack, but

Holly Kelly

she used almost all her power. It has left her helpless and unconscious.

I'm happy for the family, but thousands of Dagonians have surfaced and are now attacking all the cities across the Mediterranean.

Why can't Triton stop them?

They have Poseidon's support. Triton dares not come out in open rebellion against his father. Sara has stressed that their first priority is to free the forgotten king—and starting a war between the gods of the sea would destroy all hope of doing that. Still, Triton is doing what he can to protect the humans—as am I.

So where are you?

I'm in Naples.

Are the others with you?

Yes.

I really wish we could help. I know now how to channel Tana's power, but without a way to sustain her…

Is there no way you can leave her behind?

Drakōn looked at Tana, so weak and defenseless. *No.*

Well, we'll miss having your support, but I understand.

Drakōn could feel the connection break. Frustration bubbled inside him, and he desperately wanted to hit something.

A flash of power came from above. Drakōn looked up. There was nothing there, but wait…a flicker of something. An object with a tail fell toward him. Drakōn reached out and caught it. He opened his palm and found a black stone dangling off a thin, gold chain. Drakōn could hear…something. A song? It sounded like it came from the rock.

Have Tana wear this, and she'll always have access to the power she needs, a deep familiar voice rumbled in Drakōn's

Raging

head—*Hades?* Drakōn frowned.

What is this? Drakōn answered.

It's the stone of Orpheus.

Orpheus? Wasn't he the one who tried to rescue his wife from the Underworld and failed to do so?

You're familiar with the tale?

Somewhat.

Then perhaps you know that Orpheus had the power to charm the gods and all other living creatures. He could even charm objects— including rocks. This particular stone was linked to the Underworld. As long as she wears it, she'll have access to her power.

How do I know it won't harm Tana? You did, after all, imprison her.

Hades paused. *You don't know. But I swear on the River Styx that I mean my daughter no harm. Take the necklace and then bring Tana with you to the human world. Perhaps she can assuage her guilt and atone for her mistakes by saving the humans.*

Drakōn frowned. *Okay, I'll do it. But if you harm her in any way—*

I know, Hades said. *You'll make it your life's mission to destroy me.*

Yeah, something like that.

I'm glad my daughter has you. Your match is a strange one, but it's just what she needs.

Drakōn didn't answer. He wasn't about to get chummy with Hades after what he did to Tana, and it would take a whole lot more than words to gain his trust. Still, he placed the necklace around her neck as she continued to sleep.

Chapter 23

Tana awoke with a jolt. Taking a deep breath of water, she opened her eyes and Drakōn's face came into view. "You... wha...?" She took in several more breaths as she looked around. "Where are we?"

"We're nearing the Keys." Drakōn held her in his arms as he swam.

"Are you taking me home?"

Drakōn shook his head slowly. "The Dagonians—they're on their way here."

"To Florida?"

"Yes."

"Malia, Vin, Kai, my employees...my friends." Tana's heart clenched. "Oh, gods. But, wait a minute. Dagonians can't swim on land."

"Actually, they can."

"But how?"

"Calypso, their ancestor god, gave them a gift many years ago in preparation for a day like this."

"A gift?"

"The ability to fly."

"What—like...like me?" She paused, took a deep

Raging

breath, and glanced at her back. The wings were gone. Of course, they were gone. How could she have wings made of fire underwater?

"No, they don't have wings. Basically, they can hover above the ground. But they're fast—much faster than a human."

"Yeah, well, we've got guns," she said hopefully.

"Doesn't matter. With an army of over three million men, the odds are not good. Not only that, they will not spare the women or the young. They will kill everyone they see."

"Oh my gosh," Tana said. Her face visibly paled. "How do we stop them? Sara said we could do it, and she made it sound easy."

"I'm not sure," Drake said, "but I think I know a way."

"How?"

"The Dagonians aren't fire resistant."

"Neither are the humans." Tana scowled.

"You'll need to convince them to evacuate."

Tana's jaw dropped. "How in the world am I supposed to do that?"

Drakōn shook his head. "I don't know."

"Where are the others? Sara, Triton…"

"I'm here." A woman's voice came from behind them.

Tana narrowed her eyes at the woman floating next to a Dagonian. "And who are you?"

"My name's Gretchen, and this is Kyros. I'm…well, I'm your cousin. Your mother and my grandmother were sisters."

"You look like a Dagonian."

Gretchen shook her head. "I'm a mermaid."

"She's also another of the four," Drake supplied.

"What did you do to Malia?" Tana scowled at her.

"She saved her life," Drake said.

Tana turned in surprise. "What?"

"It was nothing," Gretchen said. "I just convinced a few Dagonians that she was no danger to them."

"Why would she be a danger?" Tana asked.

"I think we need to focus on saving her life *now*," Drake said. "So it's just you?" he asked, looking at Gretchen and the other man.

"Sorry," Gretchen answered. "The others are in the thickest part of the battle. Kyros and I just had to come here, though. I couldn't let anything happen to my family and friends."

"Your family lives in Florida?" Tana asked.

"My adoptive family lives in Miami. I grew up here. I've got friends, neighbors…most the people I know and love live here. I've convinced my family and close friends to evacuate, but their homes are here, and this is my community—where I grew up. I couldn't turn my back on it."

"I know what you mean," Tana said. She turned to Drake. "We need to protect Malia."

"Malia already has protection," Kyros said.

"What?" Tana turned to him and asked, "You know who Malia is?"

Raging

Kyros nodded. "Sara sent Pallas to watch Malia days ago."

"Why would she do that?" Drakōn asked.

"I'm not sure," Kyros said. "She wouldn't say a thing to me."

"Can we trust this guy Pallas?" Tana asked.

"I'd trust him with my life," Drake said vehemently.

"Do we know when the Dagonians will get here?"

"They won't attack until sundown," Kyros said. "The humans will be more vulnerable at night."

Tana gave a confused look.

"The Dagonians can see as well at night as they can during the day. The humans…not so much."

"Oh, great." Tana frowned.

"It's okay," Gretchen said. "We can handle them. And you and me together, we'll be unstoppable."

Tana frowned, doubtful. "So, you're a mermaid, and from the Underworld?"

"Yes. Sort of. My mother was a mermaid, and my father is the son of death."

"You mean Hades? We're not sisters, are we?"

"No, my father's not Hades. He's Thanatos. He's death."

"So, your powers are what…fire and water? That sounds like a contradiction."

"Yeah, it doesn't do much good to combine them; they cancel each other out. But you, your powers are fire and wind. It seems like they would—"

"Yeah," Tana interrupted. "They do."

"So where is Sara?" Drake asked.

"She's not coming yet," Gretchen answered.

Tana said, "How do we stop the Dagonian attack?"

"Stopping Dagonians won't be easy," Kyros said, "They are warriors unlike humans can comprehend. They're fierce, heartless, and see land-walkers as vermin needing to be exterminated. The humans may have guns, but Dagonians are much faster and more deadly than any human. By the time you see a Dagonian, you're already dead."

Tana asked. "Then what are we going to do to stop them?"

Drake pulled himself up onto a dock and helped Tana up. "I have a plan. By the way, where is your baby?"

"Safe," Gretchen answered somberly.

"Is there anywhere safe on land?" Tana looked at the sea hugging the coast and then to the town built right up against it. Would these structures still be standing a week from now, or would this be a war zone?

"He's not on land. His aunt is watching him in Triton's castle."

Tana couldn't help but notice Gretchen never answered her question. Perhaps there would be no place safe on land.

"So, what is the plan?" Tana asked Drake.

"You wouldn't believe me if I told you."

"Try me."

"We're going to create a barrier between the sea and the land. No human will be able to cross from the land to

Raging

the sea, and no Dagonian will be able to cross from the sea onto land."

"You're crazy," Tana said as she turned to Gretchen. "He's completely nuts."

Doubt flickered in her eyes as she shrugged, then surprise and shock flashed across her face as she turned to Drakōn. "You can't be thinking to—"

"Yes, I am." Drake swallowed.

"You'll be needing my help," Gretchen said.

"It's a good thing you came then," Drake replied.

"This plan better be good," Kyros said. "There are a handful of us against an army of millions. The best we can hope for is to protect the few we can."

"What if I could help?" a deep, disembodied voice asked—a familiar one.

Tana's heart lit with hope. "Zeus!"

Drake put his hand on her shoulder and whispered, "Tana, you can't trust him."

She turned and looked at Drake. Fear flashed in his eyes. "What are you talking about? This is Zeus, king of the gods. Of course we can trust him."

Tana could feel power roll over her as Zeus flashed into view. "What do you mean she can't trust me?"

Zeus looked Drake over, suspicion in his eyes. "And who have we here?"

Drake stepped in front of her as if to shield her from Zeus.

"Quite protective of her, are you?" Zeus said.

Drake didn't answer, but his muscles were so tense,

he looked as if he were about to explode.

"What's wrong, Drake?" she whispered.

He didn't answer her. He just stood, imposing, threatening, as if he were ready to lay down his life for her.

"I feel your fear," Zeus said, "but this is more than a healthy fear of your king. I also sense anger and loathing." He turned to Kyros, who kept his head down—but his eyes flashed in fury, and then he looked at Gretchen. "You all hate me, don't you? You wish me dead. All but… Tana."

They didn't answer him. Tana felt her heart deaden in her chest. Why did Drake hate the man who saved her? Why did they all hate him? If it weren't for Zeus, she might still be frozen in her prison.

Zeus' eyes were on her, and Tana's heart went cold. There was something wrong with him. Something she could see in his eyes.

"Awe, but now, she doesn't trust me." Zeus shook his head in mock disappointment, but the hint of a smile told her he couldn't care less that she didn't trust him. "You three have turned her against me. The Dagonians and the…" Zeus' voice dropped off as his eyes landed on Gretchen. He looked taken aback at her presence. Was he afraid?

If he did feel fear, it quickly turned to anger as he looked at Gretchen. "You," he snarled, "daughter of sea and fire." He took a step toward her before stopping and looking at Tana—his eyes flashing a deep loathing. "And

Raging

you, daughter of fire and wind! How could I be so blind?" With a flick of his hand, lightning struck Drake and Kyros, throwing them back against the side of a boat. They slammed into the hull and dropped into the sea.

Gretchen rushed to Tana's side and grabbed her arm. "We need to get out of here."

At that moment, a vice clamped around Tana's neck and stole her breath.

"You two are not going anywhere," Zeus spoke, his voice like thunder. His hands were at his sides, but it felt as if he had her by the throat. "Who brought you together?" The dock disappeared from under Tana and Gretchen's feet as they were lifted by some unseen force.

"Who brought you together?" he snarled.

"I did," a soft, feminine voice spoke. Tana could see a glowing woman dressed in white. Sara.

Zeus turned, his eyes widening. "You." He searched her face. "Nikoleta?"

Sara shook her head. "Nikoleta is my mother."

"No."

Sara nodded.

"And who is your father?"

"My father is Triton."

"Daughter of earth and sea," Zeus stammered, obviously caught off guard. His eyes narrowed. "Regardless of who your parents are, I know what you are, and you are not allowed to interfere."

"And why not?"

"The Fates are never allowed."

Holly Kelly

Sara stepped in front of them, her back to Tana and Gretchen while she faced Zeus. Tana could see her hands wringing behind her back. Sara was afraid.

Tana turned to look at Gretchen. A tear leaked down Gretchen's cheek. She looked fearful for Sara.

"Ha!" Sara laughed, her carefree voice at odds with the obvious fear she showed behind her back. "I've never been one for taking orders."

"What do you want?" Zeus growled as his eyes narrowed to slits.

"I'm here to offer you a chance to redeem yourself."

"Why should I need redemption?"

Sara ignored his question and said, "Return the powers to all you have stolen from, return the memories of those you have suppressed, and allow us to free the king. If you do this, all will be forgiven."

"Who are you to forgive me?"

"It is my grandfather, your king, who will forgive you. I've seen it. If you do what I ask, he will forgive."

"And what of my son? What have the Fates done to him?"

"He destroyed himself when he tried to destroy me," Sara answered.

"He's dead?"

"Yes."

Zeus snarled in anger. "I will never submit to you. I will never submit to my brother. And you will join my son in death." With those words, Zeus threw out his hand and a bolt of charged energy flashed, brighter

Raging

than the sun. It arched toward Sara. In that moment, the watery shape of Drake rose from the dock. And he was not alone. Triton, Xanthus, Hades, and dozens more appeared around Sara, shielding her from her attacker. Zeus' bolt arced around them and deflected.

Zeus shouted as the bolt disappeared. "You are all traitors!"

"We are not the traitors, Zeus," Triton snarled. "You are a betrayer and a coward. You coveted your brother's throne and took it for yourself. You take babes from their mother's arms and steal their god powers. You hide behind lies and deceptions, using your own son to fight your battles. Well, now that I've killed your son, you are forced to come out into the open."

"*You* killed my son?" Zeus shouted.

"Yes, and I'd do it again and again for the sheer enjoyment of it." Triton smiled.

"You will pay for what you've done! You think you can beat me? Do you think any of you can?" Zeus looked from face to face. "I have the power of thousands of gods surging through me. And by dawn, I will have the power of many more. And then I will see you all destroyed," Zeus snarled before he disappeared.

"No!" shouted a man wearing a helmet with wings. He looked like Thor.

"He's too powerful, Odin," Triton said.

Ah, Thor's father, Tana thought.

"We were all blocking him," a woman dressed in furs and carrying a bow said. "It just wasn't enough."

"How can we ever hope to stop him?" Odin asked.

"There's only one man who can stop him now," Triton said.

"Petros," Odin said.

Drake rushed up to her and pressed a kiss to Tana's forehead. "Tana, oh gods, are you alright?" He pressed her head between his palms and searched her face.

"I'm fine," Tana answered. "Really I am."

Drake shook his head and then pressed a quick kiss to her lips. "What would I ever do without you? I don't think I could survive losing you."

Tana chuckled. "You sound like a man in love."

He looked into her eyes without a hint of humor. "I am."

Tana felt as if someone had sucker punched her. He loved her? He couldn't be serious.

Screams and shouts erupted in the distance. The sound of a woman's voice echoed from nearby. "Please, don't hurt me!"

"Oh no," Tana whispered.

"They're here," Drake growled.

Chapter 24

Malia's tennis shoes pounded the pavement as she jogged across the Miami Beach boardwalk. The palm trees swayed in the breeze as goose bumps broke out across her arms. She had the distinct feeling of being watched—one she'd been getting a lot lately.

She narrowed her eyes and looked around. The ocean caught her attention. The waves seemed choppier than normal. In fact…something wasn't right. Her heart pounded as she thought about the near-death experience she and Tana had on the boat. She could still see the dark, threatening eyes of the man, creature, whatever it was, as it came on deck.

She felt a distant roll of thunder down in her bones. Dark clouds obscured the sunset. The near-constant earthquake and tidal wave warnings hadn't deterred her trip today. There were so many, most people had begun to dismiss them. But from the looks of the sea tonight, she thought it best to cut her run short.

"On your left," a gruff voice shouted as another runner zipped past her. Usually, she was the fastest thing on two legs on this boardwalk, but unease slowed her down. She decided not to fight it and slowed to a walk.

Pulling out her cell phone, she dialed her brother. He picked up after only one ring, "Hey, sis."

"Vin," she said, "did you see the weather report for today?"

"Uh, yeah. There's not much to report. And with the weird weather patterns and tsunami warnings lately, it's an oddly normal day."

"What's odd is the look of the ocean," she said. "I've never seen anything like it."

"What do you mean?"

"Well…" She frowned. "You know how it looks when you're pulling up a large catch of fish in your net? Right before the fish come to the surface, there's a lot of splashing."

"What does that have to do with the sea? You think a school of fish is flapping at the surface?"

"I've never seen a school of fish this big. I mean it…" Malia's voice dropped off when she saw something. A head. It was a human head. And then the rest of him rose up from the surface. "Oh, my…"

"What is it?" Vin snapped.

"It's a—" And then there was another. No, two more, no… *Holy cow!* With renewed energy, Malia took off, racing away from the ocean. "You're not going to believe this, but there are about a million mermen surfacing right here on our beach."

"You mean like the one you and Tana saw?" His voice rose an octave. He swore softly and then shouted.

Raging

"Where exactly are you?"

"No," she said. "Don't try to find me. Just stay home. I'm coming home."

"Kai," she could hear him shouting to her other brother through the line. "We've got hostiles incoming."

Malia put her phone in her pocket and ran even faster. A blood-curdling scream caused her to lose her rhythm and stumble. She regained her pace and looked back. The man who'd passed her only moments ago was in trouble. A whole pack of those monsters had swarmed him. Muscular bodies and tailfins obscured her view. One of them came up shouting with a severed arm raised in his hand. Stumbling again, she had to bite back the bile that rose in her throat.

One of them caught her watching. A wicked grin spread across his face as he shouted and pointed to her. And then they were after her—it looked like a hundred of them, flying toward her—incredibly fast.

Spinning on her heels, she bolted away, only to slam into something hard. She fell back, but strong hands caught her. When she looked up, her heart slammed in her chest. This guy stood easily over six and a half feet tall with bulging muscles. "Get behind me," he growled as he shoved her back, but kept his hand locked around her arm.

"Look," she said trying unsuccessfully to pull away. "You look pretty strong and I'm sure you're tough, but you don't stand a chance against these things."

"These *things* are my people," he answered.

Malia shook her head as her blood turned to ice. "Oh, please no. You're going to hand me over to them, aren't you?"

The man sighed. "No."

"Then what are you going to do?"

"Save you."

"Who are you?"

"My name is Pallas; I'm a friend of Drakōn."

"Tana's boyfriend?"

Before he could answer, the Mer-things surrounded them. They watched with anger mingled with curiosity. Several of them had their eyes glued to Pallas' legs—as if they'd never seen them before. Pallas spoke to them in a strange language. They didn't seem too happy with him, but they weren't attacking. Malia caught the eye of one of them. He glared at her and bared his teeth—these things had fangs!

Pallas shouted, and they backed down. He said something else, and their eyes widened in surprise. Several nodded to him, seemly satisfied. After that, they moved on.

"We need to get further inland," he said as he let go of her arm.

Malia didn't waste a moment as she sprinted away. She wasn't about to go anywhere with this man. Friend of Drake or not, he was one of those creatures. He was probably just looking for an opportunity to slice her up and eat her. That was what mermaids did, didn't they? They lured people in so they could eat them. Well, she

Raging

wasn't about to be lured to her death.

Malia had only run a few yards when she ran into him again. "How did you…?" she stammered, her words cut short by her heaving breaths.

"I'm faster than I look. Listen, I understand why you don't trust me, but I swear, I'm here to protect you."

"Why? Did Drake send you?"

"Something like that," he answered. "Listen, we need to head inland. My friends are about to raise a barrier—"

"We can't go anywhere without my brothers."

Pallas swore under his breath—at least, it sounded like a swear word. She didn't recognize the language. "Where are they?"

"They're at home."

"Do you have a car nearby?"

"Uh, not really. It's parked several miles up the coast."

"Why did you park so far away?"

"I came here to jog."

"Ah, jog. Why you humans feel the need to run with no particular destination in mind, I'll never understand."

"Humans, right," Malia said. "What are you?"

"I'm a Dagonian."

"You're not a merman?"

"Hades, no."

"So what are these Dagonians going to do to us? I mean they…they killed that guy back there. Are they going to—?"

Sounds of gunshots rang out.

"Yeah, they're going to try to kill everyone they come

in contact with."

"So how do we stop them?"

"We don't," Pallas said. "Not that I don't enjoy a good battle, but we can't let them mar that pretty face of yours." He raised an eyebrow and smirked at her.

"You're not seriously flirting with me, are you?" she asked.

"Do you want me to flirt with you?"

She looked at the guy. He was ripped like no other and his face looked like it belonged on the cover of a magazine. Oh yeah, she wanted him to flirt with her, and there were a few other things she'd be happy to do with him.

"My brothers!" she shouted the moment she remembered they might be in danger.

"You want me to flirt with your brothers?" he said as he held back a smile.

"No," she stammered, shaking her head. "I mean, my brothers are in danger. I, um, we can flirt later."

"I'll hold you to that," he said breaking out into a full smile as he stepped up to her.

His chest now inches from her face, she asked, "What are you doing?" She strained to look up to his face.

"I need you to trust me."

"Okay," she said suspiciously. His arms came around her and she was off the ground. "What are you doing?"

"Getting to your car faster."

She huffed. "This is not going to be faster. You know, I'm a pretty fast runner—"

Raging

"I'm not going to be running. What direction is your car?"

"It's that way." She gestured.

"Hold on," he said, and then they were moving. Fast. Like so fast, Malia left her stomach behind and held Pallas in a death grip. The trees were flashing by. She looked down to the sidewalk and couldn't even make out the individual tiles. Looking up, she could see the parking lot.

"Which car is yours?" Pallas asked. It sounded like he was in a wind tunnel.

"The silver Taurus," she shouted as they stopped suddenly. Her stomach did somersaults in her belly.

"I don't understand car models," he said as he put her on her feet and let her go.

The world spun around her, and Pallas' arm came around her. "Having trouble walking?" he asked.

"I didn't know I'd be riding a roller coaster." She spotted her car the next row over and pointed. "It's over there."

Pallas located the car and then searched the surroundings. Pulling her close, he said, "We'll be safer once we're inside your vehicle." Less than a second later, they were next to her car.

"You'll need to drive," he said as he let go of her and moved around to the passenger side.

Malia had her hand over her mouth as she leaned against her car and tried not to vomit. "Just give me a minute," she said, taking a few deep breaths. Her sour stomach settled a bit. The sound of screaming in the distance caused desperation to rise in her chest. Fumbling with the keys, she unlocked the door and they got inside.

"You don't look so good."

She frowned as she sped out of the parking stall. "There's a reason I don't like amusement parks."

Minutes later, she ran up the walk to her home with Pallas on her heels.

Drakōn had confessed his love to Tana. Why did he do that? Hadn't he learned a thing? Telling someone you loved them only gave them ammunition to harm you. But by the gods, he cared about the woman. He'd give his life to make her safe. He'd give his life to make her happy. If that wasn't love, he didn't know what was.

Drakōn thrust his thoughts to the back of his mind. People were dying. Now was not the time to analyze his feelings, by gods.

"Xanthus!" he shouted as he rushed over.

Xanthus turned to him. "Drakōn, it's good to see you, friend."

"So what's the plan?" Drakōn asked, getting the attention of everyone around. Silence descended, leaving only the cries in the distance. "How are we to protect these humans?"

"I don't know," Xanthus said.

"How many Dagonians have come ashore?" Drakōn asked.

"As yet, less than a thousand." Triton stepped forward.

Raging

"But there are countless more preparing to come."

"What if we could seal off the borders?" Drakōn asked.

Triton's brows rose. "How could we possibly do that?"

"How many gods do we have on our side?" Drakōn asked, looking around. Their numbers were swelling as other gods and goddesses appeared. Was someone summoning them? He looked for Sara but couldn't see any sign of her.

"Just over a hundred," Triton answered.

"And how many from each realm?" Drakōn asked.

"That's hard to say. We have gods from several pantheons—the Greeks, of course, Norse, Hawaiian, Sumerian, Roman, Egyptian, and several others."

"And the human leaders? Has anyone contacted them yet?"

"I tried to talk to the US president," Xanthus said. "Tried to reason with him. When I appeared in the Oval Office, the man panicked and called for his Secret Service. They shot me seven times before I could transport." Xanthus pulled something from his pocket and held his hand out. In his palm were several bullets. "They hurt just as much coming out as they did going in."

"It a good thing you're a god. That many bullets would likely have killed you otherwise."

Drakōn shot a glance past Xanthus to see what was happening with Tana. Gretchen had her arm around her, speaking in her ear. Kyros stood on her other side. He wondered for a moment how Tana was taking all this. Flames sprouted from her chest as her expression turned dark. Drakōn pulled Xanthus back as he prepared to run to her. He jerked to a stop when Gretchen waved her hand and calmed the flames.

Xanthus covered Drakōn's hand with his and whispered, "It looks like Gretchen has her covered."

"So," Triton said as he stepped toward them, "how do you propose to seal the border?"

Drakōn took a deep breath. His idea would be a hard sell. "We build a wall of brimstone along the shore and set it on fire."

"Bold plan," Triton said. "So, what of keeping our secret? If we do that, the humans will know we exist and will likely see this act as a threat. They may launch an attack on the sea."

"They already know about us," Drakōn said. "Poseidon doesn't care about secrecy anymore. Besides, can you think of a better plan? Either the humans are outright attacked, or we build a wall separating us from them."

"What about the Maj bands?" Gretchen asked. "Take away those and the Dagonians would be like fish out of water."

"Only Calypso has the power to remove them," Triton said. "I'm afraid she won't be much help. She was the one leading the charge against us in Naples."

"Then that's it," Drakōn said.

"What of the quest to free the forgotten king?" a

Raging

young woman with black hair and black eyes spoke. "He could stop this attack."

"Nyx," Triton said. "You know there's not enough time. The humans are dying now."

"Do we really want another king?"

Drakōn tried to find the source of that voice, but he could see nothing but shadows.

"You all remember now how it was, right?" Triton said, looking at a shadowy figure, and then turning to the crowd surrounding them. "Erobes, you remember the time before King Petros was sealed and all memories suppressed."

Erobes—the shadow—stood silent.

Xanthus stepped forward. "I hadn't been born yet, but Sara showed me. Two thousand years ago, the humans knew and respected the gods. They feared the gods enough that they dared not commit genocide against each other. But since we have been erased from memory, terrible things have occurred, the death of millions—one million Armenians, six million Jews, two million Cambodians, hundreds of thousands of Syrians, and countless more. Now, if we don't stop it, there could be billions killed worldwide. If we abandon the humans, they could be completely destroyed."

"We need to stop this attack," Triton said. "Petros would want us to save the humans. And Drakōn's plan truly is the only way. We can't stop millions of Dagonians and the sea-gods that support them if we don't create that wall. Unless we intervene, they will slaughter the human race."

"The humans will hate us for it," Xanthus said. "They will fear us. And then they will try to kill us."

"We'll need to free your king before that happens," said Odin. "He can create order once again. The humans may have once worshiped us, but King Petros is the one who created them. He understands them. He is their best hope for survival."

"Why do you care what happens to the humans?" Drakōn asked.

Odin turned to Drakōn. "I could ask the same question of you."

"I've lived among them," Drakōn said. "I've come to like many of them."

"Then you already understand."

"And that's why most of us are here," Xanthus said. "So let's get started before more humans have to die."

"Where is Hades?" Triton asked.

They looked around, searching the crowd.

"He's gone," Tana said. All fell silent at her words.

A glowing goddess with fiery red hair stepped toward her, snarling. "What do you mean gone? Where did he go?" She narrowed her eyes as she glared at Tana. "And who are you?"

Drakōn stepped to Tana's side and pulled her against him. Tana gave him an irritated glance.

"Makaria." Triton stepped forward to stand between them. "This is Tana, goddess of wind and fire, and your sister."

Raging

Drakōn could feel Tana tense.

"My sister?" Makaria's eyes widened before narrowing into slits. "I've never heard of you. But I can guess why. Well, Tana, I'm the *legitimate* daughter of Hades and Persephone. You must be one of my father's bast—"

"Makaria," Triton interrupted. "Now's not the time. We need to save the humans." Drakōn could feel heat radiating from Tana's skin. He squeezed her shoulder and kissed her temple. She relaxed and cooled slightly.

"Why *should* we help the humans?" Makaria asked as she turned to Triton. "They don't even believe in us anymore. And if my father didn't see any reason to stay, I don't either." With that said, she disappeared in a flash of fire.

"Well," Triton said. "That's disappointing." He turned to the crowd. "How many more do we have from the Underworld?"

"I am here," Gretchen said.

"And we are with her," Thane said with two other dark men at his side. "I am Thane and this is my father—Thanatos—and his brother—Hypnos."

"Any others?" Triton asked. Silence was his answer. No one spoke, no one moved.

A young god with shining, silver wings stepped forward and said. "Looks like there are no more. This plan has failed before we've even begun."

Drakōn turned to him. "And who are you?"

"Anteros, son of Aphrodite and Ares."

"Son of Ares, huh?" Drakōn eyed him suspiciously.

"Don't judge." Anteros frowned. "No one could hate that man more than me. But I do know something of battles and odds, and the odds are not in our favor. This plan can't work without more gods from the Underworld."

"We have Tana." Drakōn turned to her, noticing her flinch as she stepped back.

She shook her head. "I can't control it."

"Not alone," Drakōn said, "but with help, you can."

"How can five gods have enough power for this plan?" Anteros asked.

"Technically," Gretchen said. "It's only three gods. Thane and I are both demigods."

"Even worse," Anteros said.

Drakōn turned to him. "You're underestimating their power. It's immense. Tana alone has more than enough." He wasn't about to tell them about the Stone of Orpheus she wore around her neck, but it made success a distinct possibility.

"Thanks for *my* vote of confidence." Gretchen smirked.

Drakōn shrugged. "Sorry. I haven't seen it."

"I'd show off," Gretchen said, "but I've got a feeling I'll be needing every drop of power I have."

Tana stepped into his frame of vision, and he saw something in her face he'd never seen in her before. Hope. "Do you think we can do this?"

Drakōn nodded. "Yes." He desperately hoped he wasn't lying. He turned to Triton. "Okay Majesty, what do you want us to do?"

Triton shook his head with a smile. "This was your idea. I happily relinquish command to you."

Drakōn frowned. "Oh, thanks a lot."

"Alright!" Drakōn shouted. "What earth gods do we have here?"

"The Ourea are here," a tall man with a thick neck shouted. "I am Olympus, and these are my brothers—Helikon, Parnes, Kithairon, Athos, Nysos, Tmolus, Oreios, Aitna, and Olympus."

"I thought *you* were Olympus."

"Yeah." He shrugged. "There are two of us."

"That's not confusing at all," Drakōn said under his breath and then raised his voice. "Okay, what sea-gods do we have here?"

"Just you and me," Triton said.

"You're kidding me." Drakōn frowned.

"I wish," Triton said. "We're *fighting* the sea-gods."

"Yeah," Drakōn said. "That's unfortunate."

"I've been watching you, Drakōn," Triton said. "And—"

"You've been watching me?" Drakōn interrupted.

"Don't let it go to your head." Triton shrugged. "Together, we should have enough power."

Drakōn frowned at the word *should*. If they didn't have enough power, this plan wouldn't work. Never mind that. They would have to try. "Okay, we will need to travel along the coast. Triton and I will go first, moving back the water, then the Ourea will follow and open the earth, and then Gretchen's group will bring up the brimstone. After all this is accomplished, Tana will light it. She'll have to wait for me to return first. She'll need me to shield the humans from her fire. Those of us who can't fly will need the sky gods to help us travel. How many of those do we have?"

Dozens raised their hands. Looked like Zeus created most of his enemies in his own realm.

"You and Triton will have to separate to cover all the continents," Olympus said.

Drakōn nodded.

"Has anyone considered how bad the brimstone is going to smell?" one of the Ourea asked. "Especially once it's lit."

"Shut up, Athos." Olympus smiled. "Smelling a stench is better than dying."

Athos shook his head. "It depends on how bad it stinks. Hey…I just had a thought. What happens if the humans try to put out the fire?"

Triton shook his head. "Once brimstone is lit, it's difficult to put out. The only way to do it is to submerge it."

"How do you know so much about it, sea-god?" Athos asked.

"When you've lived as long as I have," Triton raised his eyebrow, "you learn a few things."

"Enough chitchat," Olympus said. "Humans are dying. Let's get started."

CHAPTER 25

"Who's the stranger?" Vin asked with his M16 clutched in his hand and Kai at his back with his sniper rifle. Bodies of Dagonians littered the ground around the house. Malia tried to avoid looking too closely at them. Who knew her brothers' military training would have a use at home?

"He's Pallas," Malia answered breathlessly. "A friend of Drake's."

"Drake sent you?" Vin asked Pallas.

"More or less," Pallas answered.

"Do you know how to use a gun?" Kai asked Pallas.

"I know the basics," he answered. "I'm better at hand to hand."

"Not against these things," Vin said.

"You'd be surprised," Pallas said.

"Being cocky is going to get you killed, friend."

"I'm not cocky, I'm confident."

"He's one of them," Malia said.

Before she could blink, Vin and Kai had their weapons aimed at Pallas.

"Whoa…" He raised his hands and backed away. "I'm here to help."

Holly Kelly

"Why?"

"Let's just say, not all of us agree with the order to slaughter the entire human race."

"What?" Malia's heart took off in a sprint. "You mean this isn't just happening here?"

"Incoming!" Kai shouted.

"Listen," Pallas said. "I can convince them to not attack, but then we won't be able to attack them."

"So they'll just pass us by and kill our neighbors?" Vin asked as he lowered his weapon. Malia sighed in relief when the gun was no longer pointed at her rescuer.

Pallas frowned. "Basically."

Vin shook his head. "Sorry, no deal. I grew up here. I care about these people."

"Yeah," Kai said. "We're not leaving them to be slaughtered."

"So are you going to fight alongside us?" Vin asked. "Or is this where we say goodbye."

"I'm staying."

"Right," Vin said. "Malia, go in the house. Get your friend a weapon, and then you get yourself hidden."

"No way," she said, incensed. "I'm just as good a shot as either of you."

"There's no time to argue." Vin raised his gun towards the corner of the yard and shot. The sound rang in Malia's ears.

Pallas pulled her through the door and said, "Looks like I'll need a weapon."

Shouts came from the porch, catching her attention.

Raging

Her brothers were both swearing up a streak. That didn't sound good.

Malia grabbed the nearest rifle and shoved it at Pallas, gave him the ammunition to go with it, and then grabbed her own weapon—a Smith and Wesson.

"Malia, wait!" Pallas shouted at her back as she sprinted out the front door and skidded to a stop.

Something was going on with the distant shoreline—something big.

The ground shook beneath her. She staggered, trying to stay on her feet, but fell forward. Pallas tried to catch her but ended up falling with her. When they hit the floor, she knew something wasn't right. When did they replace their wood porch with stone blocks?

The resistance the water gave was greater than Drakōn could have ever imagined. For the first time in his life, he could empathize with Atlas holding the whole earth propped on his shoulder. No matter how hard he pushed, it seemed the water pushed back with greater force. An idea struck him. He certainly hoped it worked.

Drakōn stepped into the surf and felt a surge of power. Closing his eyes, he focused on becoming one with the water. Giving himself over, he could feel more—do more. He *was* the water.

Pushing it back was easy now. As much power as he expended, it was replaced by the power from the sea. Moving with confidence, he moved the water back as easily as he moved himself. In fact, it was difficult to tell where the ocean ended and he began.

He could hear the stone breaking apart and the brimstone grating as it rose behind him. The sound at his back encouraged him to move forward. He didn't want to be overtaken.

"Drake?" He could hear Tana's voice, her tone pleading.

Drakōn could hear her, but he dared not respond. He couldn't afford to lose his concentration as he moved and swelled, pushing the water back. "I'm here, Drake." She couldn't know how much her words meant to him. They gave him the comfort and confidence to push forward—even as the stench of brimstone washed over him. The journey seemed to take years, but he knew he was moving fast—a current traveling along the coast that moved faster than any natural current. Finally, he could see the end in sight. Triton came at him from the front. Drakōn braced for impact as they collided, but instead of hitting Triton, he washed over the sea king like a wave.

"Drakōn?" Triton said, looking around at the water. "Where under Olympus are you?"

Drakōn focused on returning to his human form. *Where in Hades were his arms and legs?* Rising from the water, he found himself looking down at Triton below.

Triton swore—his eyes opening wide as he gaped at Drakōn.

Drakōn finally located his hands and looked down at his legs. He was still transparent, but he was also about fifty feet tall!

Raging

Letting the power wash away from him, he shrunk down. In seconds, he found himself a man again, standing drenched on the dock. Tana landed at his side, and she threw her arms around him. "You did it," she said. "I knew you could." She pressed a quick kiss to his lips. It came and went much too quickly.

"Yeah," Drakōn said, brushing the wetness away from his face. "It was a lot easier than I expected."

"Speak for yourself," Triton said, breathing hard. "I've never seen anything like what you did. You're not only a god of the sea—you *are* the sea."

"Felt like it," Drakōn said, still in awe of what he'd experienced. He looked back at the wall and gasped. It was bright yellow and towered above them.

Looking back at Tana, he said, "Now you're up."

She pursed her lips. "I don't really know how to control it."

Drake lifted her chin so that she was looking him in the eye. "You can do it."

She nodded and cracked a weak smile. "I'm glad you have faith in me."

"Always," he said and pressed another kiss to her lips. "It's time."

Looking up at the crowd, Drakōn shouted. "Everyone who is not immune to fire will need to leave."

One by one, everyone left until only Drakōn, Tana, and Gretchen's group remained.

Gretchen wheezed, obviously exhausted from the effort she expended. She stepped up to Tana and put her hand on her shoulder. "I can lend you…what power I have left."

Drakōn shook his head. "She won't need it."

"What…? How?"

"A gift from the Underworld."

"What gift?" Tana asked.

"Your necklace," Drakōn said.

Tana reached up and pressed her hand against the stone.

"I put it on you when you were asleep."

"Why didn't you tell me?"

"I didn't think you'd appreciate who it was from."

She scowled at him. "My father."

"Tana," Drakōn said as he took her hand. "He—"

"Don't." She shook her head. "We'll talk about it later."

"Okay, it sounds like you've got things under control. I'll just—" Gretchen began and then transported.

"Did she…?" Tana said.

"I guess she decided to leave." Drakōn shrugged. "I'll shield the humans from your fire as you light the wall."

"But you'll have to be on the land side," Tana said. "You won't be able to access the sea."

"Don't worry," Drakōn said. "I can do this."

Tana nodded. Closing her eyes, she lowered her head. She breathed deeply as she clenched her fists. Drakōn felt for the heat; he knew it would be intense. *Where's the heat?*

"It's not working," she breathed. "I can't…"

Raging

"You can do it," Drakōn said.

"No, I can't," she said as her eyes flew open wide in shock. "I don't..." She looked him up and down as realization lightened her eyes. "Drakōn, you need to hit me."

"What?" he asked as he backed against the brimstone wall. "I'm not going to hit you."

"You have to." She stepped toward him, pressing her hands against his chest. "Emotions drive my power, and right now, I'm not angry or afraid enough."

Yellow dust and rocks rained down from above as Drakōn looked up.

The face of a livid Dagonian flew toward them. The soldier missed him and crashed down on top of Tana before Drakōn could even blink. Tana lay sprawled under the Dagonian's bulk as he lifted his head. Drakōn moved to pull the attacker off but stopped short when he met Tana's eyes. They glowed orange as she snarled, "Get off me!"

The creature flew back, terror on his face. "You humans are worse than we thought," he said as rose from the ground and drew his sword.

"I'm not human," Tana said, her voice resonating with power.

The Dagonian lowered his sword and asked, "What are you?"

"I am Tana, goddess of wind and fire, protector of the human race."

Drakōn could feel the change wash over his body as

the sound of rushing water filled his ears.

The Dagonian seemed to catch a view of him in the corner of his eye and turned his head. His eyes widened even more as his sword fell from his loose fingers and clattered to the ground. "And who are you?"

"I am Drakōn, god of…oh, who knows what, but I do know two things. I am Tana's protector and you are a dead man," Drakōn said—his own voice like the sound of rushing waters. He looked over to Tana, who was now fully engulfed in flames with her fiery wings spread wide, framing her figure.

The Dagonian trembled as he backed away. "Don't hurt me."

"Leave now," Tana said, "and you'll live. Stay and you'll die."

"I'm going," he blurted as he scaled the wall.

Drakōn turned to Tana, not caring whether the Dagonian escaped. "Are you ready now?"

Tana nodded as her wings beat back and forth, driving hot wind over the ground. Brimstone dust ignited and popped—dancing embers in the swirling wind.

No sooner was Tana out of sight than she exploded in light. Flames burst from the wall and raced along the shore. Drakōn, flowing like a wave across the ground, could barely keep up with the advancing inferno. The wall blocked the flames, and he found his presence largely unnecessary, thank the gods. This was infinitely more difficult than pushing back the sea, but he wasn't about to disappoint Tana. He would live up to his side,

Raging

even if it killed him.

Mile after mile, they raced along the wall, jumping continent to continent, island to island. They met Triton at the halfway mark. Drakōn refused to let the sea king take over. Triton didn't argue, but shared his power with Drakōn, giving him the strength he so desperately needed.

Drakōn and Tana continued for what seemed like hours, but the moon remained fixed. Someone was manipulating time.

Finally, the familiar dock glowed in the distance. Moments later, they were finished.

"That was easier than I thought it would be!" Tana said, circling him in the air and landing on the wall. Her flames danced over her skin—they looked almost… happy. No, fire didn't feel happy.

"I'm not even tired," Tana said as she smiled. "Are you alright, Drake?"

Drakōn was having difficulty concentrating on Tana's voice. He'd never imagined he could be so exhausted.

"Drake?" she said. "You need the ocean, don't you?" Her tone of her voice changed. She seemed worried. Drakōn tried to be concerned, but he was just so darned exhausted.

Chapter 26

Drake's eyes closed and his breathing seemed labored. Tana shook him, fear burning inside her, threatening to ignite once again. "Oh no, no, no," she said, looking at the growing flames. "I've made enough fire." She looked up at the boats and buildings glowing orange in the distance—lit from the fire of the brimstone wall. She looked down. "Drake," she shouted as she dropped to her knees. "What do I do?"

He didn't answer her, but his breathing seemed to slow and he looked pale against the wooden planks. Was he dying?

"Gretchen!" she shouted in desperation. "What do I do?" She didn't answer. No help was coming.

Brushing his hair back from his face, she pressed her hand against his cheek—the flames licking his skin. "What do I do? I...wait a minute," she blurted as a thought crossed her mind. He wasn't just a sea-god; Triton said he was the sea itself. As the thoughts went through her mind, she knew they were true. And the sea couldn't be harmed by her fire. She could transport him. *Close your eyes and think about where you want to be, then when you feel it, grab hold and pull.* Drake's words came back to

Raging

her.

She closed her eyes, and before she could even picture the sea in her mind, she felt something. It seemed to beg her to come. Perhaps this was Gretchen. Tana wrapped her arms around Drakōn and pulled with all her might.

Tana opened her eyes, and her heart stopped. Bars crossed her vision and stone blocks pressed against her knees. "Oh no," she breathed. Her eyes searched around her. She was in a cell—a very small one. She shook her head, stood, and ran forward, taking hold of the bars.

Her cell was not the only one. There were many more circling the perimeter of a vast empty room around her—and the cells were filled with people with varying expressions from rage, to fear, to confusion.

"Oh, no you don't!" she snarled. "You can't hold me!" Anger fumed in her.

"You can't use your powers, can you?" a woman's voice asked from nearby.

"What?" She turned as her eyes landed on a teenage girl. "Who are you?"

"My name is Angel, daughter of Zeus. And I was just telling you it's no use trying to use your powers. This prison blocks gods from accessing their power."

"Are you a prisoner?" Tana asked.

"Yep, just like you."

Tana pressed her lips together, refusing to admit she was a prisoner once again. This really sucked! But at least she wasn't frozen in ice this time. "Who's holding us prisoner?"

"Zeus."

"I thought he was your dad."

"Ha," Angel answered. "I don't call him Dad."

"What do you call him?"

"I don't think you want to hear the names I call him. They're not very polite."

Tana frowned. "I know exactly how you feel."

"What? You don't like him either?"

"No. I mean, yes. I don't like him, but I was talking about my father."

"Who's your father?"

"Hades."

"Awe, so you don't have warm and fuzzy feelings for dear old Dad either, huh?"

"Nope, the last prison I was in, my dad put me there."

"You were in prison before? What'd you do to get put there?"

"I don't want to talk about it."

"Should I be afraid? You're not going to knife me to death in my sleep, are you?"

Tana cracked a smile. "Only if you snore."

Angel gave a weak smile. "You are kidding, aren't you?"

"Yes, I'm kidding."

Drake groaned and turned on his side. Tana rushed over to him and knelt down.

"So, what's wrong with your friend?" Angel asked.

"I think he needs water."

Raging

"He passed out because he's thirsty?"

"No, he's a sea-god."

"Ah," she said with understanding. She approached and looked him over very thoroughly. By the time she was done, she was practically drooling. "He's...you know."

"Good looking?" Tana asked.

"No," Angel said, chuckling. "He's hot. Like center of the sun, hot."

Tana gave a weak chuckle. "I know." She turned back and looked at her protector. She'd always felt inexplicably safe with him around. But now, he also looked helpless. This was a new look for him.

"Do they give you food and water here?" Tana asked as she laid her head against Drake's chest and listened to the thump, thump of his heart.

"I haven't been here long enough to know," Angel said.

Tana pressed her eyebrows together. "How long *have* you been here?"

"About an hour."

"Shut up," a male voice shouted from another cell. "You freaks are crazy!"

"Wait a minute," Tana said, sitting up. "Who are you?"

"Looks like I'm the only sane person here," he answered angrily. "I'm not from Olympus, the Underworld, or any other idiotic, stupid, fictional place. I'm from Wichita, Kansas."

"Okay..." Tana answered tentatively. "So who

brought you here?"

He didn't answer, but Tana could hear him pacing.

"Hey, Kansas," Angel said as she stepped up to the bars. "Who brought you here?"

"Nobody brought me here," he snarled.

"Fine," Angel said. "You want to be in denial, fine with me. Just shut up and let us talk."

Tana could hear him curse under his breath, but he didn't say another word.

After several moments of silence, another voice spoke. "My name is Lisa." She seemed to be from farther away.

"Hello, Lisa," Tana answered. "Do you think we're crazy?"

She hesitated before answering. "Maybe."

Tana smiled as Angel said, "You could be right."

Tana's smile vanished as she looked down on Drake. She leaned forward and said, "Drake, come on. Wake up." He responded with a low moan. "Gods, what I wouldn't give for some water."

"I still have some water," Lisa said.

"You do?" Tana asked.

"Yeah, I was saving it for later. You probably need it more than I do. But…"

"What?"

"I think Kansas is between us."

Tana's heart dropped as she cursed under her breath. She raised her eyes and spoke gently. "Kansas."

"That's not my name," he growled.

Raging

"I'm sorry," Tana answered. "What is your name?"

He paused before speaking. "Myron."

"Okay, Myron," Tana said. "Would you please pass the water to me?"

"Why do you need water?"

"It's for my friend," Tana answered. "There's something wrong with him. I can't wake him up. I really think the water will help."

He roared and shook the bars of his cell, and then he quieted—his deep, angered breaths the only sound to be heard. "A glass of water isn't going to help anybody. He's not a sea-god, and you're delusional."

"If we're crazy, then we're crazy, and a glass of water won't help him. But it can't hurt either."

He didn't answer, but she could hear his heavy breathing. He was afraid. Perhaps too afraid to find enough pity in himself to help them.

"Please." Tana's voice cracked. If only Drake would open his eyes. "I'm not asking for you to believe us. Just pass the water down."

Once again, he didn't answer.

"Please."

"Alright," he said softly, and then shouted, "Alright, I'll do it."

"Thank you," Tana said.

"Don't thank me," he growled. "The stupid water isn't going to help."

Minutes later, a tin cup came into view.

Tana took hold of it and knelt beside Drake. Lifting

his head, she pressed the rim of the cup to his lips and tilted. As soon as the liquid touched his mouth, he sucked eagerly, practically inhaling the fluid.

His eyes flew open just as a door slammed open somewhere in the complex. Footsteps against stone let her know someone was coming. A deep chuckle told her who it was.

Zeus.

"Where am I?" Drake said as he sat up.

Tana's heart leaped out of her chest as she whispered, "Shh! I don't know exactly. But—"

"My power."

"What?"

"I can't feel it."

"Blame Zeus," Angel said. "No one can access their power here—well, except for Zeus."

Tana felt for her power just as two more figures appeared in the cell—Pallas and Malia with their arms around each other as they fell to the floor.

"Malia," Tana breathed. "What are you doing here?"

Malia answered. "I don't know. There was an earthquake, we fell, and the next thing I know, we're here."

Pallas looked around, alarm written on his face when his gaze finally rested on Drake. "Where are we?"

"Some kind of jail cell," Drake answered.

Pallas shook his head. "Thanks a lot. I would never have guessed that much."

Tana noticed that Pallas kept his arm around Malia.

Raging

Was there something between those two?

"Who has us in jail?" Pallas asked.

"Zeus," Angel answered.

"Who in Hades are you?" Pallas asked.

Before she could answer, a voice boomed from the center of the room. "Hello, one and all." Zeus looked at all the prisoners, smiling triumphantly.

Drake shot to his feet, grabbed the cell bars, and shook them. "What are you doing with us, you traitor?"

Zeus burst out laughing. "Trust the sea-god, Drakōn, to call me out on my crimes." He looked around to all the cells and then his eyes landed on Drake's face. "Well, the sea-god is right. I am a traitor. I banished the true king of the gods to the depths of Olympus and then erased everyone's memories. After that, I ascended the throne. How's that for treachery?"

He stepped slowly toward their cell—his eyes on Drake. Tana's first instinct was to back away at his approach, but she refused to give in to the impulse and stood firmly at Drake's side.

"But," Zeus said. "I do wonder how *you* knew."

"I'm one of many who know."

"Impossible," Zeus growled.

"You made one mistake, traitor."

"And what's that?"

"You wished for everyone to forget. Forgotten things can be—"

"Remembered," Zeus growled. "You don't think I didn't realize that? Still, soon, it won't matter. After today, no one will dare oppose me. I don't know why it took me so long to shake off my conscience, but now that I have, I know what I need to do. And I'm sorry, my dears," he said, looking from Angel to Tana. "You will not survive this." He turned to the other prisoners. "And the rest of you…well, you'll see."

Drake snarled at Zeus, so livid he seemed more animal than human. "You touch them, and I swear—"

Zeus' laugh interrupted him. "Drakōn and Tana, together at the end." Zeus stopped at the bars and shook his head. "Too bad you won't have a chance to see your happily-ever-after." He cracked a wicked smile. "You won't even have a chance to see tomorrow."

"You're insane," Tana growled.

Zeus shrugged as he paced away. "Perhaps I am. With the power of a thousand gods and goddesses in me, it's hard not to give in to the madness." He turned back. "Still, my goal is worth any sacrifice."

"What goal?" Tana asked. "What do you want?"

"You, my dear. I want you." He turned to Drakōn. "And you." And then he turned his eyes on all of them, onc by one, and repeated it to each one.

There's a heck of a lot of people here.

While Zeus' attention was diverted to the other prisoners, Tana whispered to Drake, "He's crazy."

"Certifiable," Pallas said.

"We have to get out of here," Angel said, rushing to the bars.

"Who *are* you?" Drake asked.

Raging

"The name's Angel," she answered.

"She's the daughter of Zeus," Tana said.

"Yeah, a lot of good that did me." Angel frowned.

Malia shook her head. "This is all crazy. There's no such thing as gods, and Dagonians, and…and… it's all insane. I swear I have to be dreaming. I'm totally dreaming, right?" She turned to Pallas. "I should have known you were too good to be true. I mean, someone as incredibly sexy as you, coming to protect me from these flying mermen wanting to kill me. I mean, how insane is that? But I can't seem to wake up," she said, her gaze on Pallas seeming to heat. "Though, I don't know if I want to. You'd be gone."

Pallas shook his head. "I knew you were attracted to me."

"If this is a dream," Malia said, "I might as well make this dream a good one." She yanked Pallas toward her and smashed her lips against his. Pallas stiffened for a brief moment as if stunned by her action, but in a blink, he eagerly returned the kiss, picking Malia up off the floor.

Tana turned away when the kiss got so hot that she felt embarrassed watching them. She frowned at Drake. "What is it with you Dagonians?" she whispered. "Do all of you have a thing for humans?"

"You're not human, Tana."

Tana scoffed.

"Your friends need to get a room," Angel said, her eyebrow raised.

"We should probably stop them," Tana said. "Malia thinks this is a dream. She'd never do something this blatant otherwise." She turned to Drake. "Your friend is taking advantage of her."

Drake smirked. "Malia is the one who kissed Pallas."

"Yeah." Tana frowned. "But only because she thinks she's having a dream."

"This dream of hers is going to end in a nightmare," Angel said.

Drake turned to Angel. "He's really going to kill us, isn't he?"

She nodded sadly.

"Why would your own father put you here?" Tana asked.

"The same reason he put you here," she answered. "I may be his daughter, but he doesn't care. He never has."

"We have to stop him," Tana said

"And you," Zeus said, drawing her full attention when he added, "have the honor of being the first."

"No!" She heard a gasp and a hum of voices from all around. "What are you going to do with me?" the voice of a young man asked. When she located him, her heart dropped. He couldn't be more than twenty.

"My boy, Georgios," Zeus said. "Don't worry. You won't feel a—oh, who am I trying to fool? This is going to hurt. A lot." Zeus dragged him into the center of the room. He reached toward the floor and it broke apart. The stones swirled around a vortex and were sucked in.

Zeus closed his eyes and whispered.

Raging

"What is that?" Angel breathed as she pointed to the mist swirling around Georgios' head. A ghostly face flashed into view.

"I know what that is," Drake whispered, horrified. "It's a siphon."

"What's a siphon?" Tana asked, wondering if she really wanted to know the answer.

The siphon flew around the man as he screamed and cowered on the ground as he began to change. His tanned skin turned yellow, glowing as bright as the sun as it spread across his body. And then his fingertips dimmed—the darkness spreading up his arms. The shadow of blackness spread across his body as he disintegrated into smoke. Within seconds, all that was left of Georgios was a lingering haze. And soon, that too was gone. The siphon sank into the vortex and it, too, was gone.

"Ah," Zeus said, beaming with joy as his chest heaved. "There's no greater feeling than that of stolen power. What a rush!"

"Where is he?" Angel shouted.

Zeus turned to her, beaming. "He's gone."

"To the afterlife?"

Zeus shook his head. "He's simply gone. After I'm through with you, there will be nothing left to send to Hades."

Angel turned away. "I think I'm going to be sick." Her white face let them know that she wasn't just saying that.

Zeus turned his eyes on Tana. She took a step back,

nearly panicking as she considered she would be next.

"Ha!" Zeus smiled. "Are you afraid, Tana?"

Tana clenched her fists and narrowed her eyes. She wouldn't give him the satisfaction of showing fear. Breathing slowly, she calmed her temper.

"Such fire," Zeus said, "even when your powers are suppressed. I'm going to save you for last, my dear. I've already got a taste of your power, and I'm desperate for more. But there's joy in anticipation. So," he raised his voice and turned away, "another. Who is going to be my next victim?"

A girl was brought out. She looked to be about eighteen. Tana couldn't watch this time. Drake wrapped his arms around her as she buried her head his chest and covered her ears. It wasn't enough. She could still hear the tortured cries. But what was worse…the agonizing silence that came after.

"Sorry, Pallas," Malia murmured. "But I want to wake up now."

"I wish we could," Pallas answered. Tana glanced up. Pallas was holding Malia like Drakōn was holding her.

"Who are these people?" Tana mumbled in Drake's chest. She could feel him press a kiss against her head.

"I'm not sure," Drake said, "but I *think* I know."

Tana lifted her eyes and focused on his face. Drake turned her so that her back was on the scene. Still, the horror and fury in his eyes were easy to see.

"So, who are they?" she asked him.

"They're like you."

Raging

"Like me?"

"Those he's siphoned power from."

"But what about Pallas?" Tana asked. "Is he a god?"

"I'm a Dagonian, one hundred percent pure," Pallas said.

Tana looked toward the crowd and turned away as Zeus finished with another victim. "So all these people… they're like me? What did he do to us?"

"No," Drake whispered.

Tana turned her head. "What?"

Zeus was walking toward them. In a flash, Malia was outside the bars.

"No!" Pallas shouted as he rushed to the bars. "You filthy traitor. Take me instead."

"What do you want with Malia?" Tana shouted, dumbfounded.

Zeus shrugged. "It's simply her turn."

"But she's not—"

"Oh yes, she is," Zeus said, obviously relishing the situation. "Tana, I'd like you to meet the daughter of Atlas and Eos."

"But Eos is my mother." Tana swallowed a lump in her throat.

"So she is," Zeus said in mock surprise. "You didn't know Malia was your sister, did you?"

"Malia, daughter of…earth and sky," Drake said.

"Right you are, sea-god," Zeus smiled. "You're not as dumb as you look. In fact, I'll take it by that Dagonian soldier sniffing around her for the last few days," he spared a glance at Pallas, "that she was part of some pathetic plan to free the king. But I'll make things easy for Malia. Instead of dying in a battle, I'll kill her now. Nice and easy."

"You know of the prophecy?" Drake asked.

Zeus laughed and then shouted, "I created the prophecy! You think you can outsmart me? I locked my brother deep in the earth and created the conditions for his release myself. You see, if I know how he can be freed, I can stop it from happening."

"Why not just make an unbreakable prison?" Drake asked.

Zeus exploded in rage. "There is no unbreakable prison for the king of the gods!" He stood in silence. His chest heaved as he seemed to be trying to calm himself. Malia silently crawled away from him.

"So you see…" A fragile smile cracked across Zeus' face. "I had to do it. And now I'm going to destroy all the children of mixed realms."

"Children of mixed realms?"

"Yes," Zeus said. "The prophecy will never be fulfilled without them."

"What about Sara and Gretchen?" Tana asked. From the corner of her eye, she saw Drake shake his head ever so slowly. She turned to his stricken expression.

Zeus chuckled. "You mean this Gretchen?" He pointed to an obsidian statue of a woman. With her back turned, Tana couldn't see who it was. Zeus swirled his finger in the air, and the statue grated across the floor as

Raging

it rotated in response.

Gretchen's defiant expression was brought into view, frozen on her stone face. "No," Tana whispered, despair heavy in her heart. That despair quickly turned to anger. In a flash, flames burst from her—covering her entire body and casting a blinding light across the prison.

"You," Zeus said in stunned horror as he looked at her. "You are not supposed to be able to access your powers."

"You killed Gretchen," Tana said. "She's a wife. A mother. She saved my life. And you killed her. You killed all these innocent people. You want to kill my best friend. And Drake—" Her voice broke on his name.

"But…" Zeus stepped back in shock. "How are you doing this?"

"That's a question you should ask my father."

"Your father is helping you? I thought you hated your father."

"I hate you more."

Tana lifted her hands, which now appeared to be made up of white flames. At her touch, the bars melted. She stepped out into the wide, round room. Now that she'd embraced her powers instead of fighting them, she found them easy to control.

Zeus swallowed and stepped toward her. "You know you can't kill me. Not even the burning center of the sun can kill a god. You might be able to burn my body, but I will come back."

"That's what I'm counting on." She narrowed her

eyes.

"What's that supposed to mean?" Zeus took a step back.

Tana looked at those surrounding her. Most of them didn't even know who and what they were—gods and goddesses, each one, and then she looked back at Zeus. "It's not you I'm trying to kill."

Understanding washed over Zeus as he roared, "*No.*"

Tana exploded, bursting into an inferno of fire. Screams erupted around her as the rocky walls blew apart. Tana could see through the inferno to the hundreds of people burning alive around her. But they weren't just burning—they were falling. Tana hovered above them, watching them tumble down below. The prison must have been above the earth. Her fire had burst the walls. If these gods and goddesses weren't killed by the fire, the fall would do it.

Tana hovered above, her wings beating the fire into a rage. Searching the falling bodies, she could easily make out Drake's watery form, and then she found Malia with Pallas locked around her. Tana's heart dropped when she realized that Pallas likely wasn't a god.

She'd just killed him.

Malia's eyes locked on Tana's for a moment as she shrieked, falling to the earth. In a jumble of bodies and rocks, everything came crashing to the grassy ground below. And then there was silence.

CHAPTER 27

The fire calmed as Tana dropped into a crouch against the ground at the edge of the smoldering hill. Drake's watery form rose from the rubble and took shape. In seconds, his body was back to normal, but his face reflected the horror of the surroundings.

"They're dead," Drake said as he turned to her. "You meant to kill them?"

Tana shook her head. "There are only a few ways to kill a god. And like Zeus said, this isn't one of them."

"Then you—"

"Released them," she said as she made her way to the bodies.

"But Pallas wasn't a god," Drake said.

Her shoulders sank as tears stung her eyes. "I know. I would have had to do it either way. Zeus was going to kill us all."

"Including Pallas," Drake said, somber.

"I'm sorry," Tana said with tears in her eyes.

"We need to find Zeus," Drake said. "In this state, he'll be easy to subdue." Drake was all business now. Tana had a feeling he'd be mourning his friend later.

Tana blinked away the tears and tried to focus on

finding Zeus. She did her best not to step on people as she worked her way in, but it was difficult. Broken bodies and charred limbs were everywhere.

"How long do you think it will take them to regenerate?" Drake asked.

Tana shook her head. "I've no idea. I just hope everyone will be okay. I only wish I could have saved them all. The ones Zeus drained before, and then Pallas…and Gretchen. I couldn't save them."

"You did all you could."

"Did I?" Tana stopped and looked at Drake, tears stinging her eyes.

"Yes," Drake said, his voice also thick with emotion.

Tana turned her attention to finding Zeus. She wasn't ready to face the guilt of what she'd done. She searched for a long time when she finally said, "I can't find him." She shook her head in frustration. Taking another step, she froze. There was a charm bracelet. A silver dove and blue dolphin shone brightly against charred skin. It was Malia's bracelet. Tana had given her the dove charm with a diamond chip eye for her birthday last month. "Oh no," Tana said as tears flowed freely from her eyes and she turned away.

"Malia," Drake murmured as he stepped beside her. "Pallas is beneath her."

Tana's stomach lurched. "What if I'm wrong? What if they're all dead?" She stumbled forward, coming face to face with a…man? Woman? She couldn't tell; the face was burnt beyond recognition. Her body began to shake

Raging

as her heart pounded in her chest. "They look dead, Drake."

"Tana," he said as she continued to stare at the lifeless face in front of her. "Tana, look at me," Drake said, snapping her out of her trance.

Reluctantly, she turned to face him. His eyes were fierce as he glared at her. "They're not dead."

She gave him a shaky nod. *Oh please, let him be right!*

He lifted Malia up. "Let's find a better place for her to wake up." He held her so her face pressed into his chest as he made his way over to a clearing. He lay Malia on the ground and gingerly lay her arms across her chest. Tana caught a quick glimpse of what was left of her friend's face and turned away.

"I think I'm going to be sick," she blurted as she stumbled over the debris. As soon as she reached the clearing, she ran. She only made it twenty paces when she dropped to her knees and sobbed. In that instance, Drake was there, pulling her into his arms and stroking her back.

"It's okay, baby," he murmured. "It's going to be okay. She'll be fine; she'll be more than fine. She'll be perfect. Just you wait and see."

Tana cried until she had no tears left. "How do you know? How can you be so sure?"

"Tana," he said as he pressed his fingertips under her chin and lifted her head. "I saw *you* die." His eyes drifted as his mind seemed to reflect back on the horror he'd witnessed. "I'd never felt so helpless, so alone. And seeing your broken body…thinking you were dead." He closed his eyes as he sighed, a tear leaking from his eye. "I wanted to die myself."

He opened his eyes and wiped away the tear. "But you weren't dead. You healed. You came back to me."

Tana nodded, holding desperately to his words. Malia would be fine—Malia, her sister. That was hard to wrap her brain around.

She sighed, wiped her eyes, and looked up. For the first time, she noticed Drake wasn't wearing a shirt. Her gaze wandered over his muscled skin, slicked with sweat and ash, and her heart skipped a beat. "What happened to your shirt?" she asked, her voice strained.

Drake shrugged. "I used it to cover Malia's face."

"Oh," she said as guilt washed over her. She was ogling Drake while Malia's burnt and charred body lay nearby. Shaking her head, she turned away. "I wish I knew how—"

"Unhh," someone or something groaned from behind. Tana turned to see movement in the debris. A young woman staggered to her feet and looked around at all the carnage. She raised her eyes to Tana. "You…what did you do to us?" She turned once again, her eyes landing on a body that looked like a cross between a skeleton and beef jerky, and then back to Tana. "What are you?" The woman's voice rumbled. Or was it thunder?

"Uh, Drake?" Tana said, backing away. "Should we be afraid?"

"Well, let's see," he said. "If she has a similar

experience to yours, then probably."

"You mean when I was nearly killed and got my powers back?"

"Yeah."

"That didn't end very well. I killed everyone around me."

The young goddess with golden curls looked down at her hands as electricity crackled over her fingertips. "What is happening to me?"

"We need to leave now," Drake said.

"We can't just leave them like this," Tana said. "They need our help."

"They need a miracle," Drake said.

"I've never been called a miracle before."

Tana turned to the familiar voice. "Gretchen…" she gasped.

"By the gods, you had me worried," Drakōn said.

Gretchen sauntered over and smiled. "I didn't know you cared."

Drakōn grunted. "I don't. I just didn't want to be the one to tell Kyros you were dead. I rather enjoy remaining in one piece."

Tana stepped toward Gretchen. "So, Zeus didn't kill you. Did he kill the others?"

Gretchen frowned and nodded. "Yes, he would have killed me too, but I had my own personal siphon—one who was not under Zeus' control. Sara convinced her to help me fool Zeus into thinking I was dead. She knew I would be needed here."

"Needed for what?"

The goddess with the golden hair dropped to her knees—electricity arcing over her entire body. Gretchen reached out her hand as black mist erupted from her fingertips. As soon as the mist reached the distraught goddess, she collapsed in a heap on the ground. "My job is to keep these deities asleep until they can be retrieved and helped." She continued to let the mist loose and it advanced, blanketing the entire area.

"You can make people fall asleep?" Drakōn said.

"Yeah," Gretchen said. "And save the jokes."

Drake looked taken aback. "I'm not the type of person who jokes in a situation like this."

"No." Gretchen shrugged as she sighed. "I guess not. But Pallas would."

Drakōn's face fell. "Yes, he would."

"I'm sorry," Gretchen said. "I'm sure he's—"

"Don't," Drakōn interrupted. "I don't want to hear how he's in a better place. That will comfort me later. For now, I need to focus on freeing the king."

"Okay," Gretchen answered. "You need to meet Sara at the base of Olympus. Oh, and make sure you bring Malia with you."

"Malia?" Tana asked.

"Yes, she's the final one we need. I'll be coming after I'm finished here."

Drake looked at her. "Your sister is the final key."

Tana sighed, worry in her eyes. "I guess so."

"I'll go get her," he said.

Raging

She nodded, not wanting to see her charred body again.

Tana waited patiently.

"She's gone," Drake said.

Tana's couldn't breathe as she shook her head. "Impossible," she gasped.

Drake looked around—confusion on his face. "She's not here."

A rumble shook the earth, kicking up smoke off the smoldering ground. A mound of dirt lifted nearby, and a head broke the surface as a man arose. He shook his head and brushed the dirt from his body as he looked around in desperation. Strange how the dirt fell off him completely, leaving his skin and golden robe without a speck on them.

"Where is she?" he shouted, looking at Tana and then Drake.

"Who are you looking for?" Gretchen asked, and he turned to her.

"My…" His voice broke with emotion. "My daughter. I am Aeacus. And my child's name was…is Ruby." His tears fell as he spoke. "I should know what she looks like. She's my daughter, but…by gods, I don't know; I don't know anymore. She was only a baby when Zeus came for her."

"It's alright," Gretchen said, stepping forward and taking his hand. "We'll find her."

Tana rushed forward. "Gretchen! Malia is gone. She was just here. Do you know…do you think her father came for her?"

Gretchen shook her head. "No. This god is the first."

"Where would she go?" Tana asked.

"Please," Aeacus said. "I must find my daughter."

Gretchen nodded to him and turned to Tana. "I'm sorry. I have no idea where she is. Do you know who her parents are?"

"Yes, she's my sister. Our mother's dead, but her father is Atlas," Tana said.

"I'll keep my eye out for him," Gretchen said. "You should probably talk to Sara. She might know."

Tana turned to leave when Gretchen called, "Tana, Drakōn, you *have* to find her. Without her, we can't free the king."

"We'll find her," Drakōn answered as Tana clenched her fists and nodded.

Chapter 28

Zeus roared as he slammed his fist into the crystal prison. The ground rumbled as rocks shook loose from the massive cave encasing the mountainous structure and riddled the ground around him. "I should have killed her! I should have drained every last ounce of power from Tana when I had the chance." He paced as he wrung his hands together. Shadows stretched and morphed within the cavern as he moved, his light dimming from the loss of power.

He shook his head as he stepped toward the lonsdaleite wall. He could feel enormous power and rage beneath it. "No, my first mistake was not destroying you when I had the chance, brother. And now, my power is weak. I've lost so much, so much." He growled as he dropped to his knees and clawed his hair in his fists. Rocking back and forth, he continued to rant. "My plans, she's ruined them. This will take years to remedy. And now they will all know. Everyone will know what I've done."

He looked up and shouted, "You've won, brother. Do you hear me? Your rescue party is being assembled and you will soon be free and will no doubt destroy me."

Zeus dropped his hands to his side as a thought played at the edges of his muddled mind. "Unless…" The thought took shape, lighting hope inside him.

Zeus closed his eyes and searched for the first of four—the one whose importance was only just discovered.

Ah! There she was. And she was unprotected.

He pulled her to him, and the first thing he noticed was the scent of burnt hair. He opened his eyes and found the goddess—a burnt carcass below him.

He smiled and knelt beside her. "Heal quickly, young one. I need you to do what you were born to do. You and your friends will open this prison and free the king. And then I will destroy him.

"I will destroy them all."

Chapter 29

Drakōn surfaced at the shore near Olympus with Tana at his side. After the death and carnage, the sea was so welcoming. So refreshingly clean.

"When this is over," Tana said, "I'm never leaving the sea again."

Drakōn was taken aback. "What makes you say that? Not that I mind. I mean, I'd be happy for you to…"

"To what?" Tana asked.

"Live with me."

"We've only shared a kiss, and now you're asking me to move in with you?"

"Well, um, if you'd be willing, I'd like you to marry me."

Tana gasped so hard she choked. Drakōn patted her on the back while she coughed. "Is there something wrong with marrying someone like me? I know we are different. You're a goddess of fire and wind, and I'm a god of the sea, but I—"

"No." Tana shook her head. "It's just…"

"Yes?"

"We've only known each other for a few days."

"Where I'm from, that's longer than most couples

know each other."

"What?"

"It's common for Dagonian marriages to be arranged between the prospective husband and the female's father before the bride and groom officially meet. Women don't go socializing with men. So if these things weren't arranged, they'd rarely happen."

"Seriously?"

"Most males I know spend no more than a day or two deciding on a match."

"Well, I just…I think we should get to know each other better before we make that kind of decision."

Drakōn shook his head, shards of his heart chipping away with each word she spoke. "If you don't care for me, I would rather you just say it. I'm a man, a warrior. I don't need to be placated to protect my feelings."

"You think I don't care about you?" Tana's voice rose.

"I don't know how you feel."

She scowled up at him. "Well, let me show you." At those words, she pulled him down and pressed her lips against his. At the touch of her mouth on his, passion ignited. The kiss quickly became hot, carnal, and filled with so much emotion he felt as if they'd spontaneously combust. Her sweet taste made him desperate for more. He wanted nothing more than to take her—all of her. It took a tremendous amount of self-control to pull away.

"Gods," he whispered with his forehead pressed against hers. "If you don't marry me, I swear I'll…"

"What?" she asked through ragged breaths.

Raging

"Please," he asked.

"I just," she said with pinched brows. "I can't. Not yet."

"Do you love me?"

Her eyes were flooded with confusion as she looked everywhere but at him. She didn't seem to want to answer.

"That's a simple question."

She shook her head. "No, it's not."

"Tana," he said softly, his voice a caress. "Look at me."

Several moments went by before she lifted her eyes to his. Tears welled in them. "I care more for you than I ever have for any other person. I don't know if that's love."

"Sounds like love to me."

Tana continued to frown.

"Marry me," he asked.

"And if I don't?"

"What do you have against marriage?"

"You might think you love me now, but what about a year from now? What if I do something so terrible that you couldn't stand to even look at me again?"

"So you think I might turn my back on you someday?"

"You wouldn't be the first."

"Tana, I'll never leave you. What more could you do—?"

"What if I kill your daughter?" she interrupted. "If I lose control and burn her to death?"

"We'll live alone if that worries you so much."

"But—"

"No," Drake snapped. "You deserve some happiness, Tana."

"So do you," she said. She pressed her lips together and sighed. "We'd better go. Sara is waiting for us."

Drakōn frowned at Tana's back as she pulled herself out of the water and stood on the shore.

Sara, Xanthus, and Olympus stood at the head of a trail leading to the base of Mount Olympus. It towered majestically above. Tana stood in awe at the mountain range. It wasn't just one large mountain, there were many peaks rising above them in a semi-circular shape—open towards the ocean and to a small town called Litochoro.

"Tana." Sara stepped toward her. "I'm so glad you could make it."

"Um…" she smiled shyly, "thanks."

"So have you forgiven me then?" Sara asked with a smile, but there was tension in her eyes. She was seriously worried about the matter.

"Well, since you saved my life, I kind of have to."

Sara chuckled. "I was glad to do it."

Tana glanced around, her eyes widening at the men surrounding her. Big didn't even begin to describe them. They were insanely tall and ripped—each one. Xanthus caught her glance, and Tana felt a jolt deep in her bones. That man was dangerous. And then there was the guy called Olympus. He towered above all of them, built like a mountain, with brown, earthy skin and dark pupils,

Raging

black as onyx. She remembered his voice—deep, gravelly, like the sound of a landslide.

Tana caught his gaze, and he smiled. "You look so much like Eos. She was an amazing woman—full of light, with skin as soft as a dove." He cleared his throat as his cheeks glowed with a pink cast.

Looked like her mother got around.

Tana didn't know how to respond, so she simply nodded.

Sara stepped closer. "You and Malia became very close in the short time you knew each other. You both sensed your connection. You were kind to take care of her."

"Right, you're the goddess who can see everything." Tana shook her head. She looked at the goddess and was struck with how different she was from her husband. Sara was soft and elegant, and if Tana weren't feeling the immense power coming off the goddess even now, she'd think Sara was fragile. But no one with that much power could ever be called fragile. "I didn't take care of Malia; she took care of herself along with her very protective brothers."

"Ah, yes." Sara's eyes sparkled with understanding, "Vin and Kai. They are pretty amazing. They actually remind me a lot of my husband. Though I doubt Zeus was trying to be kind, I'm happy to see Malia ended up with a human family who loved and cared for her."

"Yes," she said, "they do."

"But you watched out for her too," Sara said.

"We watched out for each other." Tana swallowed and nodded. Tears burned her eyes as worry set in.

Drakōn put his arm around her. "Malia is loved dearly by all those around her."

"Yes." Sara nodded. "By the way, when is Malia coming?"

Tana looked at her; worry tinged Sara's expression. "You don't know?" Tana asked.

Sara's eyes darkened. "Know what?"

"She's gone."

"What?" Sara's eyes went from worry to frantic. "Where has she gone?"

"I'm not sure."

Sara shook her head. "No, no, no. This is not how it's supposed to happen."

Xanthus stepped up to her. "What is it, moro mou?"

"Malia's gone," Sara said, grabbing his arm and turning toward him.

Olympus shook his head and took an intimidating step toward her. "It has to be Zeus. You told me you had this under control. What else can go wrong?"

"I…I don't know," Sara said, uncertain.

"What *do* you know?" Olympus growled, and the earth shook at the anger in his voice.

Xanthus stepped into his path, power flowing from him in waves as he clasped the sword at his waist. "Keep your distance from my wife, Olympus," he snarled, his voice reverberating like the sound of a war cry.

Drakōn turned and whispered to Tana, "Xanthus

needs a reality check."

"What?" Tana whispered back, her eyes glued on the scene. "You don't think he could beat Olympus?"

"Oh," Drakōn answered. "I know he could. It's just Xanthus won't accept who he is."

Olympus took a step back. "My apologies. My quarrel is not with your wife. I only wish to stop Zeus from destroying my family."

Sara gently tugged Xanthus back. "It's alright, sweetheart. He won't hurt me." Drakōn noticed she kept her hand on Xanthus' arm as if she preferred to keep him close. *Smart woman.*

"Who is he?" Tana asked.

"That's for Xanthus to say," Drakōn said.

"Why is Olympus so upset?" Tana asked. "I thought it was only humans who were at risk."

"I think he's gotten involved with the humans," Drakōn whispered.

"You mean…" Tana raised an eyebrow. "You think he has a human wife?"

Drakōn nodded. "Children too, I'm guessing."

Sara looked toward the mountain. "I can't see what's happening. I'm too involved in these events. But I know this much. We have to free the king, now. If we allow Zeus to do it, there won't be any stopping him."

Drakōn felt power brush his back.

"What did we miss?" a familiar, gruff voice asked.

He turned to see Kyros and Gretchen approaching.

Drakōn took Kyros by the hand and clapped his

back. "Sara says it's time to save the world."

"Then what are we waiting for?" Kyros asked.

"We were waiting for you, my friend," Drakōn said. "How did you get away so soon?"

Gretchen stepped up next to her husband. "My dad and his uncle came to relieve me."

"Gretchen told you about Pallas," Drakōn said.

Kyros nodded—sadness in his eyes.

"I'd say I'm glad you could join us, Gretchen," Sara said, somberly, "but actually, I'm terrified for us all. I haven't seen anything like the events that are taking place now. Zeus has obviously changed the rules of the game, and there's no guarantee we will succeed. Even if we do, we may not all survive."

"That's never stopped us before," Kyros said. "So where do we begin?"

"Olympus," Sara said, turning to the god. "We need you to open a path inside."

"You want me to crack open my precious mountain?" he asked, horrified.

"We need to get in," Sara said. "We've been looking for an opening, but we haven't found any."

He shook his head. "That's because you didn't know where to look."

"Excuse me?" Sara said, obviously offended. "I always know where to look."

"Cocky is a new look for you, Sara," Gretchen said smirking.

"I just…" Sara looked at her best friend as her cheeks

Raging

filled with color. "Sorry. I do sound a bit full of myself, don't I?"

Gretchen laughed. "I'm not saying it's a bad look. It's just different." She threw her arm around Sara's shoulder. "I like the new, more confident you."

Tana could hear the conversation, but she couldn't take her eyes off the mountain. "We'll find your sister," Drake whispered in her ear. "She's going to be alright."

"I know," she said softly.

"Okay," Sara said, turning to Olympus. "How do we get inside?"

Chapter 30

Tana's jaw dropped when Olympus handed them each a shovel.

"Are we supposed to dig our way through the mountain?" she said.

Olympus bellowed in laughter as he leaned on his own shovel. "That's a good one, fire girl."

Tana frowned at the nickname.

"No." He smiled. "We aren't going to dig our way to the king—we are digging our way to the door."

"There's a door leading to the king?" Drake asked.

"Nope. It's a door leading to the Hu."

Triton had been silent until then. But at the mention of the Hu, he stomped forward and grabbed Olympus by the shoulder. "The Hu? The Hu are in there?"

"Yes," Olympus answered, all humor gone. "They guard the heart of Olympus."

"What is the heart of Olympus?" Triton asked.

"I'd always thought of it as the power and strength of the gods," Olympus said.

"And now?" Triton asked.

"It must be Petros."

"So will they let us through to free him?" Drake asked.

Raging

Olympus shook his head slowly. "Their job is to keep everyone away from the heart."

"How in Hades are we to get past them?" Triton asked.

"What exactly are the Hu?" Tana asked. "Why are they so dangerous?"

Triton sighed. "I've had dealings with them before. They are unstoppable. Made from the earth, they are stronger than any god and indestructible. Well, that's not exactly right. You can destroy them if you fight hard enough, but they don't stay dead. They reform quickly, and are no worse for wear."

"Can we sneak past them?" Xanthus asked.

Olympus shook his head. "There's nowhere to hide in there."

Tana felt a rumble deep in her chest as the ground began to quake. "What's going on?" she asked amid a flurry of worried shouts and words. After several seconds, the quakes stopped.

"That shouldn't have happened," Olympus said.

"Is Olympus going to erupt again?" Triton asked.

"Again?" Tana turned to Drake.

"Olympus erupted not long ago," Triton said and pointed south. "That peak, the one closest to the village."

Tana could see what looked to be a crater.

"But Pele was able to stop it," Drake said.

"What does that mean?" Tana asked. "I didn't even know that Olympus was a volcano."

"It's not," Triton said.

Holly Kelly

"I don't understand," Tana asked. "How—?"

"We don't know," Triton interrupted. "Not even Sara knows."

"Looks like the mountain doesn't show her everything," Olympus said.

Sara looked at him. "Olympus, can you tell us what's happening?" Worry clouded her face as Xanthus put his arm around her.

Olympus closed his eyes and blew out a breath. Moments later, his eyes flew open and his breathed out a name.

"Zeus."

"He's here?" Drake asked.

Olympus nodded. "He's trying to open the prison himself." He threw up his hands, exasperated. "Why would he do that?"

"He's trying to take Petros' power," Drake said, and everyone turned to him in shock.

"But he needs all four to open the prison," Gretchen said.

"And he has all four," Drake said looking from Tana to Gretchen and then to Sara.

"But he also needs—" Sara began.

"Malia," Tana said. "He already has her."

"Yes," Drake said.

"What do we do?" Kyros asked.

"We need to see this through," Xanthus said.

"But—" Kyros began.

"No," Triton said. "Xanthus is right. If we don't do

Raging

it, the world will be destroyed."

"And Malia will die," Tana said. "I'm sure of it."

"Listen," Olympus said. "It's not that I don't care, but if Zeus is here, he's already won. My family can't survive without me." He backed away, looking from face to face. "Sorry, but you're on your own," he said and disappeared.

Tana rushed forward. "No," she screamed. "You coward!"

"Tana," Drake said, stepping to her side. "It's okay. We'll save her. We'll save them all."

"I don't know how," Kyros said, shaking his head. "With Olympus gone, we can't even get inside."

Drake turned on him and snarled. "Are you a coward too?" He looked around at everyone. "Are you all cowards?"

Triton stepped forward with his hands up. "It's not courage that's lacking, Drakōn. It's knowing how under Olympus to get inside this mountain."

With that said, everyone seemed to be speaking at the same time as they all gave their opinion on how hopeless the situation was.

Despair pressed down on Tana, making it difficult to breathe. She sank to the ground as tears began to fall. The hum of hopeless voices in the background didn't help her. She caught bits and pieces of their arguments—

"...there's no way in..."

"...no getting past the Hu..."

"...we can't let Zeus win..."

...please, no, I can't..."

Tana's heart stopped when she heard that voice. "Malia," she whispered. Straining to hear, she couldn't seem to find her voice again. There was too much noise. "Shut up," she shouted, her voice ringing with power.

Everyone fell silent.

"We're sorry—" Sara began.

"Shh!" Tana interrupted. She closed her eyes and listened again.

The hum of the wind and chirping of birds seemed to be the only thing she could hear, but then very faint, she was sure she heard a voice begging. "Please."

"It's her." Tana jumped up. "I heard her. It's Malia."

Sara stepped up to her and asked, "Can you lead us to her?"

Tana closed her eyes and listened. She couldn't hear her voice again, but she...could feel her. She stepped toward the direction she felt her coming from. "I think so."

It was only a short distance into the trees when they came to a steep slope at the base of the mountain.

"So," Kyros said. "How do we find the door?"

"Tana," Xanthus said gently. "Can you tell where the door is?"

"I don't know." Tana closed her eyes and listened as she walked. Drake held her elbow and guided her.

When she found the place where she could feel Malia's presence the strongest, she stopped. "I think it's here."

Raging

"Alright everyone," Triton said as he drove his shovel into the ground. "Start digging."

Digging went quickly with so many strong men heaving shovels, but then slowed when they hit mud. Sara, Gretchen, and Tana let the men take over. Why should they wallow in the muck when there were four perfectly capable men to do it for them?

After what seemed like forever, they struck a stone slab. Clearing away the mud and small rocks, they were able to expose the entire door.

"Alright," Kyros said. "Let's open it."

Wading knee deep through the sludge, he pushed with everything he had. His muscles bulged and he grunted from the effort, but the door didn't move.

"Stop before you hurt yourself, Kyros," Drake said. "I'll get this." Drake strode confidently up to the door and made an attempt. Despite the impressive show of back and arm muscles—which Tana couldn't help but appreciate—the door didn't budge for him either. Finally, he had to admit defeat.

"My turn," Triton said as he stepped forward. He didn't have any better luck than the others.

"I think we've seen enough," Sara said. "This door doesn't open to muscle strength."

"Obviously," Kyros said under his breath. Gretchen smiled and shook her head.

"I think I should try it," Sara said.

"Sara," Xanthus said, amused. "If Triton, Kyros, and Drakōn couldn't do it, I doubt you can either."

"Xanthus, my love," Sara smiled sweetly. "What does the prophecy say?"

Xanthus frowned at his wife but didn't answer.

She must not have felt it necessary to explain as she stepped forward. Tana took in a quick breath when she saw how the mud reacted to Sara walking into it. It cleared away in front of her and solidified under her feet.

Drake shook his head, beaming. "Gods, of course," he whispered loudly to Tana. "Sara's not just a goddess of fate; she's the daughter of earth and water." He shook his head. "It would have been a lot more helpful if she'd cleared it out before we wasted an hour shoveling."

Sara looked his way, shrugged, and mouthed, *Sorry*. She turned back to the door and cocked her head to the side as if considering something. Reaching forward, she began to chip and peel away the dirt from the door. One large piece of dirt came off in a chunk and Tana held her breath as she recognized a recessed handprint—a small hand print. Sara reached forward. When she pressed her hand into the impression, it grated open. "Hmm," she said smiling. "Looks like it worked."

She took a step inside just as Xanthus said, "Sara, wait." In a flash, a large mace with four-inch spikes slammed into Sara, knocking her from view and leaving a trail of blood in her wake.

Chapter 31

Malia felt as if she'd been roasted in an oven. Every part of her burned and the smell of charred meat and burnt hair hung in the air. She should be dead. Yet, here she was, alive and doing Zeus' bidding.

"Try again," he growled.

"Please, I can't do it," Malia begged.

"You will do it, or I'll rip apart everyone you've ever loved or cared about—Vin, Kai, Tana, the humans you call your friends…I'll feed their bodies to the vultures."

Malia's stomach sickened. He would do it too.

Once again, she attempted to climb the crystal mountain with Zeus watching every move she made. The strangeness of this place overwhelmed her. This was a mountain within a mountain. She had awoken inside a cave the size of the Grand Canyon with a strange crystal mountain inside. It had a surface unlike any she'd ever climbed before. Of course, she wasn't an expert climber. But the few times she went with her brothers taught her the basics. And she had enough experience to know that climbing this crystal was completely insane! With a mixture of glassy smooth and sharp, jagged edges, it provided very few handholds. In other words, it was impossible to climb. That didn't stop Zeus from forcing her to do it.

Malia tried not to look at her skin. It was charred grey and flaking away, and it burned like the deepest recesses of hell. Seriously, she needed a burn unit in a bad way. *Could I still be dreaming?*

She had to practically do a split to make her next foothold. Just as she adjusted her weight, her foot slipped, and down she went. Her body slid and tumbled down the jagged slope—her skin slicing open with new wounds along the sharp edges. Finally, she landed in a heap on the ground.

She groaned in pain, not wanting to move for fear her pain would increase. Zeus grabbed her by the hair and jerked her head up. The pain flared so bad, she thought she might pass out—or throw up.

"At this rate, you'll never get to the top before they get here," he said. His attention turned to the broken body of a dead corpse lying nearby—Pallas.

"Don't touch him," Malia snarled, her anger rising near the surface. Her fear twisted to anger inside her gut. "Why did you even bring him here?"

"I know you care about him," he answered. "I brought him for an incentive."

"If you even think about touching him—"

"And what will you do, my dear?" Zeus interrupted. "You're no more than an animated corpse yourself."

Malia's blood turned to ice. *Animated corpse?* "So am

Raging

I dead then?"

Zeus laughed. "Malia the zombie. The humans would be fascinated to see you."

"What did you do to me?"

"I did nothing but wake you, my dear. I'd heal you if I could. You'd be more useful with your powers. I'd use my own to get what I want, but that worthless sister of yours stripped me of them. If we were outside, I'd use the wind to lift us to the top. But there's not near enough air in here to do the job, and I have no time for you to heal on your own."

"I don't think this will heal." She looked at her black, charred skin.

"Of course you'll heal. You're a goddess."

She shook her head. "You're crazy."

A grin spread across his face. "Crazy enough to dismember your precious Pallas right in front of your eyes."

"You're not just crazy—you're a monster."

"Yes, I am. And I've never felt so liberated." He stepped over to Pallas. His body had been broken and burned so badly, he was nearly unrecognizable. Malia swallowed bile as she looked at the man who had so recently captured her affection.

Zeus lifted his arm and electricity erupted from his hand, forming a bolt. He clutched the crackling rod of lightning and pointed it toward Pallas. "This will let you know I mean business…" Light arced toward Pallas and burned across his wrist. His severed hand dropped to the floor as Malia screamed.

"Hm," Zeus said, the bolt going dark and disappearing. "I don't know. That wasn't nearly gory enough." A silver sword appeared in his hand next. "This will work much better."

"Why are you doing this?" she shrieked, tears streaming down her face. "He's already dead."

Zeus smiled. "Why dear, it's because you care. And I need you to—"

Pain, greater than she'd ever felt before, flared over her entire body as Malia screamed, collapsing to the ground.

"Finally," Zeus shouted. Malia only half paid attention—her focus was entirely on the searing agony that washed over her, only to retreat and settle in her back. She could feel something sprout there, growing from within her and rising from her body.

"Brilliant," Zeus said.

What's happening to me?

Chapter 32

Tana's heart stopped as Xanthus roared. He raced inside with Triton and the others on his heels. If Sara had been human, she'd be dead. The amount of blood on the ground was proof of that. She'd been taken out in one swing of a mace. What other weapons did they have in there? There had to be some other way in. Oh please, let there be some other way. Malia's life depended on it.

Tana reached out and grabbed Drake. She shook her head. "Don't go in there."

"Tana," he said with sorrow in his eyes. "I have to. I can't leave my friends to fight alone." He brushed a kiss over her lips. For a brief second, Tana felt whole. But no sooner did that feeling come than it was gone as he slipped from her grip and ran inside, leaving her heart empty and aching.

Tana trembled as she backed away. Sounds of fighting came from inside the gaping door. Inhuman snarls along with shouts and clashes of steel reverberated in her bones. She should go in. Drake needed her. But what could she do? She could go in there and set them all on fire. But Gretchen's husband wasn't a god. She'd kill him. She just couldn't take another death on her hands. And even then, if they had to wait for the rest of them to heal, they'd be too late to stop Zeus. She needed to get to her sister before anything happened to her.

Sneaking up to the doorway, Tana peeked in.

Drake, Triton, and the rest were being tossed around the cave like rag dolls. The men doing the tossing looked like humans. Average, ordinary humans—except for the fact they were wearing what looked to be ancient Greek clothing.

I should go in there. But seriously, what could she do? They needed help.

Dad?

Tana? What's wrong?

It's the Hu. Drake and the others are being attacked by creatures called the Hu. What if they're killed?

Leave! Leave right now, Tana. Don't even look back—just run.

Do you think Drake and the others can beat them?

No. None of you stand a chance against them.

What about you, Dad? Please, can you help us?

I can't. I'm sorry—

What? Seriously? You're not even going to try? After all you did to me, you owe me.

I'm sorry, child. There's nothing I can do. There's nothing anyone can do.

No. I get it. I'll take care of it. She had no idea how, but she'd do it even if it killed her.

Tana. She could hear the warning in his voice. *I beg you, don't do anything rash.*

Raging

I'll handle it.

No. Tana, don't—

She cut off communication, anger burning inside her. Closing her eyes, she took a deep breath and calmed herself. Fire would not help them. Neither would rushing in and getting captured herself. She needed the Hu to come out. If they did, the door could be closed, locking them outside. But how did you get guards to come outside and leave the thing they were protecting?

The door rumbled, and Tana's heart sank. Running to the entrance, she pushed with everything she had, but as hard as she tried, she couldn't do it. She caught a glance inside and saw a sickening sight. The Hu were the only ones left standing. She pulled her fingers away just before they were crushed between the stone slab and the rocky doorway.

"No," she shrieked as she pounded against the door. "Let me in!"

Fire erupted from her, surrounding her in a halo as she beat against the door. Flames scorched the rock, turning it black, but the door didn't budge. Tana never felt so alone. After what seemed like an eternity, the fire died down as did her rage, melting into despair.

Finally, she sank to the ground, sobbing.

"You've got friends in low places, chick."

Tana looked up and found a man smirking in front of her. He stood amidst swirls of smoke and charred trees. She didn't care who the heck he was. He'd just insulted her friends, ones who could be dying even now.

And Drake...she couldn't even go there.

"Go to Tartarus," she mumbled.

The man had the gall to chuckle.

"You think this is funny?" The fire once again ignited.

"Whoa, whoa! Wait a minute," he said, backing away—orange flames reflecting in his eyes. "I was talking about Hades. The guy who told me you needed help."

"Hades sent you?" she asked as the flames died down.

"Yeah."

Tana looked him over, inspecting him. He was a blond-haired, blue-eyed man not quite six feet tall, with a thin build, wearing Bermuda shorts and a tank top. He definitely didn't look like he could break into a mountain. "How are *you* supposed to help?"

"I have a few surprises up my sleeves that come in handy from time to time."

"Like what?" she asked.

He shrugged. "What kind of help do you need?"

Tana frowned. "What's your name?"

"My friends call me Peter."

"That's not what I asked."

His smile widened as he chuckled. "You're a cheerful girl. You want to know my real name, huh?"

Tana scowled at him. "Yes."

"I don't know what good it'll do you. No one has called me by it in years. But if you'd really like to know, I was born Proteus, son of the pompous, full-of-himself Poseidon."

Tana's jaw dropped. "You're Drakōn's father?"

Raging

All humor vanished from his face as he took an intimidating step toward her. "Who told you that?"

"I'm Drakōn's..." She tried to think of what she was to him. He'd told her he loved her, and she had pretty strong feelings for him too. "...girlfriend."

"Do you love him?" he asked, putting her on the spot.

"I...don't know," she began. She just didn't know if she could say the words out loud. And even if she could, Drake should be the first to hear she loved him. Instead, she said simply, "I'd give my life for him."

He nodded. "At least you're honest about it. Where is he? Why did Hades summon me to come to you?"

"Drake's in there," she looked to the stone door, "along with Triton and four others. They've been captured by the Hu."

"Captured?" His eyes widened. "What has my idiotic brother gotten my son into? And what under Olympus is a Hu? Most of all, why does that name sound familiar?"

"The Hu are the guards of King Petros, Zeus' older brother. The brother he stole the throne from. You probably don't remember. Zeus erased everyone's memories of him."

"A forgotten brother." Peter sighed. "I think I can relate." He frowned at the stone door. "Still, I think you're crazy. So how do we get in there?" he asked.

"I don't know." Tana walked up to the door. "Triton tried to open it, but—"

"My little brother?" He smirked.

"Little?" Tana smiled. "I'm sorry, but Triton is built...

how can I say this nicely? Much more…substantially than you are."

"What?" Peter raised an eyebrow and his arms as he turned around. "You don't think this body looks strong enough for you? Well, how about this?"

It took seconds for his body to morph, bulge, and change right before her eyes. The man standing in front of her now looked nothing like the way he did seconds ago. This man was massive, with dark hair, bulging muscles, and piercing blue eyes. He actually looked a lot like Drake—except Drake had brown eyes.

"Okay," Tana said. "You'll be a contender now, but I still don't think you can open it."

Peter ignored her and attempted to force it open. His muscles strained and bulged as he pushed, but eventually, he had to give up. "Well, that's a first." He leaned against the door and sank to the ground, breathing heavily.

"Sara was the only one who could open it."

"Who's Sara?"

"Triton's daughter."

"I have a new niece. That's a surprise," Peter said. "Who are these Hu and what do they want?"

"They guard the heart of Olympus, but they were made to guard King Petros."

"Ah ha," he shouted. "Now we're getting somewhere. What does King Petros look like?"

"I don't know."

"Well, who does know?"

"Uh, I…I should have listened closer. Wait! He has a

Raging

daughter, Nicole!"

"Can you summon her?"

"I don't know."

"Have you met her before?"

"Yes."

"Then I'm sure you can summon her."

Minutes later, a shining, beautiful goddess stood before them.

"Proteus?" she said, surprised.

"Do I know you?" he asked, equally surprised.

"I'm married to your brother, Triton."

"You and my little brother are married?" Peter shook his head. "Did no one think to invite me to the wedding? Of course not. No one ever invites me anywhere."

Nicole shook her head in exasperation. "And this is why we don't. You always make such a big deal out of everything."

"You act as if you know me," he said.

"I do know you. Unlike you, I have my memories intact," Nicole said.

"I'm missing memories?" Peter asked.

"Yes, and don't ask me to explain. Believe me, I don't have time. Now why did you call me here?"

Peter glowered at her.

"We need to get inside Olympus," Tana said.

Nicole turned to her and frowned. "I've been trying to figure—hold on." She froze; her eyes glued on the door. "Where in the world did that come from?"

"Um," Tana said. "Olympus brought us here, and I

found the door."

"Us?" Nicole asked, her voice strained.

"Yeah, me, Drakōn, Xanthus, Triton, Sara—"

"Oh no, he did not," Nicole interrupted. "That no good son of a leech."

"Who?"

"My husband!" Nicole roared. "He did it again. He left me behind. I swear I'll kill him!" Nicole turned to Tana. She stepped back at the fury in the goddess's voice. "So where is he? And where's my baby?"

"Um," Tana said. "They're in there. They've been captured by the Hu."

"The Hu?" Nicole frowned. "Did you say the Hu?"

Tana nodded.

Nicole stepped up to the stone door and pushed.

"You won't be able to—" Peter began, but stopped talking when the door grated open. "Well, that's a blow to the ego," he said, frowning.

Nicole stepped inside, with Tana following. She wasn't about to be left behind again.

The Hu surrounded them immediately. That was not a surprise. But what did surprise Tana was that the Hu stopped, looking stunned at Nicole. Peter stepped in front—in an obvious attempt to shield them.

Tana tried to see beyond Peter and through the wall of men surrounding them. She caught a glimpse of broken bodies and pools of blood. Her heart pounded when she saw Drake. He was in pretty sad shape, but she could just make out his chest rising and lowering. At

Raging

least he was still alive. Then she saw Gretchen and Sara. They were standing, chained to the wall. Sara hung unconscious as Gretchen glared defiantly at her side. Tana clenched her fists and focused on her breathing. They really didn't need a fiery explosion right now.

"What did you do to my son?" Peter asked. The Hu didn't answer. Their eyes narrowed.

"He's fine," Tana said, feeling she was saying it as much for herself as for him. "He'll heal."

"I know he'll heal," he growled. "But it's going to hurt like Hades."

"Solon…" Nicole stepped around Peter. "I order you and your men to stand down."

The largest and bloodiest of them took a defiant step forward. "You know my name? Who are you?"

"Yes, I know you well. I am Nicole, daughter of King Petros and Queen Tyche."

The Hu erupted in a murmur as they spoke to each other—their confusion obvious. Tana could hear the name Petros mentioned several times.

"Who is this King Petros?" Solon asked. "I cannot remember, but he feels like someone important."

"Well," Nicole snarled. "If you hadn't knocked my daughter senseless, she could have shown you who he was."

He turned to another Hu and said, "Miltiades, bring the girl here."

"Which one?" he responded.

"The one who's been knocked senseless, you idiot!"

"Oh, right." He jogged over to Sara and unlocked the chains around her wrists. She slumped down, and he caught her before she could fall. Lifting her in his arms, he carried her back and laid her on the ground.

Nicole dropped to her knees and brushed Sara's bloody hair away from her face as she inspected her daughter. "Oh, baby," she whispered to her. "What did they do to you?" Nicole's eyes snapped up and the glare she gave the leader was hot enough to melt steel. "If there's any permanent damage to my child, I'll see you stripped of your flesh and your bones thrown into the pit of Tartarus."

Tana had to admit, Sara looked pretty beat up. Her head was bleeding profusely, there were wounds around her wrists from where the iron shackles cut into her, and she was so pale that she looked dead.

"Healer!" Solon said, looking at another Hu. "Heal this woman."

"As you command." He stepped to her side.

He tried to move Nicole out of the way. She looked up at him, glaring. If looks could kill, this man would be incinerated on the spot. Instead, he moved around to Sara's other side, knelt down, and pressed his palms against her temples.

Color returned to her face and her cuts closed, leaving her skin completely healed and unscarred.

Sara's eyes opened. "Mom?"

Nicole threw her arms around her daughter. "I'm here, baby."

Raging

It was strange to see this mother and daughter side by side. They looked to be the same age—more like sisters. Tana's heart clenched when she realized that if her mother had lived longer, they would have looked like sisters too.

Solon stepped forward and looked from Sara to Peter and finally to Tana. "Zeus' instructions are clear. I must destroy any and all who enter here. And do not be mistaken, I intend to carry out that order. But I will allow you to live for a moment more if you tell me why it pains my heart to hear the name of Petros." His eyes turned to Nicole. "And why is your face so familiar, yet I do not remember who you are?"

"You do know me, Solon," Nicole said. "You guarded me from the time I was a baby until I was old enough to give you grief as a youth, and then again as a married woman."

"Impossible." He frowned, but there was doubt in his eyes.

Sara stood and brushed herself off. She looked around the chamber—her eyes lingering on Xanthus lying unconscious in a pool of blood. Blinking back tears, she looked at Solon. "I can give you your memories back."

"Who erased them in the first place?" Solon asked.

"Zeus," Sara answered without hesitation.

"But…I am loyal to my king. Why would he do such a thing?"

"You'll know when your memories have returned," Sara said.

He looked around to the other Hu. "And my brothers need their memories restored as well."

"Will you promise not to hurt us if I do this?" Sara asked.

Solon shook his head. "I cannot. I must always obey commands."

"Then I won't—"

"Sara." Nicole put her hand on Sara's arm. "Just restore their memories, and I can handle what happens next."

Sara turned to her, confused. "But Mom…"

"Trust me." Nicole smiled.

Sara sighed and answered. "Okay. I'll trust you."

Sara turned to the Hu. "I need you to close your eyes and open your minds." She turned to Peter. "You too."

He nodded, curiosity shining in his face.

Tana could see doubt in the Hu's eyes, and flickering uncertainty, but eventually, all eyes were closed—and that was when it got interesting. Emotions flashed across their faces, each of them with the same expressions simultaneously—as if they were watching the same movie. The emotions ranged from fear to despair, and then finally anger, which eventually turned to what looked more like murderous rage—and then their eyes opened.

Chapter 33

Malia awoke with the strangest sensation—she had a second set of what felt like arms coming out of her back. Testing those new arms, she swung them out and pulled them back. The wind whipped around her as she glanced behind. These things weren't arms—they were wings!

"What did you do to me?" she shrieked as she looked toward Zeus, panicked.

"You have your powers back."

"My powers?" She looked down at her hands and her breath caught. They were perfect, healed completely! "But…this can't be real."

"Oh, it's real."

"I…" She blew out a breath of air. "I can't be a…"

"A goddess? Oh, you are. You're the daughter of Eos and Atlas."

"Atlas, he's the one who holds the earth on his shoulders, but who's Eos? Is she a goddess?"

"She was the goddess of sunrise. And I must say, being with your mother made me wish the sunrise would never come."

"You were her lover?" Malia scowled.

Holly Kelly

"Which is why I gave you such wonderful human lives," he answered. "I owed your mother that much."

"Lives?"

"Yes," he said. "You've led many human lives. And I'm proud to say you've been happy in most of them."

"But…wait…how—?"

"I'd love to continue this conversation, but I don't have time." He frowned, his expression turning harsh—without a hint of humanity. "Fly up to the top of this mountain, and open the chamber." He leaned over her and sneered. "Do it now or Pallas loses his head next."

"Fly… I don't know how to fly."

Zeus lifted his sword above Pallas' neck.

Malia glared at him. "I hate you."

"Whether you love or hate me is inconsequential," he said, and then shouted, "Just do it!"

Malia scrambled to her feet and backed away from the rage. "Okay, just leave him alone." Zeus continued to glare as she stood, wondering how on this green earth she could just take off and fly. She tested her wings, lifting and lowering them. Her weight on her feet diminished and within seconds, her feet left the ground. This really was easy—so far. She flew up higher—away from the psycho god. She took a few turns and relaxed when she realized how easy this whole flying thing was. Of course, now that she thought about it, baby birds left their nest and flew around like pros without a single lesson. So why should it be different with her?

The feeling of flying was exhilarating! Strange how

Raging

she'd always hated roller coasters. They made her feel out of control. But this…she was in complete control. She looked over to Pallas. Her heart ached at the sight. She could still see the handsome features in his face, and if she didn't know better, she'd swear he had more color than before. But the missing hand and the stillness of his body squelched any hope he was still alive. Still, she could make sure his body was not desecrated any more than it was—if she were strong enough. Hopefully, as a goddess, she was. If not, this plan would fail miserably.

She landed at his side and swallowed down bile.

"No," Zeus shouted as he manifested his bolt. She reached down and lifted Pallas off the ground. She was beyond surprised to see she could actually pick him up. As big as he was, and as insanely heavy as he must be, he felt as light as a child in her arms. She took off just as Zeus' bolt exploded the rocky ground beneath her.

She had to flap hard to move quickly out of Zeus' sight. His bolt hit the crystal mountain. Electricity and light exploded all around—shaking the whole cavern and causing chunks of the ceiling to cave in. Malia had to dodge rocks as they tumbled down. She hoped Zeus would be crushed by the falling boulders, but she doubted that would kill him. Finally, the rocks settled and all was quiet. Maybe Zeus was out of commission—at least for a while.

Getting the altitude she needed took a crazy amount of work. The mountain loomed high, and the air thinned. With less air, there was less lift. By the time she reached the top, she was dripping with sweat.

The top held a platform with a clear, crystal wall. This had to be the place. Her feet touched down, and she gently lowered Pallas to the floor. She turned away, her stomach queasy. Swallowing, she wiped sweat from her face. If anyone had asked her what she'd be doing today, she'd never have guessed in a million years that she'd be doing this. What *was* she doing here? And why did she feel the need to protect Pallas? He was already dead.

Squeezing her eyes shut, she choked back a sob. She knew exactly why she was so protective of him. He'd saved her life, and she so desperately wanted to be able to save his. But she couldn't. He was dead, and somehow, she just couldn't accept that. Maybe she was crazy.

Stepping toward the wall, she could see a handprint—as if someone had pressed their palm into the crystal wall and left an impression. When she lifted her hand, Malia could see that it fit perfectly. In fact, there was no way this was a coincidence. The match was too exact.

This was probably the lock. "What do you think, Pallas?" she mumbled—as if he could answer.

"I think I must have died and gone to heaven," a deep voice spoke from behind her. Malia whipped around—her heart pounding so hard her sternum hurt. She sank breathless to the floor.

Pallas looked around, confused.

Malia shook her head. "You're dead."

"Then we're both dead."

"No, I'm not—"

Raging

"You look like an angel." He stepped toward her.

"I don't understand…this can't be real. How are you alive?" She shook her head again.

"It looks like there were things we both didn't know about each other." He reached out his hand, and she took it. He pulled her off the floor.

Wait! "Your hand grew back."

"My hand?" He scrunched his brows in confusion.

"Zeus cut it off."

He narrowed his eyes. "He did, did he?"

"How—?"

"I'm a pure-blooded Dagonian."

"Which means…?"

"I'm immortal—well, basically. Most Dagonians have human blood tainting their lineage, which makes them mortal. I don't, so when I die, all my wounds heal and I wake up again. I've never tested losing limbs before, but I'm happy to see I get them back. And now, if you could please answer *my* question," he said, smiling.

"What?"

"Exactly." He stepped back, but kept her hand in his. "What are you? I swear you look like an angel with those white wings."

She shrugged. "Zeus says I'm a goddess. The daughter of Eos and Atlas."

He shook his head. "It figures."

"What figures?"

"I should have known," he said half smirking, half frowning. "Here we have a fish falling in love with a bird."

At the word love, her heart pounded in her chest. Could he be talking about them? "A fish?"

"I'm a sea creature," he said. "Remember? I was born with a tail. These legs are temporary."

"And did you say, that you…?"

"Love you? Hmm. I guess I did." He smiled. "Want to test it out?"

"How—?" she began to say when he leaned down, lifted her off her feet, and kissed her. If this was a dream, it was the best dream in the history of dreams. She'd rather die than wake up. The magic of his mouth on hers caused her toes to curl and her wings to shudder.

When he finally pulled away, she was breathless and couldn't feel her feet. Pallas tried to set her down but kept his arm around her when she started to tip. "Don't you think things are moving a little fast?" she asked. "I mean, we only just met."

"We met, we kissed, and we fell in love." He smirked. "It's every Dagonian's dream. Too bad it's illegal."

"Falling in love is illegal?"

"No." He chuckled. "Kissing before the wedding is. But I know from personal experience that the law is rarely enforced." He winked at her, and she could feel heat rise in her cheeks.

"So," he said as he looked around. "Where in Hades are we?"

"Um, Zeus brought me here to help release the king."

Pallas' expression turned dark. "Why would he want to?"

Raging

"So he could kill him."

"Hmm. Well, we'll just have to kill Zeus first."

"And how are we going to do that?"

"I have no idea. First of all, we need to find a way out of here."

"Zeus said the only way out is to unlock this crystal."

"And how do we do that?"

"I'm supposedly some kind of key," she said as she stepped toward the handprint. "I think I put my hand—"

"Wait," Pallas said.

"What?" She turned to him, confused.

"Are you sure it's safe?"

She shook her head. "I don't know, but I haven't been able to see another way out."

"Have you looked?"

"Of course I have. And unless you can punch through solid rock," she said, "this is it."

He frowned as he seemed to consider her words. "Okay, but let me stand in front of you. If something dangerous is to happen, I'd rather you not be in the way."

"But then *you'll* get hurt." She raised her eyebrows.

"Better me than you," he said.

"I don't think so," she said, shaking her head.

"And this is what's wrong in the human world." He scowled. "What kind of man would let a woman stand between him and danger? A coward, that's what kind. Well, Malia Parks, I'm no coward."

"How do you know my last name?"

He shook his head. "That's not important. What is

important is there is no way in Hades that I'll let you open that so-called lock without my protection."

"Oh, all right," she huffed and stuck out her hand.

He looked down at her hand and pursed his lips. "Okay." He took her arm, stepped in front of her as he turned his back, and pulled her hand in front of him—pressing her arm between his elbow and ribs.

She could feel the cool crystal at her fingertips and splayed out her hand. As soon as her palm touched, the entire crystal mountain began to rumble.

Chapter 34

Drakōn's eyes opened with Tana's face swimming in his vision. Gods, she was beautiful. With her eyes on him, she breathed a sigh of relief.

"Thank heavens you're alive," she said. "What did the Hu do to you?"

"They schooled me on the fine art of hand to hand. And I thought *I* was a good fighter." He shook his head as he sat up. The room spun in his vision. He closed his eyes and took a deep breath. When he opened his eyes again, the room stayed in place.

"It didn't help that they couldn't be injured or killed," he said, moving in close. Tana rocked back. He wasn't about to let her get away, so he wrapped his arm around her and pulled her in for a kiss. She seemed hesitant to kiss him back at first, but soon, she returned it—and then some.

Hades, she tasted good.

Someone cleared their throat, bringing Drakōn back to his senses. He reluctantly pulled away and looked back. Kyros was frowning at him. "Oh, don't stop on my account. It's not like we have the world to save."

"I'd say I'm sorry, but I'm not," Drakōn said.

Kyros chuckled and looked at Tana. "Who is this man, and what have you done with Drakōn?"

Tana laughed as her cheeks blossomed pink.

"Drakōn." At hearing his name, he turned to a stranger.

"Yes?" he answered, searching the large man with dark hair for any sign of who he may be.

"I'm Proteus, your father."

Drakōn's eyes widened in surprise. His eyes…the stranger's eyes looked much like his own. Was he really his father?

Drakōn frowned, not trusting this man. "You abandoned me."

Proteus nodded. "I'm sorry. Your mother said it was necessary to protect you."

"Who is my mother?"

"Nammu," he answered, "the Sumerian goddess of the sea. I'm sure she would love to meet you. She was broken with grief when she had to leave you."

"I'll think about it," Drakōn said. Keeping Tana wrapped in his arms he stood and walked away. Tana looked over her shoulder and gave an apologetic look. Had she already met his father? Regardless, he wasn't yet willing to forgive either his father or his mother at the moment. Perhaps he'd consider his relationships with them later—when the world wasn't being threatened.

A commotion caught Drakōn's attention. He looked over at the Hu. They were gathered in a circle and shouting at one another.

Raging

Xanthus stepped forward. "Solon, now that you know what Zeus did to your king, why can't you join us in defeating the pretended king?"

The largest of the Hu shook his head. Drakōn rubbed the lump on the side of his head. That Hu may only be just over six feet tall, but his kick packed an insane amount of force.

"It doesn't work that way. We are creatures born to serve our king, and in Petros' absence, Zeus is acting king, so our order still stands. You all must be destroyed."

Nicole stepped forward. Drakōn was struck by how much she looked like a goddess now. In fact, her skin seemed to glow—literally. "But Zeus is not truly king," she said. "Solon, who would be next in line after Petros?"

"Your husband, princess."

Triton stepped to her side as Nicole asked, "And what would that make me?"

"You would be my queen."

A hint of a smile lightened Nicole's face. "Well, my husband and I are laying claim to the throne until my father returns. And as your queen, I order you to assist us in freeing my father."

Solon looked from Nicole to Triton and then his fellow Hu, several of them nodding their approval.

Solon dropped to one knee. "As you wish, My Queen." One by one, each of the other Hu knelt and crossed their right hand over their hearts in a show of loyalty.

Perhaps they *would* stand a chance against Zeus and

all his ill-gotten power.

A low rumble shook the earth underneath their feet. Everyone staggered, trying not to fall. Drakōn caught a flash of darkness coming from above and pulled Tana out of the way just as a rock the size of her head smashed into the ground beside them.

"What's happening?" Drakōn shouted.

"It's an earthquake," Kyros shouted.

"No," Sara said. "It's not just an earthquake." She pulled Xanthus forward. "We need to go. Now!"

Drakōn and the others ran behind Sara just as the wall of the cavern cracked open before them. Scrambling over boulders, they made it into a colossal cave.

Drakōn gasped when he looked up. Within the massive cavern stood a crystal mountain. And the crystal was cracking, breaking off in sharp chunks and crashing to the floor below. This cave didn't seem to be any safer than the last. They all gathered against what appeared to be a stable section of the cave wall.

"Look," Tana shouted and pointed. "Up there."

High above, silhouetted against the dark cave wall, flew a shining creature with a wide wingspan—probably a harpy.

"Get behind me," Drakōn said as he pulled Tana back.

"No," she said, resisting. "It's Malia."

Drakōn looked closer at the creature. It did seem to be a woman, one with wings as white as the brightest pearl, flying and carrying someone…a man. "Is that

Raging

Pallas?"

"He's alive?" Tana said—relief in her voice. "How did he survive?"

"I don't know," Drakōn said. "I'm just glad he did."

They watched in silence for a moment before Tana spoke in a near whisper. "Her wings look just like my mom's." She turned to Drakōn. "What happens when Malia remembers? Will she hate me for killing our mother?"

Drakōn wanted to tell her no, of course not. But to be truthful, he didn't know how Malia would react when she got all her memories back. "Did Malia know your mother?"

"I have no idea. I didn't even know I had a sister. She has to be older than me, right?"

"That would be my guess. Otherwise, when Sara gave you back your memories, you would have remembered her."

Xanthus had Sara's hand in his as he made his way to Drakōn. "Keep an eye out for Zeus."

"What do we do if he uses a siphon?" Drakōn asked.

"We have a siphon of our own," Xanthus said.

"Where?" Drakōn looked around for the ghostly creature.

"Sypher is staying close to my mom," Sara said as she glanced back. "That way, she can be ready to help if we need her."

Drakōn searched his surroundings. "I don't see the siphon."

"She's um…inside," Sara said.

"Inside?" Drakōn asked, horrified. He couldn't imagine giving up his powers to anyone. Just allowing Triton to use his powers for a short time—even to save innocent humans—had been extremely difficult.

"My mom doesn't mind. She said she's used to it. Besides, it keeps her safe from someone trying to use her power to gain a wish. And after what Zeus made Sypher do, Sypher's just aching to kill him. She wants to be ready."

"What's that?" Kyros asked.

Drakōn looked back to the crystal mountain, searching for what Kyros might be talking about. The mountain was beginning to glow. Inside the base, an orange radiance rose through the center—like liquid through a straw.

When Malia neared the ground, she set Pallas down and then landed gracefully—her wings tucking against her back as soon as her feet hit the ground.

"Malia?" Tana said hesitantly.

"Tana." Malia turned and rushed forward, throwing her arms around her in a crushing hug.

"I'm so glad to see you're okay," Tana said.

"I'm fine. Different, but fine." Malia looked around at the others. "Can you believe all this? Greek gods and goddesses, they're real." She turned back to look at Tana. "And we're a part of them."

"Sisters." Tana nodded.

"Yeah." Malia smiled and shook her head. Then her

smile faded. "I really don't know who I am. Well…who we are."

"I know some," Tana said with a lump in her throat.

Malia looked up at the crystal mount, lava now oozing down the sides. "You'll have to tell me later."

Triton stepped forward. "Malia, what happened?"

"Who are you?" she asked, looking Triton over—her eyes lingering on his trident.

He shook his head. "I'm Triton."

Malia's eyes widened as she whispered, "Wow." She blinked and shook her head. "Right, what happened? Um. Zeus had me unlock the crystal mountain. He wants to free the king so he can destroy him."

"It's as we feared," Triton said. "Where's Zeus now?"

"I don't know. I haven't seen him since the ceiling started to collapse. I was hoping he was crushed under a boulder."

"That wouldn't stop him for long," Triton said. "So how did the lock work?"

"It was a recessed handprint. I put my hand in it, and the crystal mountain started falling apart."

"Just like the one I unlocked," Sara said.

"So how did Zeus get inside without Sara?" Tana asked.

"The Hu," Sara said. "They must have opened it for him from the inside."

"Do you have any idea what we do next?" Drakōn asked Sara.

"I wish I did," she answered with a scowl.

An explosion blew the top of the mountain in a fiery plume. Flames and burning debris came raining down. Drakōn braced himself, but then felt nothing but heat. He looked up. Tana had her hands out and the blazing crystals were all obliterated as they impacted her fiery ceiling. When the explosion died down, Tana lowered her hands. Drakōn could see that the mountaintop was lit with fire. The flames rose from the crater and came down like a fountain.

"I think I know who's next," Tana said. "Me."

"It makes sense," Sara said. "I was first as the daughter of sea and earth. Malia, daughter of earth and wind, was second. Now it's time for the daughter of wind and fire."

Drakōn looked at the raging fire and shook his head, his heart clenched in fear. "Tana. Are you sure?"

"I'm pretty sure I'm the only one who can not only reach the top but also survive that inferno."

"Be careful, love," Drakōn said.

"I will," she said as her fiery wings sprouted from her back and spread out.

She's really getting comfortable with her powers. Drakōn smiled proudly. His smile faded as worry crept it.

"Does anyone else feel as if we are playing right into Zeus' hands?" Pallas asked.

No one answered, but the tension caused by his words was thicker than the smoke in the cavern.

Chapter 35

Tana flew with the top of the mountain in her sights. She didn't look back. She might lose her nerve if she saw Drake watching her below. Breathing deeply, she attempted to relax. The heat increased as she neared the top. She tried to see anything that looked to be a lock. She frowned as she thought about what had happened to the crystal tower when Malia unlocked her portion. What would her actions do to it? At least Drake was fireproof, and well...everything proof, seeing as he could turn himself into water. But if Malia were anything like their mother, she wouldn't be able to withstand fire.

Tana decided she'd have to fly straight into the inferno. Taking a deep breath, she dove in. The light blinded her, and she had to blink to clear out the smoky haze scratching her eyes. Finally, the light let up and she could see something—a shadow, just ahead of her. She slowed to a stop, hovering over what appeared to be a jagged rock burning with white light in the shape of a hand. This had to be it!

Reaching forward, she pressed her hand against the shape of the palm. Like someone had just turned on a giant vacuum, the fire was sucked away—blowing her hair and snuffing out the heat. The peak of the mountain collapsed, and Tana had the sudden feeling of vertigo. The whole world seemed to be spinning.

She could hear Drake shout just as she realized she wasn't experiencing vertigo. She was falling! Her wings—where were her wings?

Her body flipped and turned, the rocky surface coming toward her. Drake's face came into view, moving fast. Seeing the shards of crystals below her, she prepared to find out what it felt like to break every bone in her body. Instead, water enveloped her. She still hit the crystals, but she felt cushioned, the impact softened by Drake. And then she was falling again. She left her stomach behind as she opened her mouth and screamed.

As they hit the bottom, she felt only a slight jarring. Lying on her back, she tried to get her bearings. She was spread-eagle in a puddle of water. Darkness surrounded her. And the smell…. Gods, she didn't have anything to compare it too, but it smelled bad. Like raw, oozing sewage.

The water morphed underneath her and before she could scramble away, strong arms came around her. "Tana, it's me," Drake whispered in her ear.

"Drake?"

"Yeah," he said, his voice grim.

"How did you get here? I didn't know you could fly."

"I can't. Triton threw me."

"He did?"

Raging

"Yeah."

"Where are we?" Tana asked as she looked up from where they'd come from. A tiny spot of light shone in the distance.

"Inside," he answered simply.

"Who are you?" An eerie voice brushed over her, raising goose bumps on her skin.

"Who was that?" Tana whispered harshly.

"I don't know," Drake answered.

"Where are we?" she asked, her voice quaking.

"We're in another cavern, below the mountain."

Tana looked around, attempting to penetrate the darkness. "Where's Petros?"

"They're from the outside," another spectral voice spoke, chilling her. She didn't need cold; she needed warmth. Fire would lighten up the darkness.

She closed her eyes and focused on the spark that always burned within her chest.

"We could use some light," Drake said.

"I'm already on it," Tana answered as she directed the fire to only her hands. Flames ignited from her fingertips, lighting their surroundings.

Fog swirled around them, and then Tana squeaked a cry when she saw a face in the mist. Ghosts surrounded them. They were everywhere—spectral phantoms. She raised her hand to light their faces and they backed away, hissing. They obviously didn't like fire.

Drake's fingers squeezed her arm until it hurt, but Tana couldn't be bothered by a little pain. She was too preoccupied by the horror that enveloped them.

"I know what they are," he murmured.

"Yeah, I do too. Siphons."

"I'm hungry…" a voice spoke.

"Yes, so hungry," another one joined in.

Tana? a familiar voice spoke. This one was in her head.

Malia? she answered.

Holy cow, it worked! Malia said. *Yes, yes, it's me. Are you alright?*

We're surrounded by siphons, Tana answered.

"*They have power,*" another siphon spoke, "*and I'm so hungry.*"

"*Sooo hungry,*" another echoed, and Tana caught sight of it moving in toward Drake. She flashed her fire higher, covering Drake with flames, and the siphon retreated.

"We need to do something about them," Drake said as he shimmered and went transparent.

"I'm talking to Malia right now," Tana answered.

They're not attacking, are they? Malia asked.

They tried, but they seem to be afraid of fire, Tana answered and looked over to Drake, who had stepped out of the flames. The siphons didn't seem to know what to do with him. *Looks like they can't penetrate water, either.*

"Tell Malia to ask Sara if she knows what we need to do," Drake said.

I hear you, Drake, Malia said.

"Do you hear her?" Tana asked.

Drake nodded.

Raging

Okay, I'll ask her. There was silence for a moment, and then Malia said, *"Sara said you need to find out where Petros is. He should be there."*

"Okay," Tana said, turning up the flames so that the siphons wouldn't have a chance to attack her while she was distracted. With light flooding the chamber, she wished she could turn down the illumination. The place was scary enough when they couldn't see where they were. Gnarled trees towered over them with slimy moss hanging from the branches.

"Who'd have guessed," Drake whispered, "that deep below a crystal mountain, it would be like…"

"Like a giant with a sinus infection sneezed down here?" Tana supplied.

Drake curled his lips in disgust. "Yeah."

Tana looked around the cavern. It wasn't overly large. They should be able to find Petros easily.

"It shouldn't be that hard to find him," Drake said, echoing her thoughts.

"Let's see." Tana racked her brain. "He's not made of fire or water, and he wouldn't want to be siphoned, but he also hasn't been able to escape." Her stomach twisted and sickened when she caught sight of something—a bog. It was only a few yards past the trees.

"Look at that," she said as they neared it.

The water looked filthy, and it bubbled and hissed, spewing out flames with spurts of noxious gasses.

"He has to be in there," Tana said.

"Oh, no." Drake backed away with a shudder. "I'm

not going in there. That looks poisonous."

"That's not just water."

"How do you know?"

"I know because it comes from the Underworld," Tana answered, frowning. "It's from the river Phlegethon. It flows to the depths of Tartarus. It's also known as the River of Fire."

"Wait a minute...fire and water," Drake said as he looked at her. "This is Gretchen. Here's where she's needed." He looked back to the river and gagged. "She's not going to like this."

"Not to mention," Tana said, "that she can't transform. She won't be protected from the siphons."

Drake shook his head, "No. But she *is* fireproof."

"She is?"

"Yeah, her father taught her how to withstand fire and heat."

"So I can engulf her in flames and she'll be alright."

Drake shrugged. "I'm fairly sure. Why don't you ask her?"

Tana sighed. "Okay." *Gretchen?*

Tana? Is that you?

Yeah. Tana took a deep breath.

It's my turn, isn't it? Gretchen spoke when Tana hesitated.

Yes.

What do I need to do?

We think Petros is submerged in the waters that come from Phlegethon.

Raging

No. Gretchen gasped. *Seriously?*

You're familiar with it.

Unfortunately. I don't have to swim in it, do I? Tana could feel Gretchen gag.

Tana empathized with her but was still relieved she wouldn't have to do it. *Yeah, you do. I'll need to use my flames to protect you from the siphons.*

Now I know why I'm the one who got the vision of the end of the world. No one else in their right mind would swim in that nasty water. But if I don't…it's a good thing I love my human family so much.

You're not worried about me burning you?

I'd rather be burned a million times over than swim in that. Gretchen paused, apparently bracing herself for the inevitable. *Okay, so what do I need to do?*

Chapter 36

Drakōn was beyond impressed with Tana. She had raised a fiery tornado with a funnel that ran from the tiny hole in the top of the cavern down to the water. Gretchen's ride should be easy—just like a ride down a waterslide tube. He didn't envy her landing, though.

Malia's shadow hovered over far above, and Drakōn could just make out Gretchen dangling below her. Drakōn's heart dropped as Gretchen fell. The fiery tunnel worked like a charm, and seconds later, Gretchen splashed down.

He didn't breathe as they waited, both of them with their eyes glued on the water's surface.

"So," Tana said, breaking the silence. "How do we protect Petros when he surfaces?"

"Oh gods," he breathed. "I really hadn't thought of that. Hades, I think of him as a powerful god, the king of all the gods. But, yeah, he may need some protection from the siphons."

"Right," Tana said.

Tana, Drake! Malia's voice rang in his head. *The siphons are escaping. They're coming for us!*

Raging

"What do we do?" Tana screeched.

"We..." Drakōn shook his head. "Hades, I don't know. We were told that Petros would save us. If we saved him, he would save the world."

"But what about Malia?"

"You need to trust that the others will protect her. Triton, Xanthus, Sara...they're all powerful and even more importantly, they're smart. They'll figure it out."

Drakōn could sense something different. Power. Enough power that he had trouble taking a breath. He had never felt anything like it. The ground shook under his feet as he stumbled.

Petros had awakened.

"I think he's coming," Tana said, looking toward the bog. It bubbled and churned.

Drakōn prepared to lift a watery shield against the siphons to protect Petros but stopped when he realized they were all pressing against the hole in the ceiling—trying to escape. There were none left to bother them.

A giant rose from the murky water—the ground rumbling as he stepped forward. He towered above them—at least fifty feet tall, with bulging muscles and slick, black hair that hung past his waist. This had to be Petros, king of the gods. And he looked furious.

"Oh, my gosh," Tana said as she backed away. "What have we done?"

Petros let out an ear-shattering roar. Drakōn slapped his hands over his ears as Tana did the same. Petros took two long strides, exited the bog, and walked up to the wall of the cavern. Lifting his fists, he slammed them into the wall—smashing a hole in the side and climbing out, not even bothering to glance at Drakōn or Tana.

"Drake!" Gretchen shouted from behind. She stepped out of the bog, squeezing out her hair and wiping the filthy water from her face. "We have a big problem."

"He doesn't look like he's coming to save the day," Tana said. "He looks more like Godzilla getting ready to demolish Tokyo."

"We made a mistake," Gretchen said, walking up to Tana. "A big mistake."

"What is it?" Tana asked.

"That isn't only water from the River of Fire," Gretchen said. "It's mixed with water from the Lethe."

"Oh, no," Tana breathed.

"What is the Lethe?" Drakōn asked, fearing the answer.

"It's a sister river to the Phlegethon," Tana said. "It's otherwise known as the River of Forgetfulness."

"So…" Drakōn said, leading them to explain.

"Petros doesn't remember a thing," Gretchen said. "He doesn't know who he is, who we are, and because he's been submerged for so long in the waters of the Underworld, all he feels is hate, anger, and a desire for vengeance."

"But if he doesn't remember anything," Drakōn asked. "Who does he want vengeance against?"

"Everyone," Tana said with a knowing look in her eye.

Raging

Screams erupted from the other room, along with a large crash—like a rockslide. Drakōn sprinted toward the commotion. Petros came into view quickly. He smashed his way through the wall as the others ran away. Nicole alone stood, not backing down.

"Father!" she screamed. "What are you doing? Don't you recognize me?"

Petros turned and snarled at her as he swatted her away like a fly. Nicole flew through the air—coming toward Drakōn. He threw up a shield of water that cushioned her fall. They both landed in a heap on the ground.

"What's wrong with him?" she asked as she scrambled to her feet. Triton immediately appeared at her side.

"He doesn't remember anyone or anything," Drakōn answered her.

"How is that possible?" Triton asked.

"He's spent the last two thousand years submerged in waters from the Lethe River."

"No." Triton visibly paled. "How can we restore him?"

"Sara," Nicole said. "She has to know what we can do." As soon as the words were out of her mouth, Sara and Xanthus were standing at their side.

"Sara," Triton said. "Petros' memories are gone. What do we do?"

"We need Tyche," she answered.

"His wife?" Drakōn said. "But he won't remember her. Besides, I thought you said she couldn't be part of this."

"Believe me," Sara said. "It's time. She needs to come now."

They rushed out through the hole in the mountainside. With his long stride, the king of the gods had already reached the town below. Smoke rose from the path of rubble he made as he demolished buildings and homes. Humans flooded the streets in an attempt to escape the monster laying waste to the town.

Nicole raised her eyes to the skies and yelled, "Mother! We need you. Father needs you." They stood in silence, waiting for the goddess to appear. "Please." Nicole's voice broke.

A breeze rustled Drakōn's hair as he felt power at his back. He turned to see a shimmering goddess with black hair and a rounded stomach.

"Are you pregnant?" Drakōn asked, stunned.

"Yes," Tyche answered, her face filled with concern, but a spark lit her eye when she answered.

"Who's the father?" Triton asked grimly.

"Petros is, of course." Tyche frowned.

"But that's not possible," Drakōn answered.

"It is possible," Tyche answered. "I remember finding out I was carrying his child just before forgetting everything. In my husband's absence, the babe refused to grow."

"How can a baby refuse to grow?" Tana asked.

Tyche shrugged. "He's his father's son."

Nicole rushed to her mother. "Mom, Dad was

Raging

submerged in the waters of the Lethe."

"So he's forgotten us all." She glowered.

Nicole nodded.

"You know what you need to do," Sara said.

Tyche looked at Sara and smiled. "Yes, granddaughter, I do." She strode toward the town, stopping when Nicole pulled her back.

"Mom," Nicole said. "Dad doesn't remember you."

Tyche looked into Nicole's eyes and smiled. "You need to trust me, daughter."

Nicole had doubt in her eyes when she nodded.

They all followed closely behind the goddess as she rushed to reach the rampaging king. Drakōn wasn't about to let Petros—king or not—harm a pregnant woman. He assumed the others felt the same as they stayed close to her.

When they were finally close enough for Petros to hear her, Tyche stopped and shouted, "Petros. Husband!"

He stopped and turned slowly. He stood, stunned at her appearance. Shock and grief flashed across his features as he dropped to his knee—the earth shaking at the impact.

Tyche approached him without fear. A single tear trailed down her cheek.

Petros shrunk down to nearly human sized as his monstrous features disappeared, leaving a man—sobbing, grieving.

"He remembers her?" Drake whispered to Sara.

She shook her head. "No. He has no idea who she

is. This is a result of the wish she made when my mother was just a baby."

"What did she wish?" Drake asked.

"That Petros would always love her."

"That's what she wished for?" Nicole asked.

Sara nodded. "She'd seen so much anger, betrayal, and treachery in her life. She wanted to be able to trust her husband would always care for her."

Drakōn smiled as Tyche wrapped Petros in her arms—but then his blood turned to ice when he spotted Zeus, just beyond, mumbling to himself.

"Watch out," he shouted just as a siphon flew toward the couple. His heart sank when the siphon entered—not Petros, but Tyche. She screamed as she dropped to the ground—her face as pale as ash.

At that moment, Sypher raced toward Zeus. The moment she reached him, he was gone. Sypher shrieked in frustration.

"Mom," Nicole screamed as she ran toward them.

Everyone followed, horror reflecting in their eyes.

Petros had tears streaming down his face as he said, "No. No! You can't leave me."

Nicole tried to put her arms around them, but Petros pulled back, confusion on his face. "Dad?" she said.

Drakōn caught Sara's movement as she waved her hand toward them. Power flowed from her as recognition lit up Petros' face. "Nikoleta?"

She nodded as she choked back a sob.

Petros reached out an arm and invited her in. Nicole

Raging

threw her arms around her father as he continued to cradle his wife in his other arm.

Tyche's color continued to gray as her skin began to harden.

"I love you," Petros said to his wife.

"I love you, Mom," Nicole added.

Tyche didn't utter a response as a tear welled in the corner of her eye. Finally, the last of her body hardened and she stood as still as death.

Chapter 37

Drakōn's heart sank as he watched the small family huddled together, sobbing. Petros continued to embrace his wife—who was nothing more than a statue. But then…there seemed to be a change.

Tyche's color seemed to warm and soften. *Was her stomach glowing?*

"Do you see that?" Pallas asked, confirming in Drakōn's mind that he wasn't just imagining it.

Petros' eyes widened—tears still clinging to his lashes as he looked in wonder at his wife.

In minutes, her color returned, and then her eyes opened as she took a whopping breath and sagged in Petros' arms. The ghostly form of a siphon misted around her for a moment and then disappeared.

Petros pulled Tyche tight to his chest and let out a sigh of relief.

Nicole shook her head. "I don't understand. Mom? You're alive?"

"I'm here, sweetheart." Tyche pulled away and sat up.

"It's the baby," Sara said, a smile tugging at her lips. "I knew he'd be powerful."

Raging

"I remember." Petros' deep voice rumbled. "We were going to have a baby. A son?" He looked at her rounded stomach. "You still carry child?"

Tyche nodded. "Yes."

Petros once again pulled his wife in for a tight embrace and he held her, mumbling words meant for her ears only.

After what seemed a very long time, he pulled away. He lifted his eyes and looked taken aback at finding an audience. "And who are the rest of you?" Petros' deep voice rumbled as he looked around. "I recognize my daughter, son-in-law, and my guards, but you others…"

"I am your granddaughter, Sara," she said, performing an awkward curtsy.

Petros gave an amused smile. "Nice to meet you, granddaughter."

There was a moment of silence. No one seemed to want to be the next one to speak to the king. Sara broke the silence as she went ahead and introduced everyone.

Petros turned to Xanthus. "It pleases me that Ares has been destroyed and my granddaughter is married to the god who has taken his place."

Xanthus nodded with his head down in reverence. "I will spend my life proving myself worthy of her hand."

"I'll hold you to that." Petros smiled and then turned to everyone. "You have all proven brave and loyal to me and as such, you will be rewarded. As for Zeus, he will pay for his treachery."

An ear-piercing shrill rang the air. Drakōn looked up

to see what appeared to be thousands of siphons coming like a tidal wave toward them. Before he could act, a fiery dome erupted—surrounding the entire group.

Drakōn spotted Tana. She was standing at the edge of the group—her red hair like flames blowing as she held up her hands, supporting the barrier.

"Zeus sent them," Drakōn said.

"Obviously," Petros said. "How long can she hold the barrier?"

"Indefinitely." Drakōn frowned. "But it's not something she'd be happy doing for long."

"We can't stay in here forever, anyway." Petros looked around. "I'm not about to trade one prison for another."

Drakōn looked at Tana. She was standing with her eyes closed—concentrating on keeping the barrier up.

"What has my brother been up to while I've been gone?" Petros asked grimly.

"He's murdered countless gods and goddesses and retained their power for his own," Nicole said. "And then others, he simply drains continuously, leaving them living like humans with no memory of whom and what they are. In fact, that's what he did to me for two thousand years. I was his first victim. If it weren't for Triton, I would still be lost."

Petros glanced at his son-in-law, appreciation in his eyes. "How many gods has he killed and how many are living among the humans?"

"We don't know," Triton said.

"He's killed twenty-nine gods and goddesses, and

then there are 1,574 living as humans all around the world," Sara said.

Petros' eyes widened as he looked at Sara. "You have a powerful sight. In fact, you look like one of the Fates."

Triton spoke up. "The Fates bow to her. They say Sara *is* fate."

Petros lowered his head. "Then I submit to your judgment. What should we do?"

"Not to brag," Sara said, "my sight *is* pretty clear, but unfortunately, not for events I'm personally involved in. I'm completely blind to this situation. Sorry."

"Never apologize for having limits," Petros said. "It's what keeps a god humble."

"A humble god?" Pallas asked.

Petros chuckled as he shrugged. "Maybe humble *is* a strong word."

"Humble is definitely a strong word," said a familiar voice. Drakōn's hair rose on the back of his neck.

"Brother," Petros said with a growl in his voice.

Drakōn turned to see Zeus standing among them inside the fiery dome.

Xanthus charged him as he shouted. Zeus raised his hand and Xanthus stopped—frozen mid-run.

"And now the mystery of where my son has disappeared to has been answered." Zeus spoke softly, but his threatening tone was unmistakable. He stepped toward Xanthus and stopped when they were nose to nose. "I can feel Ares' power emanating from you. You killed him."

"No," Triton said casually. "I did. And I must say it was extremely satisfying."

Zeus spun on his heel to confront Triton. "You've just signed your execution order."

"You forget yourself, brother," Petros roared. "Only the king can order a god executed."

"Well…" Zeus laughed. "I guess it's a good thing I am king."

"You are not king," Petros growled.

Zeus narrowed his eyes. "I say I am."

"Are you challenging my authority?" Petros said.

"Yes," Zeus said.

"Then I say we settle this the way we settled things with Father."

Zeus' eyes lit up. "Gladly."

Petros ground his teeth. "Fine." He looked around and said, "My brother and I will fight. Whoever survives intact, wins."

"And takes the throne," Zeus said. "Right, brother?"

"I didn't say that." Petros narrowed his eyes.

"It doesn't matter," Zeus said. "Once you are defeated, no other will challenge me. I guarantee it."

"But," Nicole spoke up, "Zeus has an unfair advantage."

"I'd say it's the other way around," Petros said.

Zeus laughed. "Things have changed while you were cowering in your hiding place."

"I've known you for a long time," Petros said. "You haven't changed as much as you think. In fact, I'd ask

Raging

you to call off your siphons, but I know you can't be trusted. You'd stab your own mother in the back—oh right, you've already done that."

"I've done nothing to Mother," Zeus said.

"I feel the earth groan beneath my feet," Petros said. "I feel the turmoil. Our mother is suffering, and what have you done to help? You've abandoned her to fulfill your own desires for power."

"Enough talk," Zeus snarled. "It's time to settle this." He raised his hand and manifested his bolt. It was the size of a tree trunk, arcing out and striking Petros. The electricity crackled and slammed into the ground below his feet. Petros seemed unfazed.

Petros rushed Zeus like a freight train, slamming him back as he raised his hands—that looked more like boulders—above his head and slammed Zeus to the ground, crushing him.

For a moment, Drakōn thought that was it. The false king was dead.

The ground exploded from under Petros' hands, shooting rocks and debris in all directions.

The light dimmed, and Drakōn looked up. Tana's fire had darkened to a deep orange. *Are you alright, love?* he asked Tana in his mind.

Sorry, she answered, her eyes wide. She closed her eyes, and the light brightened once again. *I was distracted by the fight.*

"I understand," Drakōn said, wishing he could embrace her, but not wanting to distract her further.

Besides, his body would likely cool her fire.

"Shouldn't we help Petros?" Pallas asked, his eyes on the battle.

"Absolutely not," Triton said. "If we directly intervene, Petros would forfeit."

Zeus reached his hands to the ground and lifted them up, with apparent effort. The ground rose in mounds and lava leaked and oozed across the floor.

"I sure hope we can survive this battle too," Pallas said, pulling Malia back from the advancing magma.

Petros stomped through the molten lava and raised his fist. His fist flew, but Zeus ducked before it could strike him in the jaw.

"I can feel your power, brother," Petros said.

"It's immense, isn't it?" Zeus answered, beaming. "Even with the loss I sustained today, I'm much more powerful than you."

"It's out of balance," Petros said.

"What does it matter? I'm the most powerful of all the gods."

"The power you stole left voids in the balance. In the wake of those, there will be destructive events."

"Affecting humans only," Zeus said. "Who cares if one human dies, or even millions?"

"You're only as powerful as your weakest point. And...I can feel the weakness in you. It's the power of the sea. You never did like the ocean much, did you?" Petros looked at Drakōn, his gaze sharp and poignant. He was trying to give Drakōn a message. What was it?

Raging

"Ocean dwellers are barbaric, uncivilized," Zeus said as he raised a mist. Drakōn recognized it immediately. It looked just like the mist Gretchen used to put the gods to sleep. Drakōn could feel the effects. His eyes drooped. He had an insane urge to lie down and go to sleep.

He noticed several of his friends topple over. Drakōn himself closed his eyes.

No! His eyes flew open. He had to fight it. What did Petros need? Zeus lacked power from the sea, but Petros was an earth god. He didn't have power from—

Wait a minute. Drakōn was able to transfer his power to Triton when they saved the humans from the tidal wave. But he had to be touching him.

That's it! Drakon could help the king.

But would his help cause Petros to forfeit? No. Lending his power to the king is not directly intervening. It's just giving him a more even playing field. Besides, Zeus is getting help from the thousands he's siphoning. If that didn't cause Zeus to forfeit, then this definitely wouldn't pose a problem for Petros.

With confidence in his decision, Drakōn directed his body to stay solid—all but the bottom of his feet. Water flowed in a trickle over the rocky ground until it reached Petros. Drakōn could feel the drain of power immediately—much more quickly than when Triton had drained him. Drakōn fell to his knees but kept contact with the king. Now he was not only fighting sleep but also physical exhaustion.

Petros rushed Zeus, slamming him to the ground

as he shimmered, translucent. He had transformed into water. Zeus was covered in a layer of water as he slid into the fiery wall. Repelled by the liquid, the fire retreated, and Zeus and Petros found themselves outside the dome. Drakōn kept contact with the king, which allowed him to stay in liquid form, but Zeus was now completely dry. Vulnerable.

"This was your plan?" Zeus stood and belted out laughter. "I control these siphons!" They swirled around him like ghosts.

"And how did you gain control over them?" Petros asked.

Zeus narrowed his eyes and sneered.

"You happened upon them accidentally, didn't you? They treated you kindly and allowed you to visit them from time to time. Until…until the day you learned how you could exploit them."

All humor fled Zeus' face and he seethed in anger. "Who told you this?"

"Now that my memories have been restored, I recall much of my imprisonment. And I heard a lot over the years while I was trapped beneath the siphons.

"I know that they are peaceful, symbiotic beings—unique in the universe," Petros continued. "The females are called siphons and the males are dynami. The males generate life force and the females siphon it, use what they need, and then return it back to their partner. They are wholly dependent on each other for their existence. If you separate them, the females will die without a

Raging

surrogate host. However, they can also be suspended within lonsdaleite, which gives off enough energy to keep them from dying.

"The males…you probably don't know and don't care what happens to them. But I do and I tell you, it's not good. With that much power and no place for it to go, they've probably experienced destruction in their realm that dwarfs what is happening to the earth. Good thing they live in a different dimension. Right?" Petros smirked.

Drakōn couldn't ever recall seeing Zeus afraid, but right now, he looked terrified. "Why are you telling me all this?"

"I know about this world—a place called the Aether. It is ruled by a man named Aether and his wife, Sypher. I can only imagine how much Aether is missing his bride.

"You used Aether's queen to drain the powers of my daughter because you knew only a powerful siphon could handle her. But you didn't count on Sypher being released. And let me tell you, since her release, she's been very busy—finding out what happened to her husband. Finding all the other siphons. Plotting their reunion, and along with it—your destruction."

"It's impossible!" Zeus said. "I've sealed the boundary between our worlds. Even Aether himself cannot unseal it—not without the help of his wife."

"Right, because it takes the power of a complete aether to do it. But wait a minute…" With a glint in his eye, Petros turned toward Zeus. "What *is* the power of aether?"

"It's the power of all the elements—refined and enlightened," Sara supplied with a smile.

"Well," Petros said. "Look what we have here. The daughters who join the four corners have all the power of all the elements. And with the help of Nikoleta—"

"No!" shouted Zeus as he slammed against the wall of fire that still separated them. "Let me in! I'll kill them; I swear on the River Styx, I'll see them dead."

Sara stepped up to Gretchen and Malia, taking their hands. She turned to Nicole. "Mom, we can't do this without you."

Nicole gave a quick nod and ran forward.

Hand in hand, they rushed to Tana.

"We need to all be touching," Sara said, and they wrapped their arms around Tana.

"We're going to open the door to the Aether?" Gretchen asked.

"That's the plan," Sara said.

"I don't know what to do," Malia said.

"I sure hope Sara does," Gretchen said.

At the same time, Sara said, "I do."

Sara closed her eyes and said, "Tana, when I tell you to drop your barrier, do it. Gretchen, Mom, Malia, and Tana, when the barrier is dropped, you need to give me your power."

"I don't know how," Malia answered.

"You can feel the power inside you, right?" Sara asked.

"Yes," Malia said.

Raging

"Just visualize giving it over to me, and I'll do the rest." Sara frowned in concentration. "Is everyone ready?"

They all answered yes.

"Okay Tana, drop it now."

The fiery dome disintegrated in smoke just before a bright beam of light shot out from the group of women, piercing the sky. Drakōn had to close his eyes against the brilliance.

Thunder rumbled and a sharp crack, like a lightning strike, slapped against Drakōn's eardrum. After several long minutes, the light dimmed, and Drakōn chanced opening his eyes.

Drakōn's blood turned to ice when he saw what surrounded them.

An army of muscled men in silver armor had their weapons drawn and were snarling at them. They looked fiercer than any other army Drakōn had ever seen. The siphons flew toward the men and one by one, the ghostly figures materialized into shining, statuesque women, each of them embracing their partner. Many of the women were sobbing. Drakōn was surprised how beautiful the siphons were. But the men...he didn't know if they could ever be called handsome. They were almost too terrifying in their anger to look at—with one hand raising a sword, and the other holding their mates possessively.

Drakōn rushed to Tana's side, not trusting that these soldiers wouldn't attack them. Xanthus, Pallas, and Kyros must have felt the same because they were there beside him, guarding their own women.

"Brother," Zeus snarled at Petros. "Do you have any idea what you've done?"

"I know exactly what I've done, traitor," Petros said. "Meet your executioner." Petros glanced at the tallest of the soldiers who was walking toward him with a stunning blonde at his side.

"Aether, I presume," Petros said, bowing his head in respect. Aether nodded in return but kept his eyes glued to Zeus.

"And Sypher," Petros continued. "It's good to see you back in your whole form. You've spent some time with my daughter, I understand."

"We've become very close," Sypher said, smiling.

Aether turned to Zeus. "I feel the power of many gods in him. He has been manipulating and abusing his ill-gotten powers to an extent even I couldn't imagine." He turned to Petros. "He deserves to die for his treachery."

"No," Zeus shouted, raising his hands. He turned to Petros. "You can't let him kill me. I'm your brother."

"You are no brother of mine," Petros said before turning to Aether. "You understand that balance must be restored?"

Aether nodded. "I will allow you time to choose the vessels for the power he gained by killing gods and goddesses."

"Are they truly dead? Is there no getting them back?" Petros asked.

Aether sighed, sadness clouding his face. "I'm sorry to say they are lost forever, but those of yours who still live linked to this wretched creature," he said, giving Zeus a sideways glance, "can have their powers restored and their siphon will be free to return. And I ask you to do this quickly so they can be restored to their husbands' sides."

"That will take some time."

"Why wait?" Aether asked.

"Those gods and goddesses have no control over their powers. They would be a danger to the humans surrounding them," Petros said. "Please, let us find them first, and then I'll promise to release them."

"I will allow one week."

"That may not be enough time," Petros said.

"That is all the time I'll allow. We have waited for what seems like an eternity for the better half of our souls. You cannot imagine the torture we have gone through being separated from them."

"Okay," Petros said. "One week."

"And then," Aether said, turning a murderous glare at Zeus, "he is ours to do with as we please."

"Agreed," Petros said, frowning. "It has been an honor to meet you, Your Majesty." Petros bowed.

"And it is good to meet you also," Aether said, inclining his head in return. "I am forever grateful for your help returning our wives to us. You have an ally among the realm of the Aether."

"As do you, on Olympus."

Nicole approached Sypher with tears in her eyes.

"This is not goodbye, Nikki," Sypher said, taking

Nicole's hand. "You can visit me whenever you wish."

Aether frowned at her words.

Sypher turned to him and narrowed her eyes.

Aether sighed. Closing his eyes, he kissed the top of her head and squeezed her tight. "*You* are welcome anytime, daughter of Petros."

Sypher smiled as she closed her eyes and seemed to relish the show of affection. She opened her eyes, which were shining with moisture as she looked at Nicole. "Thank you," she mouthed. And then the entire army of soldiers and their wives disappeared in a shining pillar of light.

EPILOGUE

One month later

Drakōn lay back in a lounge recliner next to Xanthus, Pallas, and Kyros. They were as far from the ocean as you could get—high on Olympus, in a shining atrium. The clouds floated lazily across the sky.

Tana stood with her sister, Malia, and her newest friends—Sara and Gretchen. They were laughing and carrying on like school children. He cracked a smile at seeing Tana so happy. These four women seemed to become fast friends overnight.

"I still can't believe Petros made me a god of the skies," Pallas said, earning a sigh from Drakōn.

"Oh, stop complaining," Kyros said.

"It's easy for you to judge, god of oceanic volcanoes." He made quotation marks with his fingers in the air as he said Kyros' official title before slamming back down to recline in his chair.

Xanthus frowned at Pallas. "Aren't you happy with Malia?"

"Of course I am," Pallas said. "She's amazing. And gods, when she wraps her wings around me when we kiss…" He sighed. "I just can't get enough—"

"Too much information, bro," Drakōn said. They all mumbled in agreement.

"Isn't it crazy?" Xanthus said. Drakōn looked at his friend, who was watching his wife with a smile on his face. "First, we fall in love with goddesses, and then we're made gods ourselves."

"So you're finally willing to admit it, god of war?" Kyros asked.

"God of peace," Xanthus insisted. Kyros gave him a sideways glance and burst out laughing. Drakōn and Pallas joined in.

When they finally quieted, Pallas said. "Well, I guess it's not all bad being a sky god."

"You mean the god of love?" Kyros quipped and chuckled.

"Shut up," Pallas snapped and elbowed Kyros. "You're just jealous that you can't fly."

"What do I need wings for?" Kyros asked. "By the way, where are your wings?"

"It's like my tail; I only have them when I need them." Pallas shrugged.

"How is it working with Hera?" Xanthus asked Pallas.

"She's surprisingly amazing," Pallas said. "Now that everything is back to normal in the human world, and the human's memories have been erased, we have our work cut out for us. Hera is determined to see the divorce rate not just fall, but plummet."

"So you bring them together, and she keeps them together?" Kyros asked.

Raging

"Basically." Pallas raised an eyebrow.

Kyros laughed. "I tell you, when Petros announced he was giving you Eros' power, I was…gods, I was…"

"What?" Pallas snapped as he glared.

"Never mind," Kyros said, holding back a smile.

"So…how is it going with the baby?" Pallas narrowed his eyes as he smirked.

"Donovan?" Kyros said, surprised at the change in topics. "Oh, he's finally sleeping through the night. I tell you. I never knew it was so hard taking care of something so little."

Pallas chuckled.

"What's so funny?" Kyros frowned.

"Don't tell him," Xanthus said, giving Pallas a pointed stare. "Give him a few days of peace."

"What?" Kyros sat up, all humor gone.

"It's not *my* fault I know things," Pallas said. "It comes with being the kind of god I am."

"What do you know?" Kyros asked.

Pallas tried to force his smile into a frown, but he didn't succeed. "I know you'd better get as much sleep as you can *while* you can."

"What?" Kyros looked out at Gretchen. "No!"

Drakōn had to admit she looked like she was glowing.

Xanthus laughed. "I guess he figured it out."

"I wouldn't laugh, god of war," Pallas quipped.

Xanthus turned to him. "Why?"

Pallas raised an eyebrow.

All color drained from Xanthus' face. "Sara?"

Holly Kelly

Pallas nodded. "Two times over, dude."

"Twins? But she didn't—"

"Goddesses have their own time table." Pallas shrugged.

"No," Xanthus breathed. He seriously looked like he was about to pass out. Xanthus shook his head. "They always have to do everything together. But two…"

Drakōn burst out laughing. "So when are you going to give your wives the happy news?"

"Oh, no, no, no!" Pallas sat up. "You can't ever let them know you know. They have to be the ones to tell you. You can't take away their moment. Can you imagine the tears, the heartache, the regret…and when did I become such a sap?" He raised his eyes to the castle atop Mt. Olympus and shook his fist. "Why did you do this to me?"

"Just be glad you'll always know what to give your woman for her birthday, anniversaries…" Drakōn said.

"Yeah." Pallas frowned, and then looked out to watch Malia. His expression softened immediately.

"You love her, don't you?" Drakōn asked him.

"More than anything," Pallas answered and then looked at Drakōn. "And I don't need to ask you how you feel about Tana. God of love, and all."

"She's my life. She has my heart. Gods, I'd die for that woman." Drakōn looked around, suddenly uncomfortable at declaring his feelings to his friends. He smiled when he saw them watching their own women in adoration. They were all lovesick fools. And they'd never been happier.

ACKNOWLEDGEMENTS

I want to thank my publisher, Clean Teen Publishing, and the lovely ladies I work with there—Rebecca, Courtney, Marya, and Melanie. I'd also like to thank my editor—Cynthia Shepp and her helpers; my cover designer Marya Heiman (yes, you're worth mentioning twice); my beta readers—Mom, Dad, Lisa, Becky, Natalie, and Sherry; my fellow authors and friends; and the amazing reviewers/bloggers who have written nice things about my books.

But most of all, I have a tremendous and unabiding appreciation for my fans. You are the most incredible group of readers I've ever had the honor of associating with! This journey started out as a lonely one—just me, my laptop, and my characters. But now, you are in my thoughts and mind every step of my journey and I must say, the whole process is so much better when I am able to share it with others. Thank you, a million times over!

ABOUT THE AUTHOR

I'm a mom who writes books in her spare time: translation—I hide in the bathroom with my laptop and lock the door while the kids destroy the house and smear peanut butter on the walls. ;) I was born in Utah but lived in Salina, Kansas until I was 13 and in Garland, Texas until I was 18. I'm now back in Utah–"happy valley". I'm married to a wonderful husband, James, and we are currently raising 6 rambunctious children. My interests are reading, writing (of course), martial arts, visual arts, and spending time with family.

CPSIA information can be obtained
at www.ICGtesting.com
Printed in the USA
FSOW02n2256210617
35477FS